I0745362

Published by: Cinnabar Moth Publishing LLC
Santa Fe, New Mexico

Cover Design by: Ivan

ISBN-13: 978-1-953971-20-3
Library of Congress Control Number: 2021944984

A Cold Christmas and the Darkest of Winters

Content Notes

If you would be triggered by, find disasteful, or be negatively impacted by any of the following subject matter, please refrain from reading the contents of this collection. The following is a list of the types of subject matter contained in the story or stories you are about to read.

Adult language   Postpartum depression
Depression   Mental health
Death   Death of child
Suicide   Maiming
Immolation   Sexual assault
Animal cruelty   Murder
Murder of a child   Massacre
Emotional exploitation
Abuse of elders   Alzheimer's
Torture   Starvation
Apocalypse   Hospitalization
Gender bias   Bodily fluids
War   Abuse of POWs
Kidnapping   Climate Damage
Abandonment of a Child
Self Harm   Gore

The Epiphany of a Family Man in Solitude
By
Angelo Lorenzo

Niccolo Quijano believes Christmas is best spent with the family. Like many seniors in their sixties, he was looking forward to celebrating the season with his daughter this year. After all, she is all that he has left. But a voice message on the Viber app from Camille last month has pulled all hope away. *Sorry, Pa. I wish I could be there with you, but I don't know how that would be possible given the circumstances. I'll call you on Christmas. I promise. I miss you.*

He understands her decision because he also cares about her health and safety. He understands that she is much needed where she is now. Miles may have set them apart, but this year has made him realize that nurses from anywhere in the world are among the modern-day heroes. Her concern and regret were evident in her voice, and he didn't want her to worry about him. He did manage to reply based on how she had taught him to use the app. *It is okay, Camille. I'll be fine. Stay safe. I miss you, too, Anak.*

Circumstances have been difficult this year. But like many who are trying to survive the ongoing global health crisis, he wishes not to dwell too much on what happened. When the news bluntly delivers statistics involving the rise of infected cases and deaths, anyone who is vulnerable has every right to worry. The flu poses a major threat, and the consequences are lethal. It affects not only people's health.

Tonight, he feels Christmas would not be complete without visiting Lenora. He is standing over the spot where she rests. The love of his life had met her fate earlier last year after an artery had burst when she was boiling the *camotes* in their kitchen. He had heard the pot rattling on the floor while he was in their home's drawing room, adding the finishing touches on the image of a bouquet on the card. Copies had later been reprinted and sold at the Lasting Memories Gift Shop just in time for Mother's Day. But the day he had lost her was a day he would never forget.

He leans over his folded umbrella, using it as a cane to support his stance. The tip digs into the soil beneath the trimmed grass. The night brings cold winds, and solace that hovers over the memorial park prompts memories of days past. Not all Christmas Eves were spent in solitude. He remembers Camille coming home during her mother's wake and funeral. That was the last time he had seen his daughter except for the virtual calls they made through the mobile device, which she had taught him to use. Perhaps, that was the last time his family would ever be complete again.

If Lenora were here, he would tell her everything that happened this year. *I could have spent this Christmas with you,* he says in his thoughts, and he gazes over her name engraved in cursive letters on the surface of her shiny marble headstone.

I have more free time now. He thinks about this new phase in life. His monthly pension and savings support his daily needs now after the Lasting Memories Gift Shop made major changes in the summer. The shift to digital cards meant they had to take on board a new crew who can handle digital graphics and layout. Letting go of their former artists was a tough decision to make for the business, but printed copies of cards for special occasions didn't sell well when the majority of people's attention had shifted to online and digital media.

All the while, he thinks of Lenora and Camille. On the usual Christmas Eve, they would all be in their dining room with a plate of sliced apples, a bunch of grapes, cubes of cheese, and the tray of baked macaroni spaghetti Lenora would prepare for them. The family would discuss what happened in the year behind them. In recent years, Camille would engage the discussion about her experiences abroad.

His eyes do not sting and his vision does not blur as

he gazes over the basket of roses standing beside Lenora's name. But a soft drop trickles over the lines on his cheek. He looks above and sees more drops coming from the dark sky. He unfolds the umbrella, knowing that it does come in handy. Rain is common in December. Though he wishes to stay longer, he doesn't wish to catch a cold.

In the cab that will take him home, he sees the streets outside and notices that they are less crowded than a usual Christmas Eve. It hasn't always been like this. Rain or shine, Filipinos would always find a way to go out and enjoy the season. These days, however, fear has become an obstacle, especially when the peak number of infected cases has reached three hundred thousand barely two months ago. Not to mention the deaths associated with the pandemic.

Through the rain-speckled tinted glass, Niccolo sees shops and restaurants with their lights on, the glare visible beyond the streetlamps that outline the sidewalk. On their windows are posters and signs that say, "No Mask and Face Shield, No Entry." Others present the words: "We Only Provide Take Outs and Delivery."

He sighs after seeing them and leans further back into his cushioned seat. "Not much of a *Merry* Christmas, is it?" he mutters, almost to himself.

He doesn't expect the cab driver to hear what he said because he is wearing a mask that covers the lower portion of his face. Yet, the cab driver behind the wheel grunts as if he agrees. He looks like a man in his prime, Niccolo observes from the passenger seat at the back. Contrary to Niccolo's gray thinning hair and the deep lines on his face's loose skin, the driver has let his black hair drop over his shoulders. It is quite an unusual hairstyle, but Niccolo knows that barbershops have mostly ceased operations due to the social distancing regulations.

"Going home to your family after this?" Niccolo thinks it's polite to ask.

In the rearview mirror, the cab driver's eyes flick at him once. "Yes, Sir," the driver says. "Got my kids some presents," he adds excitedly. "Giving each of them new phones I saved up for. It'll be good for their online class once the Christmas break ends."

A memory visits Niccolo. It is clear as day. He sees Camille in their living room one Christmas morning, still in her pink Hello Kitty pajamas. She had just woken up with her hair in disarray and her eyes still squinting as if the rays of sunshine beaming through their wide-open curtains were too bright for her. Yet as soon as she saw the box beneath the Christmas tree, his daughter gasped. Together, he and his wife gave their joyous *Merry Christmas!* greeting.

She tore the wrapping of the box beneath the Christmas tree in their living room while he and Lenora sat beside each other on the sofa. When she opened the box, her eyes shone with joy at the new Nokia 3210 in her hand. Camille was thirteen, and that was many years ago.

"That's good to know," Niccolo says, after listening to the

driver talk about how his role as a father involves providing the needs for his children. The rain strengthens outside. Large drops pelt over the cab's roof. Streams cascade over the windshields like a transparent curtain, blurring the view. They stop at a traffic sign.

"How about you, Sir? Are your grandchildren coming to see you?" the driver asks.

"I still don't have any," he says. "My only daughter's passionate about her career."

"Oh, there's nothing wrong with that. What's her job?"

"She's a nurse at a hospital in London."

"Oh! A frontliner then?"

This prompts Niccolo to smile. "Yes," he says, beaming with pride. "A hero in the family."

"You and your wife must be very proud of her."

"We have always been."

Frontliner, he thinks. The term has become associated with professionals risking their lives so others can live theirs. He considers this guy as one of them. The fact that he's still running his cab at this time of night to earn for his family is already proof of his courage. Perhaps, the scarcity of passengers may be a challenge to earn like normal, since the pandemic forces people into their homes. But exposing himself to different encounters every day takes risk. Someone has to take people to places where they wish to go. How else can people who do not own vehicles get home without public transportation?

Once this pandemic is over, Niccolo hopes society will regard these frontliners as the noble heroes in this day and age; to see them not merely as essential workers but as the valiant champions who kept fighting.

We're fine, Papa, Camille once said in a call back in April when the pandemic began to spread throughout different countries. *We'll have to stay in the hospital for some time so we can treat the patients directly. But we're being properly accommodated.* Along with this message, she sends photos of herself in her personal protective equipment. It was difficult to recognize his daughter beneath all the blue scrubs and gloves, the mask and eye shield, and the head cap. But he relied on the tone of her voice which reassured him that she was well. There have been nights when Niccolo couldn't sleep just thinking about his daughter. But her profession was a decision that was hers to make.

He remembers the conversations he had with Lenora when Camille was bound for the working opportunity abroad. In one of them, his wife lay awake in their bed, her sighs slowly turning into sobs. *What's wrong?* he asked when he turned on the lamp on his bedside table. He could see fresh tears gleaming in his wife's eyes.

I'm going to miss her, Nick, Lenora said. *She'll be miles away.*

He recalls wrapping his arm around her, hoping the gesture would soothe her. He could feel her body trembling, and he reassured his wife that Camille was going to be fine. *It's about time,* he said. They both knew that day would come.

At some point, parents know their limits: when their children can decide on their own. Through the years, their hard work had supported his family quite well. His commissions as a painter and his wife's career as a restaurant cook had made them stay afloat even in trying times. But they both knew the day would come when children have to grow up. That night in their bed, he'd promised they'd still be together no matter what. Every year since then, it has become a joy to see Camille coming home, especially during the holidays.

The traffic light turns green, and the cab takes a turn to the left of the intersection. There are a few vehicles on the road. A couple of jeepneys pass. They have only a few passengers in the backseats. They pass along a strip on the road where golden trumpet trees stand with their yellow leaves. Globular lanterns hang from their branches, their lights shining with different colors.

"Do you think all of this will end by the new year?" Niccolo asks the driver.

"It's hard to say, Sir," the driver says. "Back in March, I didn't think the pandemic would reach December. Now, January is just a few days away."

While he wonders, he feels his belly grumble. He realizes that he hasn't had a meal since noon. Ordering out a full meal that would suit the Christmas Eve occasion didn't appeal to him. With perfect timing, the road leads them to the city's downtown center. The cab has to pass through Plaza Divisoria.

By this time, the rain has eased. Translucent beads speckle the cab's windshields. Niccolo gazes through the window and sees the road leading to an expansive square surrounded by more shops and restaurants on the base of buildings. The structures stand side by side, making up the congested cityscape of a Philippine metropolis. In the center of the square, an elevated park is situated where stone monuments stand amid trees and benches.

An immense Christmas tree towers above the park. It is a man-made structure made of dried banana leaves stacked together to form the shape of a cone. Bamboo poles bundled together serve as its trunk. A series of lights adorn the edges of the leaves, flickering in golden hues that brighten the vicinity. On the Christmas tree's topmost tip, a star shines the brightest. Niccolo is amazed by the sight.

There are a few people on the sidewalk, mostly men and women in sweaters and raincoats walking with boxes and bags containing their recent purchase. Masks and face shields complement their protection against the weather.

He sees a row of tents standing along the sidewalk. On one of the tables, red apples are displayed. Its arrangement resembles a Christmas tree. Beside it is a table where a bunch of purple grapes rises in a mound.

He tells the driver to park right at the front of the tents. This is his new stop before going home.

"Why the sudden change of mind, Sir?" the driver asks him.

Tradition stays the same, he thinks. "I just remembered to buy some stuff I need for Christmas," he says instead. He looks over the meter then reaches for his wallet. He hands out a bundle of bills to the driver.

"But, Sir, this is too much," the driver says as soon as he sees the amount.

"Don't worry about it," Niccolo reassures him. "It's Christmas. Your family is waiting for you."

The driver finally accepts and gives his heartfelt thanks. The cab drops Niccolo off at the sidewalk in front of the tents. The rain has entirely stopped, yet the ground remains slippery. Fresh puddles form over the concrete.

Despite his family's absence, Niccolo wishes to observe the holiday on his own. He buys bags of apples and grapes from the sales lady whose face reveals the weariness and frustration of not being able to sell the fruits on display. He greets her with a sincere *Merry Christmas* and tells her to keep the change. This makes her smile, and as soon as he leaves, she calls for her daughter who was staying behind the tent. Whatever they would use the change for, he hopes it would add more to what they have prepared for Christmas.

With his bags of apples and grapes, he gazes outside and sees the stark brilliance of the towering Christmas tree. But when he steps onto the street from the sidewalk, he feels someone tugging the hem of his red polo shirt. He sees a child who carries a star-shaped lantern. Its frames are made of thin bamboo sticks while the gaps are covered with colorful plastic.

The boy has a shaved head and a dingy shirt. His shirt is too large for his thin and frail body, and the hem reaches his knees. Like the usual Christmas season, there are plenty of children selling items on the streets that fit the occasion. While child labor laws discourage this system, some children did their part in supporting their family, while some have been forced to work by illegal syndicates. It's a sad reality, Niccolo thinks. But even though he pities the child, whose eyes now gleam with hope as he looks at him, he doesn't find any use for a lantern. The child's little mask is beaded with drops, suggesting that he must have been out in the rain not too long ago.

Christmas is tomorrow, Niccolo thinks, and most families are in their homes to welcome the holiday with the traditional *noche buena* dinner that leads towards midnight. Decorations would not be important now.

He waves his hand to the child instead, gesturing his polite refusal. Then he crosses the street and proceeds to the park at the center of the square. He sits on one of the benches beneath the Christmas Tree. A few people are spending their time at the park, most of them street vendors selling key chains, glittering balls, socks, and shirts – all of which comprise Christmas decorations and last-minute gifts.

He misses his wife. He misses his daughter. As he sits and takes a bite of one of his apples, he thinks about how this year has changed a lot of people, how the events have shifted the way of life for most of them. The park used to be filled with people. But now, the vendors struggle to find anyone who wishes to buy their products.

The child from a while ago enters the park, still bringing with him his lantern. He sits beside a woman on a bench across Niccolo. Over the woman's lap is a tray of toys in colorful plastic bags. Despite his mask, the boy reaches to kiss the woman's cheek. The woman pats his head. Niccolo presumes the woman is the child's mother, or aunt, or sister.

It is Christmas Eve, and this family of two is spending this precious moment outdoors. There might be more of them in the family. He sees this kind of family on a night when most families would spend meals within the comfort of their homes together. He remembers Camille's promise. His daughter is going to call him tomorrow. Christmas may be different this year, but families stay the same, no matter the distance.

Niccolo decides not to let more time pass before going home . He finishes his apple and tosses the core into the trash bin a few steps away from the bench. Then he rises and carries the bags of fruits with him. With his umbrella as his cane, he walks towards the woman and the child. He hands them the bags.

The woman and her son look at him. It's not much, he thinks, but he hopes it's enough to complement their celebration.

"Thank you, Sir," the woman says after she receives the bags.

Niccolo crosses the street with his folded umbrella supporting his pace. He hails for a cab. A new cab comes after a while. In the backseat, he glances at the park, wishing to see the Christmas tree again. Beneath the brilliant lights, he sees the woman, the boy, and the rest of the vendors on the park. They have apples and grapes in their hands. They may not have customers tonight unlike the usual Christmas nights, but there they are sharing what they have with each other.

Perhaps celebrating Christmas can look like this, Niccolo realizes. He settles in his seat and thinks of home.

-End-

The Black Tree
By
Vashelle Nino

I did not flower in my mother's womb, live and make love in this skin, give life, *survive* life to be flung onto the pavement of this intersection like rock salt before a snowstorm. I'm impaled, barbed by metal and glass. Skinned by this cold rugged asphalt.

The sound of chaos roars in my head. Loud sirens and people shouting. The involuntary groan coming from deep within my body.

I feel like I should be in pain, but I'm not. I simply cannot move.

This might be a while. I need someone to call Mateo so he can pick Lynn up from choir. He'll have to take Anthony with him, but shit—I have his booster seat. Maybe this can be resolved faster than I think. It's not like I'm hurting. It's just loud and chaotic. And we still have to pick up pastry flour for the cookie recipe Lynn wanted to try. I can't wait to taste them.

As soon as I can get out of here.

If I could just move. Make love again. Hear another song. Pull these shards out of my body, one by one.

I'm not in pain.

I'm not in pain. I just…

A row of naked maple trees stands in the median near the intersection where I took my last breath. Their bare branches reach out to one another, the most outstretched branch about one meter from the other. Knobby twigs fan out from their arms and tremble in the cold wind, appearing to wave at all the passersby. But the intersection is fast and busy during the holidays, and people don't seem to admire them in the winter the way they do in the other seasons. No time to slow down and acknowledge waving trees.

Except for the black one.

Some people choose to ignore The Black Tree. They stop at the intersection's red light and keep their eyes fastened ahead or look down, faces to their phones. Some look to the right where the town shopping center is situated and follow patrons walking in and out of stores. Anything not to face the left and be reminded of their own mortality.

The curious ones try to make out the tree's accoutrements: little greeting cards and tattered letters pinned to the trunk, stuffed animals tethered by twine, deflated mylar balloons anchored by a raw wooden cross. They might say a quick prayer under their breath or unconsciously finger the cross necklace around their neck.

Although the townspeople call it The Black Tree, only one side of its trunk and the lower half of its crown burned. The rest of it managed to survive both the impact and fire and—by some miracle— still flourishes on its good side during spring, summer and fall.

Despite remaining alive, albeit scarred, it stands as the town death totem.

Summertime brings warmth and company. People are happier and slower. They crawl through the intersection light, windows down. The sound of music and laughter invigorates before evaporating into the heavens. They admire the trees again—even the black one. Its leaves, as sparse and one-sided as they are, inspire perseverance. *Look at that,* they say. *It survived.*

I don't resent the tree for surviving. There is no envy in this state. *Here* is everywhere, at once. Aware and wise. Trees are stationary, anchored. Restricted in their dance. I always loved dancing with my Mateo on summer nights. Now I dance with him as often as I like.

Then comes autumn, the pinnacle of maple tree adoration. Commuters at the red light pause to study the foliage. Some think about how the black tree looks like it's on fire again. Others remember the color of fresh blood smeared across the pavement. Even then, the allure of that color against an azure sky remains irresistible.

My Anthony was born on Halloween, right at the peak of fall. On our way home from the hospital three days later, I cried quietly in the back seat watching leaves fall from the trees. I never did well postpartum. New life always felt too fragile to me, and I was afraid I'd do something stupid or careless to compromise it. Something unforgivable.

But I had a revelation that late November as I walked a wooded trail with Lynn while she pushed her brand new brother in his stroller. (She has always been a good big sister.) Trees impart gifts of shade and picturesque sights most of the year. When the wind waves and troughs through their branches, the trembling leaves mimic the sound of the sea, reminding us of warm summer days. They give us so much knowing they will have to surrender the most beautiful parts of themselves: let them fall to the ground, only to be walked upon thoughtlessly by those who once revered them. And still, they resolve to bud again. Forgiveness is omnipresent. Everywhere. In all things.

The beauty of autumn is nature's parting gift— unnecessary atonement for the harshness of an upcoming winter.

And then it arrives.

The nakedness, the disregard. The residual memory of that cold, caustic night when my car bludgeoned into the tree and severed me from my earthbound life.

The Black Tree recalls the acrid smell of burning flesh and rubber and bark, and it writhes with grief in the bitter wind. Its neighboring trees tremble at the recollection and bend in its direction, a fruitless attempt at consolation. It pines for the company of moths and maple worms, *anything* to be seen as something other than the emblem of eternal ruin. It wants to be fed upon, useful. Not a mere pin board for sympathy notes and pity.

My accident occurred a week before Christmas Eve two years ago. A light powder of snow veiled the town the day before, but the roads were as occupied as usual, if not in a Yuletide frenzy. People out in hordes buying last-minute gifts, preparing for parties, traveling past the perimeters of town for another destination. They hurtle through yellow lights, honk at one another, risk their necks to arrive somewhere three minutes sooner. Quick strokes of acceleration and escape. Gritty textures of steel and asphalt moving within the frame. A proper illustration of human insolence devoid of the wisdom of the trees in the median, which discreetly form their spring buds during the previous summer. They defer until the 11th hour, as preparedness would in some way acknowledge life's uncertainty. Most people don't want that revelation hanging over their head.

When the last of the responders and spectators left the scene of the accident and quiet befell the row of trees, the onset of snow flurries hissed as they landed on the blackened bare arms of the unlucky maple. The rest were haunted by the song it made, and they grieved not just for me, but for humankind: *they don't realize how fragile they are in this world, like seven billion dandelion seeds with fates decided by a spontaneous puff of God's breath. Please be still. Stillness is not a prelude to death.* The snow fell around me, yet all I felt was warmth. By then I knew my place.

The Black Tree against a winter backdrop reminds me so much of having my Lynn.

She was born in the bitterness of January, when the remnant of a joyous December is replaced by post-holiday depression and bleak overcast. Stretches of snow smother us into the brooding cabins within our minds. The bones hurt. The heart hurts. Whiteness feels black and heavy.

Her birth was emotional and laborious. When she came out of me and I saw her swollen purple face covered in my blood, cord wrapped around her neck like a tree twisted in its own vines, winter seemed to be the only season befitting for her ushering into this life. That's when the fragility of existence struck me. That's when the blizzard filled my soul, hindered me from providing my firstborn, my baby, the love she needed to thrive. It was in there, to be sure. A hearth, a warm kindling that grew inside me, buried by life's cold mysteries. I tried in vain to shovel my way out, to create a path that led to her. But I existed only on the surface. A warm body. A shell of a mother even when she suckled from my breasts or cooed as I held her in my arms.

Mateo did everything to make up for what I lacked. He understood how to love whole-heartedly—it was the very reason I fell in love with him. He never lived in fear of what ifs. He never considered things like rejection or changes of heart. To him, vulnerability was a mansion sitting on fifty acres. His heart was an estate. I admired him for all of it. I was undeserving.

Early February brought on a wicked winter storm. Mateo went out before its arrival to stock up on batteries, canned food, bottled water, candles, and such. He called to tell me how crazy the stores were and that he'd have to stop one more place to see if he could find a case of water. Lynn, just a few weeks old, napped in her frilly white bassinet. I peeked at her in there, and she looked like a single bald hatchling cradled in its nest. So fragile and helpless.

I walked to our kitchen window and stared out into the white. I knew it was soon to be infinite. The thought overwhelmed me. A bright red cardinal perched on a bare branch of our crape myrtle. Their colors contrasted. White, Red. White. I imagined the cardinal's mother crushing twigs with her beak, carrying bark and grass back and forth to build a perfect nest as high up as possible to keep her eggs safe. Surely, when her eggs became hatchlings, she didn't cower in fear. She foraged and sang for them.

I was an awful mother bird.

The cardinal red made me think of blood. *My* blood. The blood covering Lynn as she transitioned from the safety of my womb into this unpredictable life. I knew there was a possibility I'd make it worse for her. As a mother, you either heal or kill.

Kill.

Maybe I should kill myself.

I turned my attention from the window toward the knife block. It would be painless and quick if I slashed the seven-inch Santoku right across my jugular. *Her life would be better for sure,* I thought.

Then I heard Lynn stir the way babies do when they're about to wake. I hesitated, gripped in the tandem of life and death. *Should I go to her or go through with this? Mateo will be home any minute, so she wouldn't be left alone very long.* But then I heard the garage open. The clanging of its metal track pulleying up the door shook me out of my thoughts. It was too late. *Maybe next time.*

Next time never came. Busy days became weeks and weeks became months. I surrendered to the distraction of life as mother. The feedings, the diapers the laundry, the pumping. Wake, rinse, and repeat.

Meanwhile, Mateo's love for us sustained me until, one day, I realized I wasn't buried in cold anymore. Only guilt.

Lynn was a quiet baby who grew to be a docile child. She never challenged, never caused a ruckus.

"What a well-behaved child," people would say.

Part of me wondered if she had simply resigned; a wounded bird whose mother once abandoned the nest.

"Thank you," I'd say with a smile.

Deep inside the Santoku knife slid against my jugular like a snake wrapping around a trunk, slow and punishing.

As an early teen, she was a lot like The Black Tree. Parts of her were solemn and dark, but once she began to flower, she'd bloom over and over again. A winter baby dancing toward spring. We bonded over her interests—baking and music, and we'd spend time together in the kitchen, getting doused in flour, dancing to our shared favorite songs. We had yet to experience the mother/daughter contention you hear about at that age. It was all love. Unspoken love, subdued and cherished. Like so many other things, I knew I didn't deserve it.

She was sixteen when I died in the accident. I was on my way to pick her up from choir rehearsal for the winter concert, and we had planned to pick up pastry flour on the way home. That year, she had chosen chocolate crackle cookies as her Christmas cookie of choice. The bark of The Black Tree reminds me of them. I had pinned the recipe in my phone earlier that day to ensure we didn't miss an ingredient at the store. I wish we could have made it, but it's okay.

There are no *what ifs* here. Only *what is*.

She visits the black tree often now that she has her driver's license—mostly at night since the intersection is so busy during the day, and without all the commuting voyeurs and pity, the tree becomes less of a death totem and more of a makeshift memorial. The letters pinned to the trunk are mostly from her with a few scribbled words at the bottom from my Anthony. *I love Spiderman. Bye, mom.* and such. Those are my favorite even though they don't last in the elements very long.

Yesterday was Lynn's 18th birthday, and the three of them stopped by the tree long after dinner at her favorite restaurant. Mateo laid a chocolate crackle cookie at the base of the trunk and tidied up that area of the median, popping what was left of the deflated mylar balloons and stuffing them into a plastic bag. He gathered the potted poinsettias and straightened out the wooden cross staked there by a local church the day after my accident. I don't always recognize everyone who comes by, but I know some people find solace in grief. They revel in the participation of the only guaranteed thing in life—death. Even as a mere bystander.

The surrounding trees, stripped of their green regalia, danced in the nighttime breeze. They were happy to see my family. They were happy to feel me. *Be still,* they said.

Happy Birthday, my sweet baby.

"I miss you, Mom," Lynn said under her breath.

I imagined her as the featherless hatchling in her little bassinet, oblivious to the inner life of her struggling mom. The wounded bird, oblivious in her own right. *Forgiveness is everywhere, silly.* That's what I would have told that incarnation of myself if I could. Then again, maybe I did.

"It's cold," Anthony protested.

His teeth chattered and he hugged himself for warmth. It was January. Lynn's birthday. Snow flurries fell in slow motion like silver confetti against the night sky.

Lynn pulled her baby brother close for a warm snuggle.

"You know, there was a time—I think I was in second grade—mom was walking me home from school and it was so, so cold. She pulled me close to warm me up. I remember feeling embarrassed cause she was rarely the touchy type, and neither was I. I looked up at her, and she had a tear rolling down her face. 'What's wrong, Mom?' I asked. 'Nothing's wrong, sweetie. It's just so cold and windy it made my eyes tear up.'"

A light wind pushed some of the branches of the black tree, and it appeared to lean into the story.

"I always wondered what was wrong that day. I knew it wasn't the cold cause I could just feel her. I always felt her."

"Your mom struggled sometimes. Things made her sad and overwhelmed. But she loved you two so much."

"I know she did. I never felt otherwise. I hope she knew that."

I didn't know it then, but of course I know it now.

Lynn gave Anthony a tight squeeze, and a tear rolled down her face. She wiped it quickly, embarrassed and cognizant of how it might make her brother feel.

Mateo walked over and reached out his arms, pulling in the two of them toward his trunk. He looked like a snowy owl with a massive wingspan looking after its delicate hatchlings. Warm. Wise, Protective.

Look at that, I think. *We survived.*

-End-

The Christmas Tree
By
Kisstopher Musick

Louis Armstrong's *It's a Wonderful World* started to play on the radio. "Nope" Lilly said as she changed the station with her toes. She knew Suzie hated it when she put her feet on the dashboard and waited with anticipation for the playful smack on her feet. Suzie was right on cue.

"Hey, stop that! I was listening to that. Put your feet down. You know I hate it when you do that, and I just got my truck detailed!" Suzie said, half irritated and half amused.

"Come on, you know you love my feet" Lily said as she wiggled her toes and giggled.

"You're going to make us crash." In truth, Suzie knew they were not in any danger. Suzie and Lilly played this game often, and she contemplated grabbing Lily's foot and biting it then thought better of it. If they were going to get to the tree lot before it closed, they didn't have time to pull over and play. Suzie knew how much this Christmas meant to Lily. It was their first Christmas as a married couple, and only chosen family were coming. This was big for Suzie as well. It would be her first Christmas without her mother in attendance shooting her disapproving looks every time Lily was affectionate. This would be the first Christmas where she could be herself and just relax.

Suzie was brought back to the moment when she realized that Lily had been talking. Lily was so focused on the gifts that she hadn't noticed Suzie had stopped listening. Lily wanted everything to be perfect, which meant having an extra gift for unexpected guests. "Should we just go with gift cards? This way, if we don't have any unexpected guest, we can use them ourselves, but I don't like the idea of anyone knowing how much their gifts cost."

Lily had been planning this Christmas for a year. All the presents were perfectly matched and a dream item each person had told her about. Jeremy was getting a Chanel broach. His whole life, he had wanted one but always felt they were too extravagant and that money could go towards something useful. Earnie, a few years back, had mentioned wanting a full-length leather trench coat. Lilly was especially pleased with herself for how she had wrapped it. Lilly had put the coat in a big bin and covered it with wrapping paper that was crumpled up and had glitter in it. Lily and Ernie had been giving each other cards and gifts with glitter in them for years. Caroline and Linda were getting matching Velour track suits; Debbie, boxer shorts; Lena, empty photo albums; Leslie, a vegan leather bag; and Charlotte, a pair of pearl drop earrings. Debbie was going to start their transition and announce their new name at the party. Why Debbie wanted their birthday to be on Christmas, no one knew, but there it was. Debbie had decided he was a boxer man, and Lilly bought him an array of boxers that had different themes. One pair even had a snow globe with a snowman and snow on the front covered in plastic so you could actually shake the globe and make the snow fall on the sow man.

Lily had only invited couples and felt a little guilty not inviting Ryan, Melvin, or Robert, but she knew they would kill the family vibe she wanted. This just had to be perfect because it was the first Christmas Suzie was going to be out and herself. Lilly always hated the way Suzie's mom made snide remarks whenever they were the least bit affectionate in front of her. It wasn't homophobia. It was straight up loneliness and jealousy. Still, it made Suzie tense and far too aware of herself. Lily wanted this to be the best Christmas of Suzie's life, and that's why she'd been working overtime to be able to afford a spoiler kit for Suzie's truck. Suzie had a ton of truck magazines and could go on and on about her truck.

To be fair, it was a really nice truck. Lowered to the ground with tinted windows and a custom stereo system. The spoiler kit was the finishing touch to all of Suzie's hard work. Lily wanted to help Suzie fulfill her dream of entering her truck in car shows and competitions. To be competitive, Suzie needed the custom spoiler kit. As they pulled into the tree lot, Lily couldn't help but giggle when she saw how muddy it was. Suzie swore under her breath. She washed and detailed her truck once a week rain or shine. Now she was going to have to spray it and wipe it down once they got home. Suzie always wiped her truck down after being out but having to spray it down was a lot more work than a quick wipe down.

Lily grabbed Suzie's hand and guided her through the tress all the while chatting away. After a few moments, Lily's chatter drifted away as she contemplated the trees. Suzie, seeing this as the perfect opportunity, walked ahead and turned the corner. Lily looked up and noticed Suzie was gone and hurried to catch up. Just as Lily turned the corner, Suzie jumped out and Lily shrieked. She was furious with Suzie. Suzie new how much she hated being scared. Suzie couldn't stop laughing. She had always found Lily's scream to be hilarious. Lily was shaking from the adrenaline flooding into her body. Suzie tried to put her arms around Lily and give her a kiss while mumbling a weak apology in between chuckles.

Lily pulled herself out of Suzie's arms and stormed off. Suzie called after her, "Come on don't be like that. We're even now for your footprints on my radio, and you know if we come back without a tree Ernie is going to kill us!"

Ernie and Jeremy had stayed behind to decorate the house. Suzie's truck had an extended cab, but the back seats were cramped and uncomfortable. It made more sense for Lily and Suzie to get the tree on their own. Ernie had a great eye when it came to decorating, and Jeremy was good at following orders. Lily also had a creative streak. Thinking about the party they had planned, Lily felt all of her anger melt away. In short order, they were walking around the tree lot, and Lily was standing back while Suzie and one of the lot employees navigated the tree they had chosen into the bed of the truck, which was protected by a liner.

Mariah Carey's new song *All I Want for Christmas Is You* came on the radio, and they began sing to each other. At the end of the song, Suzie leaned in for a kiss and, as her lips touched Lily's, the whole world went dark.

Lily opened her eyes, and she was under a hair dryer at the salon, and her scalp was burning. Ernie walked by, holding up his hands to indicate she'd be under the dryer for another ten minutes. Lily was dying her naturally brown hair turquoise, and that meant she had to bleach it blond first. Lily, Ernie, and Charlotte chatted about random things as Suzie sat next to them casually turning the pages of the latest issue of Vogue. Charlotte's station was next to Ernie's, and things were slow today. Lily was always intimidated by Charlotte and was briming with nervous excitement at the opportunity to talk to her. Ernie had finished cutting and styling Suzie's hair while Lily was under the dryer. After Ernie finished styling her hair, Lily went to pay for both haircuts. Even as she wrote the check, she knew it would bounce. She was hoping to be able to kite enough checks to trick the back into thinking she had enough in her account to cover the check. As Lena took the check from Lily, the whole world went dark.

It was dark out, and Lily felt exhausted. They had been helping Jeremy paint the interior of his house all day, and everyone one was feeling it. Just as they began to pull the tape off of the walls that was protecting the trim, there was a knock at the door. When Jeremy opened the door, he was surprised that he was eye to eye with the man at the door. They were both an imposing six foot two. Debbie had told them she was inviting a friend over to help. Jeremy motioned and said, "Come on in you must be Debbie's friend. You're a bit late to the party if you're here to help us paint."

"Hi, I'm Ernie and actually, I'm here to talk to Lily. Debbie told me she'd be here helping you paint." Ernie replied.

Lily's blood ran cold as she recognized Ernie's voice, and she looked over at Debbie and whispered, "Why didn't you tell me you were inviting Ernie?"

Debbie replied, "Because I knew you would flake or leave early if you knew. You need to talk to him. What you did was wrong. You need to pay him and pay for the bounce check fee."

Just then, Ernie entered the room, "Hi Lily, can we talk for a minute over here", he asked as he motioned to the hallway.

Before Ernie could speak or move into the hallway, Lilly start to make her apology, "I'm really sorry about the check. I thought I could make enough deposits before your bank tried to clear it. I'm totally broke and can't afford to pay you."

Ernie looked mad but said, "If you had told me you couldn't afford to get your hair done, I would have done it anyway."

Lilly seriously doubted that. Debbie started inviting Ernie to join them, "We're just finishing up painting and then we're going out to the city. Do you want to come? I think Lily can get you a gold card so that you can join us in the VIP."

Lily and Suzie were dancers at the hottest club in San Francisco, aptly named The Box. The Box was notorious for long lines, and the door man would often send people away if he didn't like their look. Leslie was a great DJ, but more importantly, an excellent businesswoman. She was the driving force behind the genius that was The Box and all of its mystique, including gold cards. She didn't give them out lightly, and Lily wasn't sure she could get one for Ernie. Lily had given Jeremy and Debbie cards in exchange for them alternating designated driver duties. Now it seemed that Lily would be wrangling one for Ernie.

"We would need to put him on the guest list for tonight, and then I can get him a gold card from the office." Lily was hoping Ernie couldn't tell she was unsure.

Ernie saw an opportunity to get paid for his work and would have been more than happy to accept a gold card to the Box, but, just in case it was one-off, thought he should get as much as he could this time around. He started his bargaining, "Could you add two more to the list? I want to invite a couple of friends. If you can, I'll consider the debt paid."

Lily agreed. She couldn't believe her luck, "Sure what's their names?"

"Linda and Caroline."

"Because it's going to be a group of us, it'll be easier to get everyone in if we all go together. I need to take a nap before we go." Lily walked towards the bedroom with a sense of relief. Little did she know this was the night that would make them family. She fell asleep as soon as her head hit the pillow.

Lily opened her eyes and felt overwhelmed by noise and commotion. There were in their usual spot at the back of Hamburger Mary's posing for a picture. It had become their twice weekly routine. Ernie and Lily were now best friends, and it was a couple's clique. The same couple's clique that would be invited to the Christmas party many years later. Every Thursday and Saturday, they would go to the Box and then out to eat at Hamburger Mary's. They'd fight over who got to keep the polaroid of the night, order too much food, talk too loud, and leave a generous tip. After Hamburger Mary's, they would either head out to the End Up or hit up the garage sales, swap meets, and flea market circuit before deciding whose house to crash at. This week, they decided to skip both and instead go crash at Caroline and Linda's place. Their house was by far the most comfortable place to crash because all the couples could have their own rooms. The group often joked about everyone moving in. A joke Caroline never found funny. She was far too afraid that if she entertained it even a little, Linda would talk her into letting everyone move in. They were always at each other's houses, and everybody had a key to everyone else's house.

When they arrived at the house, Lily ran to unlock the door because she wanted first dibs on the shower and sauna. Lily liked to take a steaming hot shower, sauna, and then bed. Suzie was quick to join her in the shower, and they chatted while washing each other's bodies. This was a ritual of theirs whenever they stayed at Caroline and Linda's house because they had a walk-in shower with panorama water jets so no one was in the cold. They took their time and made sure they were sparkling clean before going into the sauna. Lily leaned back against the wall and let out a long, satisfied sigh.

In the blink of an eye, Lily jumped out of bed and went downstairs. "Why didn't you wake me up?"

Earnie and Jeremy exchanged knowing glances that said *no thank you*. Lily was a bear when she woke up. Suzie walked over to her, "Here's your morning coffee, my love." And leaned in to give her a good morning kiss.

"Eww, no, morning breath." Lily said, talking about her own.

"Let's go brush your teeth and have a proper good morning." Suzie said while playfully grabbing handfuls of Lily's butt.

Earnie and Jeremy called out to them in time, "Make it quick, we don't want to be late. Earnie added "It's already 10 give it a rest, newlyweds." It had only been three months since Lily and Suzie had been married and it showed.

It wasn't legal, but the ceremony, legal or not, still held meaning for them. They had a large photo of themselves in their matching wedding dresses on the beach dancing in the waves above their fireplace. They were both laughing. It had been one of the best days of their lives.

It was a little after noon when they came back downstairs and were met by a very angry Earnie. "We're going to be late. There's no way we're going to finish everything by the time everyone gets here. You know how important this is to Debbie. Who waits until Christmas morning to buy a tree anyway?"

Lily couldn't stop laughing, so Suzie replied and tried to sound sincere, "We're sorry, and you know why we waited. We waited so that we could all decorate the tree together."

Jeremy mouthed the word, "go" while making a shooing hand gesture. A bit louder he said, "Why don't you and Lily go get the tree while Earnie and I finish setting everything up here?'

Earnie and Jeremy had arrived the evening before. Everyone had their own reasons for wanting this Christmas to be special. Earnie was planning on proposing to Jeremy and wanted the decorations to be perfect. Being in charge of the decoration allowed him to create a little nook where he intended to propose. Earnie knew that the reason they hadn't bought the Christmas tree was because he had asked them not to because that would allow him to create the nook and pass it off as one possible place to put the tree.

Suzie was leaning over and kissing Lily just as Lily heard a loud sound that she couldn't quite place. She took a big gulp of air as if she had been holding her beath for some time and tried to focus her eyes. The room was brightly lit, and everyone was standing around her in a semi-circle. Everyone but Suzie. Her blood ran cold because she was able to place that sound. It was the sound of metal hitting metal. She felt sick and knew the answer to her next question. She knew Suzie was gone and wondered... if she just didn't speak. If no one spoke. If no one said it out loud, then maybe it wouldn't be real. As long as she didn't know for certain and was only guessing from the look on their faces and tone of voice as they asked how she was doing, Suzie would be alright.

The moment Lily locked eyes with Suzie's mother, Karen, she felt her heart sink and would do anything not to feel the pain written all over Karen's face. Karen started to speak and before she could get a word out Lily said, "No not yet.," and everyone respected her request.

Just then, the doctor entered the room. Lily imagined that someone must have called for him when she woke up. May be that's where Karen had been. The doctor removed two discs from her temples. He held them up and explained that they were memory buds as Lily wiped away a river of tears.

Lily eyes gazed around the room. It was full of flowers, cards, and balloons. The flowers had begun to wilt, and the balloons were beginning to deflate. "How long have I been here?"

"You came in two weeks ago. The first week, we focused on stabilizing your physical condition and this week we have focused on restoring your memories." The doctor replied.

"Did I have amnesia?' Lily asked.

A tenderness came over the doctor's face and voice as he explained, "No, quite the opposite. You kept reliving the crash and begging us to kill you. You were convinced the accident was your fault."

Lily had no memory of the previous week. She remembered the kiss in the car, the crash, and everything that happened before and began to sob inconsolably as she asked the doctor, "Why? Why would you want me to remember all that I've lost? Suzie was my everything. How am I going to go on without her?"

At any other time, the doctor's response would have felt trite, but to Lily it was profound. She looked out the window in her room that faced the hallway, at everyone standing there with expressions of grief and concern, as the doctor said, "So that you would remember all that you have." The doctor motioned for everyone to come back in

As they all gathered around the bed again Lily sobbed, "What are we going to do without her?"

Suzie's mother was the first to respond, "We're going to love each other as much as she loved everyone in this room."

Every Christmas without fail, they all gathered and began the day with a remembrance of Suzie. As much as they would pretend, Christmas was never truly merry for any them after the loss of Suzie.

-End-

Patient, Marley
By
T. War Powers Tilden

Here was that man again. The doctor. One of them, but he wasn't really his real doctor. *His* doctor was old and pudgy with a shiny head poking through the rest of his hair, and he wore square glasses, and he listened to him with a for real, "How are you feeling today?" *His* doctor always said nice things about how big he was growing or how he would like all his patients to be healthy, strong boys like him. He liked his doctor. He did not like this man. He hated him.

The doctor stood at the foot of the bed and smiled before returning his attention to the clipboard of charts in his hand. He talked to himself while reading them. Then he looked up from the charts, walked around to the side of the bed and placed a kind hand on the patient's forearm.

"How are you feeling today, Mr. Marley? I'm Doctor Emus."

This is what he always said. It was the same every time, as if the patient would not remember him from one visit to the next. And, yet he, Dr. Emus, never once got the patient's name correct, and he wouldn't either because he wouldn't listen. A know-it-all, stupid doctor man! Instead, Dr. Emus would make a sort of empathetic moo-moo face while jotting something on the paper.

He had grown tired, so physically tired and drained, from yelling his name was *not* Mr. Marley. It was like sitting through a boring car ride that was still ongoing even after you went to sleep and woke up. The patient resigned himself to a smoldering quietude toward this man, and all the rest of them, until strength enough returned.

The question went unanswered. Just the effort of thinking up a reply was flummoxing and tiresome.

"Your vitals have normalized since your," Dr. Emus caught himself, "the last…episode. That's extremely good. It means we are back on track." The corners of his mouth curled upward, but the patient absorbed no comfort from the update because there was nothing good about it.

There was nothing good about none of this. If he would just wake up! Back to normal. Out of this bad dream. Back at home with mother and auntie and sister. They were going to pick dad up from the terminal. And dad was bringing back a new piece for their train set because Christopher knew he was a good boy, for sure this time, because he climbed and got Mrs. Dodson's cat down, and then she baked him a whole lemon pound cake as thank-you, and he wouldn't have to explain anything to dad because mother told him all about it over the phone and how it was even in the local evening paper. He wanted to be back at school with his friends and teachers and eating his mother's and auntie's food and playing with his toys in *his* house in *his* room in *his* own....

The patient sunk deeper into the pillows. His head lolled lifelessly to the side like a sandbag slipping off the wall, too powerless against the force of gravity and too battered by the harshness of Nature. The face was worn and heavy, too, like everything, for that matter! Head, face, neck, nose, arms, hands, back, belly, eyes, legs–especially these legs!– so worn and heavy and old and useless. He was in a bed under a pile of coats. He wept angrily. *Why?* That's all he wanted to know: *Why won't this end already?!*

Dr. Emus perceived a new depth of silence in the air and looked up from his clipboard. He was a little surprised at being met by the back of Mr. Marley's head. For one, he thought the patient was looking at him and, for another, because he could see the head was quietly trembling. The doctor felt awkward.

"Mr. Marley, sir, you're crying?"

The head refused to convey one way or the other. Dr. Emus peered over. Neither the streaks of tears running from the man's leaden lids nor the patient's ruddy complexion, he knew, were signs of joy at the improved prognosis. Mr. Marley, ensconced in crisp white linen, striped in faint teal, and surrounded by a flotilla of pillows, looked a sight of comfortably bound hopelessness.

"But Mr. Marley this is good news, sir. Very good news." Dr. Emus injected lightness and expert assurance into his voice. "The alteration of your hypertension medicine unfortunately tends to make us a little… blue" —*There he goes again with that us stuff*, thought Christopher, leagues beneath unyielding torment—"but, Mr. Marley, it was necessary to bring you back on track. *Was*, Mr. Marley. That's behind us now. You are doing very well, sir, so very, very well. There really is no need to cry." Then the doctor's tone became buoyant with genuine glee, relief and awe.

"Ah! I almost forgot: the children's choir is coming to sing this afternoon, after lunch. Would you like to go? You can if you want. The choice is yours. I really think you will like it. It's quite a nice little holiday concert. It is nice to have the children visit us and sing. And afterward there will be cake and tea and punch served!" Dr. Emus spoke slowly, over pronouncing his words. "Do not worry," he added helpfully, "you will be back in time to watch your TV program before bedtime."

A monotone murmur issued from the hospital bed.

"I want…I want to wake up. Want my mommy…."

"Of course, Mr. Marley," Dr Emus promised, half hearing what was said because he was only too glad to hear any response at all. Any sign of non-combative engagement was a good thing. "Yes. There, there," he said conclusively. "You may rest now, or watch TV, but if you fall asleep, not to worry, the nurses will be sure to wake you and check if you'd like to join us when the children come."

The children's choir affected Mr. Marley poorly. His reaction was unforeseen and, in a word, alarming. In another word, frightening.

The choir appeared excited but at ease. When they sang, their tiny heads uplifted to the director like baby birds at feeding. A soft and warm stirring filled the air. Each song was promptly rewarded with warm and encouraging applause, plum with grandparently praise and admiration. It was not until around the third or fourth number, Dr. Emus would later record in his notes, that the episode occurred.

Three soloists moved to the front of the choir to lead. It was then that a kraken awoke within the old man's forlorn indifference, and he became animated, finding new life.

"Jenny!" he called aloud.

Sometimes "Jenny" and sometimes "Christopher," among other utterances, grew quickly and incrementally louder.

Dr. Emus was present. He initially could not tell what stimulated Mr. Marley, nor would he have noticed it had not one of the trio soloists broke ranks and stammered, ambushed by the sound of her name thrown from the audience.

The little girl strove to harmonize against the distraction. She squeezed her eyes closed and soldiered on by rote, but the feat was more than the child could pull off.

A nurse deftly swooped in with hushed assurances and entreaties, but Mr. Marley would not be placated. He'd have been regarded as lucid if he was not already clinically demented.

"It's me, Jenny: Christopher!! Jenny!" was the gist of his lamentable chorus.

He wanted to point, *You there. Yes, you girl I'm calling you,* but Mr. Marley forgot that his arm was stricken by a stroke and as incapable of movement as he was desperate to reach her.

It wasn't too long before several gray and hairless, liver spotted heads suspected something was amiss, that some action was taking place away from the makeshift stage. Staff had to act quickly. They were afraid the erratic display would not only disconcert the visitors, and possibly traumatize the children, but, worse, also 'catch' among the other patients and trigger a rash of senile rants, remembered grievances, and grumpy bitterness. With as much dignity and speed as they could muster, the nursing staff wheeled Mr. Marley out of the salon. He cried fitfully the whole way.

The pair of nurses and volunteer orderlies who had escorted him back to his bed would later agree the inside of the elevator was sad and claustrophobic. It felt, shared one of them, like being locked in a trunk lost overboard.

"Poor man. I think he frightened that girl. All of the children, really, but especially that one he was looking at so...."

"Maybe she reminded him of someone back in the day," suggested the male orderly. "A sister or playmate...." He was still, unconsciously, inhaling big lungfuls of fresh air as he spoke.

"No, not a sister," the other nurse corrected. "There's just the one brother. His brother and sister-in-law, they come visit around twice a month." She glanced sadly at Mr. Marley's closed door. Then she looked to the other doors that ran along the luminously white hallway with its immaculately buffed floor gleaming like ice. "It is such a shame," she added generally. "It's such a shame this condition...," then paused, uncomfortably aware of her emotional vocabulary.

The orderly said it was cruel when you thought about it. How it happens towards the end of life, and you have to lose track of "millions and millions of things and people you knew, including your own self! And to live with it. Why don't it strike when one is still sort of young, y'know what I'm saying? Can forget what little he's learned. Leastwise he can afford to have brand new days each new day, right?" The orderly tended to think along such veins. He was a philosophy student. But the others were not.

The first nurse remarked, "No lost memories to confound and confuse? Outside of an obvious need for survival, y'know like don't turn down that street after dark or eat that plant, then really what is the receipt of life *but* our memories?"

A squeak on the linoleum stole their attention.

"Shhh," whispered the second nurse, who was even less inclined to wax philosophical. "Here comes the doctor."

Dr. Emus recorded in his observation log:

Patient: Marley, Warren. Patient vitals (heart rate, blood pressure, pulse; see chart 1) returned to normal per last recording (3/11/90) following violent episode for which Physician ordered sedative, IM; diet alteration, frequent nurse monitoring (5/20/90); Patient displayed flat affect to progress report; upon closer look, Physician observed Patient in state of quiet distress vis-à-vis crying w/expression of sadness; Physician suggested Patient attend the afternoon's special entertainment (free singing concert by the Horta Pentecostal Church Youth Choir). Roughly 15min into concert, Patient suddenly exhibited agitation, distress. To assist future counseling (i.e., psychologist, family therapy) Physician makes specific reference to the afternoon's incident:

Following first couple of numbers, 3 female adolescents (9-12 yrs) jointly led in song ("Smile on, brother. Smile on, sister"; folk song w/upbeat

tempo & humanist/non-denominational overtones).
Two soloists were dark haired, the third, blond;
all children dressed uniformly in white tops/dark
bottoms (boys, pants; girls, skirts). Patient agitation
gradually increased, displaying apparent fixation with
either of the dark-haired trio. Patient repeatedly,
and directly, called to girl "Jenny!" Hospital staff
promptly, professionally attended Patient as discreetly
as possible in order to preserve decorum of event &
minimize escalation of disruption. Before eventual,
and unavoidable, removal Patient revisited his familiar
identity dissonance: Christopher. Patient shouted,
"Look Jenny! I'm Christopher. It's me, it's me!"
Behavior was insistent, markedly earnest. Behavior
reflected 180 degree reversal from the morning's
melancholy (this Physician recommended Patient
attend the musical event for that very reason). Patient
was more demonstrably animated–more alive, if I
may–by presence of this "Jenny" (note: said name
has never been mentioned previously). Conditions
suggestive of progressing senility. No documented
family history of it nor schizophrenia; no causal
incident of PTSD. However, Physician leaves such
diagnosis to certified mental health professionals.
Physician administered 1cc of—.
Back in his bed, Mr. Marley wept bitter, furious tears
whose acrid saltiness tasted of despair and impotent rage.

Yes, he had a hate figure in Dr. Emus. But it was not only Emus; it was all of them. All of them and everything. It was everything which made it impossible for him to wake up; everything which made God ignore his prayers; everything which made his mother forget to wake him for school. Hadn't he been sleeping for a long, long time already?! Longer than ever, ever before in his life?!? He was trapped in this bed. In this hospital. In this body. In this stupid bad, bad 'Mr. Marley' nightmare.

A nurse looked in on the patient. She asked if he would like to have the television turned on. His head, with thoughts still dazed and wounded from the painful tangibleness of Jenny, weakly moved in a way the nurse took for a nod.

She walked over and took up the remote control, attached to the undercarriage of the bed by a thick crème colored cord, and turned on the television. After a few clicks, she stopped on the evening news show, a safe bet in her mind, and went away with a kind word that he missed but a pitying smile that he did not.

The tail end of *Small Wonder* played on the wall-mounted monitor. It was one canned laughter before the images froze, and the show's theme song ran while the program credits quickly scrolled up. Then the paused image suddenly slid to half of the screen, and an anchorman reminded viewers to stay tuned for the following Five o'clock News coming up next. No sooner had the scrolling fine print reclaimed the entire screen did the news show trumpet in with a montage of local scenery spliced with grinning newscasters. The top story concerned the Pope's farewell from South Korea.

Then Mr. Marley's blood froze.

He saw himself on television grinning vacantly. He was in a hospital bed, under white sheets run over with yellow stripes. On either side of him was his mother and his sister and, between them, on his lap, a shiny new engine with CHRIS painted across it in his favorite color. The accompanying story was about a little boy whose miraculous recovery from possible electrical shock was the "Miracle of the Week" feature. As images of the grateful family beamed, an unseen woman's voice narrated:

"Here is Christopher Kaufman Jr., today, smiling with his new train engine, a gift from his father, Army Sergeant Christopher Kaufman Sr., stationed in the Balkans, amid hugs from his mother, Bobbi, and big sister, Jennifer. Earlier today, Jennifer performed with her church choir for senior citizen patients at St. Luke Hospital-Irvine.

"But two and half months ago, the Kaufmans had little cause for smiling. That is when, in September, five-year old Christopher fell into a month-long coma from mysterious circumstances. His sister found his unresponsive body near a power outlet. Doctors said, however, the boy showed no physical evidence of electrocution. While the younger Kaufman sometimes exhibits confusion and difficulty recognizing family and friends, doctors caution it may take several months, or years, before Christopher's central neurological system functions in a healthy, unimpaired state. For now, though, Christopher Kaufman, Jr. is one very happy and very, very lucky young boy and our *miracle of th–.*"

Staff on the geriatric ward scrambled towards the crazed and inhuman screaming from Room 243, Patient, Marley.

-End-

I Just Want to Spend Christmas With my Girlfriend
By
A.M. Weald

Maggie glowered at the cartoon yeti on her Christmas sweater.

"We meet again…"

She laid it on the bed, then peered at the open bedroom door, listening. Elin was still downstairs, readying the house for their vacation.

From the closet, Maggie pulled out a black leather pouch. Inside was her folding sword—perfect for travel. The handle and blade each spanned nearly the length of her forearm. She unfolded it and swung at the air, testing the tightness of the hinge. Satisfied, she hastily slid the sword into the pouch, wrapped it with her Christmas sweater, and closed her suitcase.

Eyes closed, Maggie took a deep breath and tried to shed the guilt that weighed on her conscience.

"You done yet?" Elin asked.

Maggie jumped, then smiled at Elin as she entered the bedroom. "Yeah, I think so."

Elin gave Maggie a gentle kiss. "C'mon. I can't wait to meet your folks."

At the midway rest stop, Maggie said, "I'll get the snacks and you get the coffee?"

Elin shot finger guns with an exaggerated wink.

At the coffee stand, a strong breeze brushed Elin's cheeks and tousled her golden-brown curls. A snowflake twinkled down. Another. More. Elin squinted up at clear, bright blue. The other patrons in line didn't seem to notice or care that snowflakes were falling from a cloudless sky.

Coffees in hand, Elin made her way to the car. Ahead, snowflakes swirled into a tiny twister that made its way toward her. A tendril of snowflakes reached out to her as she passed, grazing her neck and tugging her hair.

Then came the whisper. "*Ellliiin…*"

Elin fumbled the coffees and one fell, splatting onto the pavement. She ran the rest of the way to the car and shoved the remaining coffee into the cup holder.

"Um…" Maggie gestured to the singular coffee.

"I… I don't think I should have any."

"Oookay." Maggie started the car.

As Christmas music jingled from the car's satellite radio, Elin said with a laugh, "I think I'm nervous. Was hearing, seeing things at the rest stop."

"Seeing things?"

Elin waved it off. "I'm just nervous."

Maggie smiled. "Don't worry. My parents will love you."

An hour out from Maggie's parents' house, the sky clouded over, and it began to snow.

"That's weird," Elin said, and took off her sunglasses. "It's supposed to be sunny all week."

A chill ran across Maggie.

"It flurried at the rest stop. Was weird. No clouds. And I saw a snow devil."

Maggie shot a surprised look at Elin. "Snow devil!?"

"You know, like a dust devil. But snowflakes."

The blizzard worsened, and the highway's sudden whiteout demanded Maggie's attention. She turned on her fog lights but, failing to see where she was driving, decided to pull over.

"What the hell?" Elin said as she checked her phone. "There's nothing on the radar."

Maggie glimpsed a shadow in front of the car, cloaked in whirling snow. The shadow crept closer. The steering wheel squeaked under Maggie's grip. "Elin," she said, "I need to tell you something—"

"What is that?" Elin sat forward, peering beyond the windshield.

Maggie eyed Elin, confused. "You can see her?"

The shadow, a condensed swirl of snowflakes, grew bigger by the second. "It's the snow devil again."

Maggie frowned and whispered, "That isn't snow."

Elin trembled. Her fingers pressed to her neck, to the place the tendril of snow had touched.

In front of the car, a girl appeared: young, expressionless, silver and luminous, dressed in white furs. The blizzard swarmed around her, obedient.

Maggie let go of Elin's hand, reached under the dashboard, and unsheathed her emergency dagger.

Elin lurched away. "The hell!?"

"Whatever happens," Maggie said, holding Elin's gaze, "don't leave this car. If I don't come back, go to my parents."

"What's going on!?"

"Promise me!"

"Okay!"

Snow swirled into the car when Maggie opened the door. Black tresses of her hair whipped about in the wind, framing her soft, fearful smile. "I love you," she said, and exited the car.

Elin yelled for Maggie and tried to grab her, but the seat belt brought her to an abrupt halt. Maggie slammed the door. Elin unbuckled then watched, heart pounding, as Maggie disappeared into the blizzard.

Her fingernails dug into the dashboard as she leaned forward, watching, waiting.

Two minutes. Five.

Maggie hadn't told Elin how long to wait.

Just as she thought to climb over to the driver's seat, the snow stopped, and the clouds faded. The sky was blue and bright again as if nothing had happened. Other travelers had also pulled over during the squall and were now continuing on their way. Elin scanned the stretch of highway ahead. Maggie was nowhere in sight.

The driver door opened.

Elin screamed.

"Jesus." Maggie put the dagger under the dashboard and caressed Elin's cheek with her icy hand. "Are you alright?"

Elin nodded.

"Okay," Maggie said as she started the car, "let's talk." She pulled back onto the highway. "I'm sorry I waited to tell you. I didn't think I would have to, so soon. It isn't something we just tell someone. But with everything that's happened…"

In a hushed tone, Elin said, "I wasn't just seeing things at the rest stop, was I."

"I… I'm not sure. I thought only people like me and my family… What did you see, just now?"

"A blizzard. And a pale girl." Elin looked at Maggie. "Why was there a girl?"

Maggie tapped on the steering wheel. "It wasn't a girl. Not anymore. She's a spirit. We call her the Snow Maiden. Russians call her Snegurochka." Maggie glanced toward her hidden weapon. "The dagger is silvered iron. Scares away spirits. I ran her off. But she'll be back."

"A spirit," Elin whispered, and watched the roadside trees flick by. "Are there others like her? Other spirits? Other things?"

"Yeah," Maggie answered gently. "There are others."

Elin had fallen silent. The annoyingly perky *Jingle Bell Rock* blared over the radio, and Maggie turned it off. She wanted to reach for Elin's hand but thought better of it.

Another mile stretched by until Elin spoke. "So... what are you, exactly? Some kind of superhero?"

Maggie cracked a small smile. "Kind of. But not like in comics or anything. We're human. Some of us are stronger than others, physically, and others can manipulate the elements. Create blizzards, rain, fire. My mom can heal wounds. I guess you'd call it magic. People like my mom, they've been called witches. Me, I'm not all that powerful, can't use magic or anything, but I can fight. People like me, and my dad, we're hunters." Maggie glanced at Elin. "You know all those times I went to krav maga class?"

"You were really fighting demons in an alley?"

Maggie almost laughed. "I was training. It... just wasn't krav maga. Self-defense classes, mainly, and weapons training. Taught by another hunter."

"How many people like you are there?"

Maggie shrugged. "A few, here and there. We find each other through networking. It isn't easy. Though, easier now with the internet, my parents tell me."

Elin fell silent again, and Maggie considered her words carefully. "I'm sorry I kept this from you. I should've told you about my family, prepared you for this. Our first winter together, I knew this could happen."

"What? *What* is happening?"

Maggie let out a great sigh, and with it, most of her nerves. "Every year, wherever temperatures get to freezing, me and my family and others like us, we have to be prepared. The Snow Maiden is just the harbinger. It means Father Winter is coming."

Elin's face scrunched. "Father Winter. Like… Santa?"

"No." Maggie shifted in her seat. "*Not* like Santa. Some people think they're the same, but they're not. They all just got lumped together in stories over time. Father Winter, Jack Frost, Ded Moroz…. If anyone ever fails to ward him off when he arrives on the winter solstice, that area of the world gets devastated by winter storms. Buildings destroyed. Plants and livestock killed. But beat Father Winter in battle, and he goes away until the next winter solstice. But we can never know where he'll show up again." Maggie peeked at the rear-view mirror. "I guess this year, it's our turn."

"Is he a spirit, too?"

"He's more like a god. Old as winter itself."

"And… these things are hunting you?"

Maggie gave a stiff nod. "Yeah. Kind of. It's like they can sense us. My parents raised me to be ready. For Father Winter and others like him."

"And you're gonna have to fight him."

Maggie nodded again, then asked, "Will you call my parents for me?"

Maggie's mother, Nora, waved Maggie and Elin inside. "I hoped this day would never come for you," Nora said to Maggie as she cradled her face between her palms, "but you've trained for this."

Thom, Maggie's father, took Elin's offered hand between his in not so much a shake as a consolation. "Maggie said you had quite the introduction to our family secret. Come on, we'll have a nice chat about it over coffee."

The hallway sparkled with holiday decor—tinsel, garlands, fairy lights, candy canes. The aroma of mulled wine filled the house.

"Are you trained in combat, Elin?" Thom asked as they entered the kitchen.

"Um." She looked nervously at Maggie. "No."

"There's still time to get some lessons in," Nora said, smiling warmly, her gaze lingering on Elin. "I'm sorry we had to meet under these circumstances. But I'm glad you're here, with us."

After a quick but thorough briefing, Thom opened one of the locked cabinets in his office to unveil an arsenal of modern and medieval weaponry. Elin gasped and took a step away from the double-bladed great-axe, the scimitar, the javelins. Thom set out several weapons on a tall, central table.

"I've used one of those before," Elin said, pointing at a crossbow. "My brother uses one to hunt deer."

"Oh?" Thom placed a case of bolts on the table next to the crossbow. "Then I guess we know what your weapon will be. We better start training—solstice is tomorrow. In the morning we'll head out to the forest to cut down a Christmas tree. We always do that the day of the solstice." Thom stuck his hands in his pockets and chuckled. "If Ol' Jack does come, at least it'll be away from the 'burbs. Somewhere he'll do less damage."

"You've fought him before?" Elin asked.

"Nora has. And she's got a gnarly scar on her back as a souvenir."

Nora rolled her eyes at her husband.

Elin frowned, and turned her gaze back to the weapons.

"You don't have to do this," Maggie said to Elin. "You don't have to fight."

A warmth washed over Elin as fear, anger, and love rose within her in equal measure. She approached the table and picked up the crossbow, learned the weight of it. "Yeah," she said. Turning to Maggie, she added, "I do."

"Are you mad?" Maggie asked Elin after they tucked into bed. "I'd understand if you're pissed."

Elin pressed her lips together. "Honestly? I'm just scared that you have to fight these things if they come for you, and there's really nothing I can do to help. I'm okay with the crossbow, but..."

"You're good with the crossbow."

"With stationary targets."

Maggie pulled Elin close. "I feel better knowing you'll be with us. Maybe it's just peace of mind, but... You make me feel safe."

Elin buried her face in Maggie's curls. "I feel safe with you, too."

Nora led the way through the forest while Thom hummed a pleasant tune. It was chilly, and the snow was knee deep. Elin was thankful for her tall boots.

She carried the crossbow on her back via a thick strap that crossed her chest. The large, bladed weapons were illegal, Thom had explained, but a hunting crossbow no one would question. Their other weapons, silvered iron daggers, were concealed.

As Thom searched for the perfect tree, Elin glimpsed the tail end of what she assumed was a deer.

"Not many dryads this year," Nora remarked.

"Nope," Thom agreed.

Elin looked to Maggie and mouthed, "Dryad?"

Maggie grinned and said, "Tree spirits. Last thing you want is to take home a tree with a sleeping nymph in it. Dad sings the song, they wake up and leave the tree."

Something darted across their path. Elin halted and clung to Maggie. Thom and Nora stopped too, but then chuckled and carried on.

Maggie turned to Elin. "You saw her?"

"Here we are!" Thom called, hands hovering in front of a fir tree not quite six feet tall. He hummed his tune, and the delicate crunch of galloping footsteps on snow faded into the distance.

On the way back to the SUV, Thom dragging the felled tree behind him, it began to snow. A cloudless snow.

The hairs on the back of Elin's neck stood when Nora said, "They're coming."

Flurries multiplied rapidly, and a strong wind gusted between the trees. Icy needles stung Elin's face as everyone raced back to the SUV.

Thom popped the trunk and pulled out a warhammer. Nora chose a longsword. Maggie retrieved her folding sword then pulled a dagger from her boot.

A wisp of snow lashed at Thom's cheek. He cried out but shook it off and slammed the trunk closed. An angry red gash, frostbitten at the center, marred his face. To the wind he shouted, "Come on out, kiddo! And bring that old bastard with you!"

The wind carried delighted giggles, and a swirl of snow condensed and took form as the Snow Maiden, silver and glowing. Clouds covered the sky, and the blizzard grew violent.

Across the field, deep thuds sounded every few seconds. Louder, louder, like thunder from the ground. Maggie raised her folding sword to the Snow Maiden, and Elin turned toward Thom and Nora.

The thuds crescendoed, and through the blizzard's veil emerged a growling giant with white fur, curled horns, and massive claws. As the yeti-like beast neared Thom and Nora, it roared, sending a blast of ice toward Elin, stinging her cheeks.

The Snow Maiden giggled, and in a lilting voice teased, "Grandpapa's here."

With new ferocity, the girl flung icicles at Maggie and Elin. They ducked, but one sank into Elin's shoulder, and she yelped. Maggie lunged at the Snow Maiden, who giggled again and dissipated into a burst of snow. The icicle embedded in Elin melted, leaving a small, frostbitten wound and a hole in her jacket.

The Snow Maiden reappeared a short distance away, and Maggie ran after her. In the other direction, Father Winter took a swing at Nora and Thom. They dodged the attack and each took a swing at his legs. The beast roared again and lashed with his claws.

Elin waited for a clear shot, aimed, then watched crestfallen as the crossbow bolt shot into the deep snow. She cursed, then reloaded. The second shot went wide.

Maggie and the Snow Maiden fought behind Elin as she took aim again. As she pulled the trigger, the weapon encrusted with ice, jamming, and the mechanism snapped.

"Goddammit!" Elin hollered as she threw the crossbow to the ground.

Thom and Nora ran further away.

"I just…"

Father Winter stomped after them.

"…want…"

The beast roared, and the air shook.

"…to spend…"

The Snow Maiden giggled.

"…Christmas…"

Elin turned to the Snow Maiden.

"…with…"

Her fingertips tingled.

"…my…"

Flames ignited in her palms.

"…girlfriend!"

The Snow Maiden's eyes widened in shock as two fireballs shot out from Elin's hands, whizzing past Maggie and hitting the Snow Maiden in the chest. The girl's scream was cut short when she poofed into a cloud of steam that rose to the sky.

Elin stared at her hands, then caught surprised looks from Maggie and her parents.

Father Winter swatted Thom. The force sent him flying, and his body slammed into the side of the SUV. Nora screamed, and Maggie charged.

Elin's hands were hot. She again looked at her unburnt gloves, then removed one to find her hand to be completely fine.

Maggie's shout pulled Elin's attention back to the fight. Father Winter had conjured a spear of ice. As he drew back, aiming at Elin, Maggie leapt into the air with her sword, slicing open the beast's neck. Father Winter did not bleed but exploded, sending a blast of ice shards everywhere, nicking clothing and flesh.

The blizzard cleared. A bird chirped. The snowy field glowed beneath the sun, highlighting small patches of bright human blood.

Nora ran to Thom, pressed her hand to his chest, and sent out a golden healing glow.

"I'm fine, darling," he insisted, though his grimace said otherwise.

Maggie ran to Elin and grasped one of her hands. She examined it as Elin had, then squeezed it tight. "Are you injured?" Maggie asked.

Elin nodded to her shoulder, then looked at her hands again. "What happened? Did I… make fire?"

"I don't know." Maggie pulled Elin close. "We'll figure it out."

Nora checked Maggie and Elin for injuries and healed Elin's small icicle wound. She then took Elin in for a long, tight embrace. "I knew it," she whispered. "I sensed it the moment we met." Nora pulled back, gently grasping Elin's shoulders. "Welcome to the family."

Elin never knew her birth parents. Closed adoption when she was a newborn, no contact. Her birth parents could be anywhere, or nowhere. Perhaps they'd been young. Perhaps they'd been terrified. Were they hunters, too? Had they faced demons and spirits and monsters and ghosts? Certainly at least one of them could manipulate the elements like Elin had. Like Nora. This trait was inherited.

Elin had seen the Snow Maiden. Seen the dryads. Maggie should have realized Elin was one of them before the fight. She wished she'd known sooner. Months ago. She wouldn't have had to keep her real identity a secret.

Maggie thought about this instead of sleeping, as she watched her girlfriend sleep. Elin had been exhausted and it was no wonder: she had *created fire*. Fire! As if the universe decided there was an imbalance between elemental hunters and malevolent winter spirits. Maggie didn't personally know anyone who could create and manipulate fire. Only energy (her mother), wind, and ice. Manipulating ice was useful when fighting Father Winter—shattering their ice spears or turning the frozen weapons against the spirits. But fire...

Maggie leaned in close to the sleeping Elin, lightly brushed her nose against Elin's forehead. "I love you," she whispered, "my fire goddess. Sleep well."

Late on Christmas Eve, sat by the fire, Maggie presented Elin with a leather case. Elin opened it to find a folding sword similar to Maggie's. She carefully unfolded the blade from its wooden handle then looked at Maggie, uncertain.

"Dad and I are gonna train you to use it," Maggie said. "If you want to, that is. And Mom can help you with your magic. And, here..." Maggie pulled from the case a small stack of pamphlets. "These were written by people like us, including my parents and grandparents. Guidebooks on how to use magic. How to fight."

Elin bit her lower lip. "You think he'd come back here? Not go somewhere else?"

"He's vengeful." Maggie took Elin's hand and traced the lines of her palm with a fingertip. "And if he returns, we'll be ready."

Elin's worry faded, blooming into ardent determination. She wrapped her hands around Maggie's and nodded. "We'll be ready."

On Christmas morning, Elin unwrapped her gift from Thom and Nora: an ugly Christmas sweater, bright greens and reds and shiny gold, and a cartoon snowman winking, unafraid of the snowflakes surrounding him.

-End-

A Taste For Reindeer
By
Chad Musick

And the shoes, I had told Bigman five days ago, when he'd agreed to the shirt, the jacket, the hat, the belt, the pants. *It doesn't look right without the shoes.*

He'd clicked on the shoes and snorted. "Too much money."

How am I going to be an elf without elf shoes?

"You're making me regret the offer," he'd said. "You're being greedy."

What if it snows tomorrow? I'd looked at him out of the corner of my eye. He had promised it wouldn't. In my whole life, it had never been a snowy Christmas or even a snowy December, but if he wasn't going to cooperate, I could change that. Bigman needed reminding sometimes that I am the one who decides.

Just because someone is bigger doesn't mean they should be the one in charge.

I had reached for the mouse when he hesitated. His fault that he rushed to click but too late and got a little cut on the back of his hand. It had stopped bleeding after a few minutes.

And now the cut is healed, and the packages have arrived, and everything in the world is about to be right, maybe for the first time.

Bigman drops my presents onto the table in the main room and carries his own treasures up the stairs.

Up the stairs I go, to the top of the tower where I live. The windows look out on the ocean. On days the wind blows, it rattles them, but today is bright and sunny. Up North, they are in the middle of blizzards, too cold now for apple picking and too windy for sleigh rides.

At least, Bigman says so. I've watched the Christmas specials already. Only a few of them are still coming.

The boxes are hard to open. My hands are too small and my claws too dull. They should be sharp like razor blades, the way they are when I dream, but they are dull and stubby things.

I bring a knife from the kitchen. *Don't see me,* I tell Bigman as I pass his room, where he is deeply interested in the contents of his glass. The spirits of the season. Bigman doesn't see me.

The knife makes short work of the packaging, and I am skilled enough that I did not damage the clothing. Practice has helped.

Because Bigman had to go to the post office this morning, we didn't go fishing, and so I am dressed still in my pajamas.

I shed them like a snake shedding an old skin. The new clothes are a little too big at the ends, but the knife makes short work of the extra as easily as it did the packaging.

The shoes are perfect, curling back on themselves just a little. They jingle when I test them.

In the mirror, I see the elf I had hoped I would be. Others should see it, too. Some will see a child. Others will look and see that I am a creature of legend.

It's hard to remember whether I'm young or old. How long is a thousand years to an immortal? Are they still young?

This year, I will have my vengeance. Bigman doesn't know it yet, but he will be the tool of destruction for my enemy. Or he will be my enemy, maybe, but that would cause other problems.

Don't hear me, I tell the tower as I clamber down the stairs to Bigman's library. The bells on my shoes and my clothes still themselves in fear. Bigman doesn't hear me.

Like a red and green and black panther, I crouch behind the chair where he sits playing a game. He is shouting into his headset again.

I am death and fury! I leap and cling to the back of his chair, and he is startled by my sudden appearance. The chair tips back onto me when he stands.

"Why do you do that!"

He shouts it at me, not even caring that I'm probably bleeding and his chair has probably crushed my spine. *Help. Ouch.*

Bigman picks up his chair, but only to set it down and go back to playing. "Let me get safe before you throw a fit."

I can be patient, even as I lay here dying. I pat myself and can't find any wet places. Maybe I'm not bleeding after all. But if I were covered in blood, the red parts of my costume would disguise it. As I wanted.

When Bigman is ready to pay attention, I make my demands. *Take me to Fatman and his hounds.*

"You want to go see Santa and the reindeer?" He laughs a little. If I had brought the knife from upstairs or if my claws were better, I could open his guts and see if he still mocked me.

Instead, I nod. *Yes, please.*

"Will you behave? Nothing like last year?"

I'll behave.

But curse him for mentioning last year.

It takes him at least twenty years to put on his outside clothes, even though he has already gone once.

Are you safe to drive? He smells a bit from his drink, and it would ruin things if we crashed. *I can drive us instead.*

"You can't even reach the pedals," he says, and snatches the keys from my hand.

The shows on tv say that he shouldn't drive at all because of his drinking, but I can use my magic to keep us safe. It's beneath my dignity to use it in that way. It should be used to bring storms, sink ships, set the neighboring fortresses on fire with my lightning. But this is important.

We leave the tower, ignore the mess that is the trees dying in our yard. Bigman opens the truck's door for me even though I could do it myself if he didn't forbid me climbing onto the roof and leaning down from there. I spring into the cab and buckle myself in. He slams the door.

The day is brutally hot. Even for summer, this would be too hot. With my elvish garb, I am already sweating. *Cool me off,* I tell the weather, and start to feel better as a little wind finds its way through the window of the moving truck.

The day is searingly bright, but I have my goggles on, and the world is darker and bluer than it would be without them. I can feel my skin burning as the window focuses the sunlight onto it. If I were scaled like a lizard, like I ought to be, this would not burn.

Bigman has a blanket behind the seat, and though he squawks a little when I unbuckle myself and fetch it, I feel better almost immediately.

"Quit squirming," he chides me. Too late. I am done squirming and say nothing. We drive on the outskirts of town until we arrive at the lot.

"Stay. Don't move." He hops out of the truck and heads toward the big sign that says, "Christmas Trees & Reindeer Rides."

My door is too heavy to open, maybe he has it locked, but I am small enough and clever enough to fit through the window at the back of the cab. The bed of the truck is empty but dirty, evidence of the last time Bigman he tried to fix whatever is killing the trees by bringing in fresh soil.

I leap to the ground like a superhero except quietly.

Don't see me, I tell the people around me. Bigman had been ignoring me, but now he doesn't know where I am. He doesn't see me as I sneak up to listen to what he is saying.

Money changes hands, and I can hear Bigman wince even if nobody else can. He never likes for money to go out, only to come in. Unless it's something he wants. He shades his eyes and looks back toward the truck, not seeing me even though I'm standing just behind him, invisible in my red and green outfit with my jangly shoes. Before he stomps back to the truck, I let him see me.

"Follow me," he grunts at me, but we both follow Fatman. He is not the same one as last year. I know from my movies and tv shows that he is probably not the Real Fatman but just an imitator set up here to make money. But there's a chance, even so. I could figure it out from his smell if the stink of reindeer were not so strong here.

Around us, Christmas trees are stuck in holders to spread their branches in hopes people will buy them, and more Christmas trees are already bound up. The most expensive trees have signs above them declaring that they are $200. Bigman will never pay that much. Not for yet another tree that will just die. He still hopes some of the trees on our grounds will make it. They are just as doomed as these trees.

The stink of poop and wet fur is getting stronger, and though the reindeer are cowering in fear, knowing a monster comes: they nicker loud enough they could be found in the dark. None has a glowing red nose.

Fatman stops us in front of a horrifying sleigh. Instead of skis, it has wheels, and the sides are cheaper felt than my costume. Before I can object, Fatman has seized me and thrown me roughly onto the seat.

He will pay for that. He will wake up with me inches from plucking out his eyeballs with my claws, biting off his nose with my fangs. Later, though. The seat is more comfortable than I had expected, and I grant him mercy.

"Stay in your seat," Bigman tells me. He points a dirty finger at me and climbs into the sleigh and sits next to me. When Fatman sits, I can still see out the front, but Bigman's view must be blocked. His own fault for not thinking in advance. The reindeer move slowly but steadily, taking us on a route they already know well through the trees that mark the edge of the lot and through a field of dry grass.

"That's a cute costume," Fatman says to me. Fake Fatman. That's clear now. The real one would explode me for pretending to be one of his elves. People think he's nice, but he's not at all nice. For at least two years, but maybe two hundred, I have gotten lumps of coal from him even though I have been good. It's not like anyone has died.

The red will hide the blood of my enemies, and the green will tell the trees I am their savior. I glare at him, and if it weren't for my goggles my gaze would probably set him on fire or turn him to stone.

"Knot says thank you," Bigman lies.

You know that's not what I said, I tell him.

"Can't you just ever be nice or at least normal?" He whispers it to me, but I know it's loud enough that Fatman can hear it.

No!

Faster than Bigman can move, I spring up from the comfortable seat, throw myself over the ridge of the seat separating my bench from the front. Both adults reach for me, but this is just the distraction that I wanted. I am aloft and screaming my victory before they have finished objecting.

The bells on my shoes alert the reindeer to the death swooping down on them from above. I forgot to make them quiet, but my magic probably wouldn't have worked on them anyway. Animals can be tricky about being told what to do. Reindeer are probably smarter than fish. Fish don't object.

Reindeer do, and the one I have landed on starts trying to throw me off. If my claws were sharp the way they should be, I could slit its throat and let the trickle of blood slow it down. As it is, I am stuck hanging onto the harness and hoping not to be trampled. My shoes are too curled at the ends to help me get untumbled, but my arms are strong, and I will not fall.

I could use my magic to save myself, of course. But the way the reindeer are snorting and bucking and being way too wild is distracting. Bigman is supposed to be a magician. He could use his own magic here and maybe earn a reward from me. I hear him crying out in terror, though. Something about the way the reindeer are screaming makes it sound like laughter, but I know the impossible has not happened today.

The reindeer are calm enough now that I let myself down gently. *Don't see me,* I tell the people who have gathered to watch me, but they are too far away to hear me and keep staring. Bigman and Fatman are both moving toward me now, and I have only moments before I lose my chance at vengeance.

Opening my mouth as wide as it goes, I sink my fangs into the nearest reindeer. The taste is gross and furry. Fish are just the right texture. They taste best fried in oil, but the taste when they're still squirming is delicious. I bite down harder. When I am through the fur, the good taste will reward my persistence.

Donner, it can be no other, tries to kick me for no reason, and I am forced to open my fearsome jaws. I dodge feeble kicks while trying to wipe the fur from my mouth. There's no visible blood yet, but Donner is probably feeling his life slip away now. That's why he's calming down now. He awaits the inevitable, and I prepare myself to launch again. I will bring down the mighty beast and show everyone I am a dangerous predator.

When I leap, something yanks me back. Bigman has grabbed the wide belt I had begged for, and he is holding me captive. He grunts as I struggle.

"Stop fighting," he hisses. His tone is the kind he uses when he is going to cheat. Maybe the drink has made him lose his temper at Fatman, and now he's taking it out on me.

We can go after we pick a tree, I tell him.

"We're not getting a tree now. We're just leaving." He gives Fatman even more money and drags me all the way back to the truck. I will not give him the dignity of walking. He has made a grave mistake, and we will settle this score later, when none can interfere.

"Have something to wash out your mouth," Bigman tells me when we are back at the truck. He hands me a bottle of water, and I drink some of it and use the rest to wash my mouth. It tastes terrible, but that's probably the reindeer blood. My goggles have made it invisible, but I know it's still there, polluting the water I spit onto the ground.

The warmth of the day and the low growl of the engine and the energy I expended making my magic work on the reindeer has tired me out, and I am feeling so sleepy.

I wake and find myself in my bed. Bigman is not to be seen, and I still feel more tired than usual. The sun has not even set, and already I feel ready to sleep for the night.

Christmas Eve, and we have no tree because Bigman is selfish. We should have bought one while we were at the lot. It was rude of him to leave so abruptly.

When I wake up again, it is the deep of night. A stranger has invaded our tower. I know Bigman's nighttime noises, the way he wanders when the drink has made him relaxed but before it has set him to snoring.

My stomach growls at me. Maybe I should go fishing. Bigman doesn't like to go in the dark, but the night has always been a friend. It would be easier if there is something in the fridge, though.

Don't see me, don't hear me, I say to whoever is skulking downstairs. For extra safety, I take off my belled shoes and go barefooted. Down the stairs, past Bigman's bedroom, past his library, and finally down to where he holds court with those who come seeking his services.

The light from the fireplace is harsh and wrong. The most wrong thing about it is that we don't have a fireplace. Unless it is a dragon, there is only one who could bring fire to our tower. I am the only dragon here, so it must be him.

Fatman, I call to him. He doesn't hear me because I have

made myself invisible. *It's okay to see me and hear me now*, I tell the world, and try again.

Fatman! You are a fool to invade our tower.

Finally, he acknowledges me.

"Merry Christmas, Knot." He chuckles and his belly shakes like a bowl full of jelly. "Come sit next to me."

Only to get closer, beneath his guard, I sit on the couch. Close enough for him to grab me, yes, but also close enough that I will be able to kill him when the time comes. Curse my useless claws. I should have brought my knife.

The fire is gone, but nothing has burned. His magic is powerful indeed to trick me into seeing a fireplace.

"Have you been a good," he starts, and I wait for him to make the mistake of calling me a boy or a girl, but he pauses only a moment before finding the right word. "...dragon?"

I sigh. Much as he deserves a swift and ugly end, he is one of the few who will admit what I am. Who I am.

I don't think so, I say quietly. *I have been an awful dragon.* I have learned enough from Bigman to apologize if it will benefit me later. *I'm sorry for trying to eat your reindeer.*

"Oh, that one wasn't mine," he says and smiles. There is blood on his teeth. "We used to be friends, you know."

When were we friends?

"Centuries ago. When you were bigger and older and remembered things properly. Now, tell your old friend what you want for Christmas."

Claws, I tell him.

"Soon," he assures me. "Want some of this meat?" He points to a plate with a pile of meat in front of him.

I take a piece and slurp it down, and then another and a third. *You aren't mad about the reindeer?*

"The elves have to eat something. You think we live on cookies and milk?"

He stays until I'm full and happy and have fallen asleep. I wake to a lump of coal in my stocking. I will put it with the others, knowing there will be a year we have a glorious feast and a fire roaring from my stockpile of sooty gifts.

-End-

Smuggler's Blues
By
Cynthia McDonald

Draxil paced the width of the icy cave, his heavy boots kicking up snow near the entrance. Jade had told him she would meet him here before sunrise with a bounty that would make them both a fortune, but the first rays of the sun were already streaking across the sky behind the mountains.

The sound of gravel tumbling down the narrow path leading to the cave brought Draxil to high alert. He peered around the edge, trying to see in the dim light. A figure could be seen struggling up the path, working to drag a large sack behind them. Heavy exhalations floated up on visible fog in the cold morning air. As the person approached, Draxil recognized Jade's slim figure and long blonde braids swinging from the deep hood.

He scrambled down the path, reaching to take hold of the bag.

"Let me help," he said gruffly. "You've done all the work so far."

"Gladly," she panted. "Careful, it's heavy."

Draxil expected to lift the sack. He was a big man, broad across the shoulders with plentiful muscles. However, the bag was much heavier than expected, and he found himself jerked back down.

Jade chuckled at his discomfiture. "Just drag it. You'll hurt yourself if you try to pick it up. It's heavier than it looks." She angled around him, making her way to the cave. Draxil wondered what could possibly be inside the sack that was so valuable. He'd been expecting gemstones or something similar. Shrugging, he dragged the bag the rest of the way to the cave.

Once inside, he set the bounty off to one side. Jade had removed her heavy coat and shirt and was rinsing herself off with the water from her canteen. Draxil tried to turn his eyes politely away from her exposure. They were partners on this venture, nothing more, and he was surprised by her brazen behavior.

"Damn, it's cold," Jade said, shivering as she reached for her shirt to dry herself off. "Wish we could light a fire, but we can't risk being found up here with that." She waved a hand at the bag as she pulled another shirt from her pack.

Draxil relaxed as she put the new shirt and her coat on. He had never worked with a woman before, but Jade had a reputation as a successful smuggler and was quite dangerous with the short sword that hung from her belt. Draxil needed the money from this venture; his wife was about to give birth to their third child, and things were getting tight. Lida wanted him to work an honest trade, but he couldn't live as a laborer or a farmer. Backbreaking work to barely scrape by? He couldn't handle it. Giving up the thrill of smuggling and the boon of a big score was never going to happen.

Jade walked over to the sack and rolled the coarse burlap down. Thick padding surrounded the object it contained. As she pulled the padding apart, Draxil's eyes widened.

"What is that?" he exclaimed.

"Keep your voice down!" Jade said harshly over her shoulder. "This is a hideout, right? We're trying to *hide.*" She turned back to her task of peeling off the protective padding.

The object revealed was oval shaped, dark green with bronze splotched across the thick, scabrous surface. It stood about two feet tall. Draxil walked over and stroked the egg with one hand.

"What is it?" he asked. "And how is it going to make us money?"

Jade looked up at him, still crouched. "It's a dragon egg."

Draxil scoffed. "There aren't any more dragons. You seriously dragged me all the way out here for a joke?" He was getting angry. This waste of time was going to cost him. Maybe Jade hadn't been worth the risk. Draxil was well-known and could choose any smuggler for a partner, but Jade had promised a big score. This was starting to look like a scam.

"I'm not kidding, Draxil." Jade's green eyes were deadly serious. "This commission will make us both rich for the rest of our lives. I know you need the money."

"Where would you find a dragon egg after all this time?" Everyone knew the last dragon had been hunted down years ago.

"You can't always believe the stories. Where we are, this is just the edge of an extensive mountain range. It's inaccessible to humans, but dragons like it just fine. People believe just because they don't see dragons, they don't exist anymore. Well, dragons aren't stupid, Draxil. When people figured out how to kill dragons, dragons moved away from people."

Draxil rubbed a hand across the curly black hair that coated his jaw. It made sense, in a way. No one went into the mountains; they were cold, snow-covered, and difficult to traverse. The few people who had tried had never returned.

"Who wants a dragon egg that will pay so much money for it?" he asked Jade.

"Someone rich who wants to remain anonymous," she replied. "That's all you need to know. I need you to help me get the egg close. I deliver it, and after I get paid, I'll split it with you."

Draxil grinned widely, exposing his teeth. "Nice try, Jade. I'll be coming to the payout with you. I learned a long time ago not to trust anyone."

Jade thought for a minute. "That's going to be difficult. The buyer trusts me to bring the egg, but he's not going to like anyone else showing up." She rose to her feet, tapping a finger against her lips. "Fine. I leave the egg with you and go let him know we have it. He'll come with me to get it and pay us and take it back it himself."

"Great," Draxil said. "We have a deal. Now how do we get this heavy egg to him?"

Jade crossed the cave to his sleeping furs. "I need to sleep first, and we need to stay here until dark. Dragons are active during the day, but they can't see well at night. This one's mother will be looking for it. I'm exhausted from dragging that thing all night. It's really cold in here. Come lay with me so we can share body heat and get some rest."

Draxil shifted his feet uncomfortably. He hadn't anticipated this kind of closeness with Jade. She was supposed to be just another smuggler, another partner to work with and make some money.

Sitting on the furs, Jade sighed as she took off her boots. She looked up at Draxil and rolled her eyes.

"Look, Muscles, I just want to stay warm while I sleep. I don't want *that*, even if you are good-looking with those big brown eyes. Get over here, take off your boots, and get under the covers."

Feeling reassured, Draxil sat down to remove his boots. He clambered over Jade, accidentally kneeing her in the thigh in the process.

"Ouch, you clumsy oaf! Just lie down." Jade huffed as she rearranged herself under the furs and waited for him to lie down behind her. Draxil pulled the fur over himself and lay as close as he could without touching her body.

"Wow, you're a prude," she said. "Guess this'll have to do. At least we'll share *some* heat this way." Then she closed her eyes and fell immediately asleep. Draxil waited a few minutes, and then clamped his own eyes shut and tried to do the same. After a long night of waiting in the cold cave, it wasn't long before exhaustion and warmth overwhelmed him, and he slept.

Hours later, Draxil awoke. In her sleep, Jade had scooted back and was pressed tightly against him from chest to calf. Draxil had inadvertently draped an arm over her in his own unconscious state. It was comfortably warm under the furs, and he found himself unmotivated to get up yet.

Jade moved in her sleep, putting a loosely curled fist under her chin. She looked softer when she wasn't awake, the lines in her face relaxed. Draxil thought she was almost pretty.

Her eyes opened.

As soon as Jade woke up, Draxil leapt to his feet, not caring about the chill in the air. Grabbing his boots, he ran across the cave and sat down to put them on.

"Let's get the hell out of here," he said, tying the laces.

"Gotta eat first," Jade said. She pulled travel rations out of her backpack. "I'm assuming you have your own?" she asked, gesturing toward him with the roll of preserved meat in one hand.

"Yes." He grabbed his own pack and pulled out food, eating without looking at her. He was impatient for this job to be over. If it weren't for the promise of so much money, he would have left yesterday.

After they had eaten, Draxil rolled and tied his furs into a bundle at the top of his pack. He and Jade fashioned a sling out of the bag she had carried the egg in, cushioning it in the padding. They each grabbed an end of the sling and hoisted it, heading down the path.

Draxil was thankful for the faint light of the moons. Both were crescent, so there was not a lot of light to see by, but at least it was something. He wasn't thrilled at the thought of making this entire trip at night. Typically, during a smuggling operation, he and his partners would stop along the journey at an inn to enjoy a hot meal and comfortable bed. This time, they would have to avoid people, sleeping rough *and* during the day, making things complicated and uncomfortable, especially in the cold of winter.

The path down from the cave was difficult. It was narrow, covered in gravel and ice that was hazardous underfoot, and hard to follow in the dark. Twice they nearly wandered right off the edge and over a precipice that would have plunged them hundreds of feet to their deaths. Only Jade's previous experience saved them.

Even working together, the egg made a heavy load. By the time they reached the bottom of the mountain, they were exhausted. It had taken most of the night, and they would not have much time to find a place to bed down. Fortunately, Jade already had a place in mind, since she had planned their course.

After several nights of traveling, Draxil was already sick of dragon eggs, sleeping during the day, snow, and Jade. He wished he had never heard of her. She complained every morning when he refused to sleep next to her to share body heat. On the sixth day while carrying the egg, they had both worked so hard they sweated through their clothes. When they stopped at first light, the chill overcame them. They were both shivering violently.

"Come *on*, Draxil. We can't keep going like this. Neither of us is sleeping worth a damn, it's so cold. We can't light a fire, someone will find us. Just one warm day to sleep. Please." Jade stared earnestly into Draxil's face with her green eyes.

"Fine," he agreed, teeth chattering. He untied the furs, barely managing the knots with fingers stiff from the cold. As he laid them out in the dilapidated house they had found in the woods. They each stripped off their clothing, hanging each piece over broken pieces of furniture in the old house. Hopefully, everything would be dry by the time they woke up. They both dove into the furs, where Jade was already curled up, shivering. As they huddled together, they gradually began to warm up. Their shaking gradually stopped as the heat sank into them both and they were able to relax. Both were soon asleep.

When he awoke, Draxil rolled onto his back, careful not to lift the furs away from their bodies and let cold air in. Their body heat made the furs comfortable and warm, and he'd slept like a rock. It was still light outside, so there was no rush to get up yet.

It took another hour for Jade to roll over and open her eyes.

She smiled and looked at him, "All right, time to tuck back into those cold clothes."

Draxil agreed, and they both put on fresh clothes, tucking the dirty ones away. Then they ate a quick meal. Draxil noticed that he was getting low on his supplies, and asked Jade about hers.

"I don't have much left," she said. "Good thing we're getting close. Once we get paid, we can buy whatever we want —food, clothes, and you can do more for that family of yours." She winked at him.

It was getting dark outside, so they packed up and lifted the sling again.

While following Jade through the snowy woods, Draxil heard an odd noise. It sounded like light tapping.

"Do you hear that?" he asked Jade.

"What?"

"That noise. Stop."

They stood still, listening.

"There it is again," he said. The tapping repeated, followed by a loud scrape. Jade turned to look at Draxil.

"Where is it coming from?"

"SShhh…." Draxil shushed her, one hand in the air. He cocked his head. "It's coming from the egg!"

Jade's eyes widened. "That's impossible!"

They lowered the sling, setting the egg carefully on the ground between them.

"Why is it impossible?" Draxil asked. "How long ago was this egg laid?"

"How should I know? I just stole it from a nest when the dragon was gone! I don't know anything about dragons!"

"Then how did you know there were dragons left, or where they lived?" Draxil asked scornfully.

"The buyer. He just told me where they were, and to travel at night."

"Oh for- seriously, Jade!" Draxil was interrupted by a loud cracking sound. He noticed a piece of the egg's shell had broken away from the rest, exposing a thick membrane inside. He crouched down in the snow, seeing movement beneath the cloudy substance.

"Don't touch it!" Jade cried.

"Why not?" he asked. "It's too late now. We're not going to have an egg to deliver."

A bulge appeared in the membrane, pushing but not piercing the thick material. Draxil heard a cry from inside, muffled by the coating. He pulled out his belt knife.

"What are you doing?" Jade exclaimed.

He looked up her. "Helping it. Clearly it can't get through." Then he bent back to his task, slicing through the membrane carefully.

As the layer parted beneath his blade, a tiny black claw poked through. Scaled red toes raked the membrane aside. They curled around the opening in the egg. The egg gave another crack, the shell shattering. A miniature dragon tumbled into Draxil's lap.

The damp creature looked up at him, jaws open in an inquisitive expression. It had enormous dark eyes, black wings crumpled to its back, and a waving red tail. Its wobbly legs couldn't hold it up.

Draxil picked up the baby dragon.

"Look at this, Jade!"

"Draxil." Jade said flatly. "Put it back in the sling and push that eggshell into the dirt."

"What?" he looked up at her, dismayed.

"That's our payday you're snuggling with there."

Draxil felt something he couldn't explain. It was the same feeling he had when his own children were born and he just knew he had to protect them.

"We- we can't just give this dragon to that guy. You don't know what he's going to do to it!"

"What the hell, Draxil?" Jade snapped. "This dragon has been in the egg this entire time. We were going to *sell* it to him in the egg, and we're going to sell it to him now that it's out of the egg." She snatched the dragon out of his arms.

He punched her in the face. Jade collapsed, the tiny dragon tumbling to the ground. A piercing shriek drilled through Draxil's head. Then he grabbed the dragon and cradled it to his chest.

"You're okay," he said, inspecting it all over to be sure. He didn't see any injuries. Jade lay on the ground, stunned. She slowly pushed herself to her knees, shaking the snow from her braids.

"I can't believe you did that," she said. "I am taking that dragon to my client. I'm collecting that bounty, and you'll be dead."

Draxil suddenly felt nervous. He knew how good Jade was with her sword, and he relied more on his strength than his stealth. Now he would have to protect himself *and* the dragon.

As Jade got to her feet and drew her sword, Draxil stepped back, cradling the infant dragon in one arm. It cried out again, making both humans wince.

This time, there was an answer. A blistering roar sounded from the distance. Draxil looked up, seeing only the two waxing moons in the sky, Jade leapt at him, swinging her sword. He barely jumped out of the way in time.

"Almost got you," Jade laughed. "And I wasn't even trying. Do you think you can beat me?"

"I think you're going to have a lot more than me to worry about," Draxil replied.

A shadow flitted across the clearing, momentarily blocking out the light of the moon. Jade glanced up and cried out.

"No!"

Draxil, keeping an eye on Jade, looked up quickly to see the enormous dragon circling above them. He felt terror chill his bones. He kept his hold on the baby. If he didn't, Jade would seize it and run away.

Jade was circling around behind him while watching the dragon. Draxil turned, keeping her in front of him. Abruptly the dragon landed in the clearing.

It was a huge beast, the same bloodred color as the baby, with black wings arching over the clearing to block out much of the light. Its head darted toward them, yellow eyes glaring. Its nostrils flared as it took in the scent of the humans.

Draxil held the baby out toward the massive dragon. He was so afraid, he had to fight not to drop it.

"Here's your baby," he said.

The dragon hissed, lowering her head.

Jade screamed as she darted around him, thrusting her sword at the dragon. The tip pierced the dragon's jaw, blood instantly flowing down the blade and covering Jade's arm. The dragon jerked her head up, pulling Jade off the ground until her sword slipped from the dragon's flesh and she dropped back to her feet.

The dragon lashed out with one massive claw, knocking Jade backward almost all the wat to the tree line. As she forced herself to her feet, she started toward the dragon again.

"You stupid dragon, I'll – "

The dragon loosed a jet of fire, burning Jade alive. Her screams of agony filled the air for only a few minutes, but Draxil would never forget that sound or the stink of burning flesh filling the air.

He looked up to see the dragon eyeing him closely. The hot breath steamed from her nostrils and blew his hair back from his face. He had pulled the baby back to himself, trying to protect it from the violence. Now he carefully set it down on the ground and slowly backed away, praying the dragon wouldn't blast him with fire next.

The infant looked back at him, then craned its neck up to look at the enormous dragon in front of it. It mewled. The dragon lowered her head and nosed the baby. Picking her young one up in her mouth, the dragon placed the baby near Jade's still smoking body, then nudged it. The baby crawled onto the body and began to eat.

Draxil shuddered. He looked up at the immense dragon in front of him. It looked at him, blinked, and made a huffing noise. Then it looked back at its baby.

Slowly, Draxil began to trudge through the snow back down the trail the way they had come. He knew no one would ever believe him. He had no money for his time on this job. Hopefully, Lida would forgive him.

Maybe it was time to make an honest living, after all.

-End-

The Heart of Winter
By
Archita Mittra

On the stormiest of nights, three knocks sounded upon the door.

Not loud enough to break it down, so certainly not one of the village men who like to beat up old witches; but the pounding was insistent, each hit louder than the last. Someone desperate, then. The witch put down her knitting and hobbled to the door, wondering if it was a traveler lost in the snow and if he would be sturdy enough to make a good dinner.

But, opening the door, she saw that it was only a girl. A twinge of disappointment passed over her ancient eyes. Then, an icy blast of wind nearly toppled them both over, the girl stumbled into the witch's patchwork apron, and it was then that she realized that the child was weeping profusely.

The witch had cried a lot too when she'd been young;

cried so much that she was sure that all her tears had since dried up and her heart was an ugly desiccated thing, beating by the sheer force of magic alone. Tossing the girl onto a bearskin rug, she went over to the fireplace and sprinkled some herbs over her evening tea until it came to boil. By the time she poured the tea into porcelain cups, the girl had finished weeping and wrapped the bearskin around her like a cloak. It confirmed something about the girl that the witch had suspected the moment she'd set her eyes upon her.

"So, what is wrong, Myra?" asked the witch rather kindly, handing the girl a cup.

The girl didn't seem surprised that the witch knew her name. It pleased the old woman how everyone assumed witches to know things that they had no way of knowing. Myra drank the hot tea without complaint until flushes of color returned to her cheeks. Her eyes were bloodshot - perhaps from crying, or lack of sleep, or hunger, or a mixture of all three.

"I lost my brother in the snow," Myra confessed. The witch's creased face remained impassive, although the image of a young boy floated up and misted her eyes.

"We were running away from home," the girl continued. "Our harvest wasn't good this year. We were starving. Daddy was planning to sell us off…so we fled into the woods. We heard there's a town on the other side of the forest where things are better."

She nodded sadly at Myra, stroking her cheeks and her mop of inky-black hair, and did not tell her that the crops had failed in the other town too.

Myra took another cup and went on, "We didn't know how long we'd been walking. Perhaps a few hours or a day. But we were so tired and hungry. And we were so cold. We could barely see anything through the snow. We found an old tree stump and decided to rest against it for a bit. Kay was so afraid. He kept saying there were monsters after us, that he could spot yellow eyes watching from the shadows."

A wistful expression crossed Myra's face that made the witch think of Josef, her first-born son who she'd buried on a stormy night like this. There was an old ache in her chest. She pushed away that feeling, paying attention to the girl's story.

"But Kay was always like that, a little different, seeing things that we couldn't. Even when we played in the snowfields or near the woods, he had so many imaginary friends with him. Moash, the silver-antlered stag. Peckins, the phoenix. Bumbly, the Great Black Bear. That was his favorite…"

The girl was getting teary-eyed again, so the witch lay a reassuring hand on her shoulder and asked her gently, "Then what happened?"

She knew what had happened of course, but it was important that the girl say it.

"Kay kept saying that the Winter King was near, but I

didn't believe him. I told him to go to sleep, and when I awoke, he was gone. No footprints. I've been wandering since, trying to find a trail when I saw the smoke and lights of your cabin. You're the witch who lives in the woods, aren't you?"

It was always good to have a reputation. "Yes," the witch answered, simply.

"Then you must help me!" cried the girl, tugging on the witch's wrinkled arm. "You must help me find Kay again!"

"Aren't you afraid I might eat you? Isn't that what witches do in the fairytales they tell in the village?"

Myra looked unfazed. "Only some of them, not all. Mama was a witch too. She told us to not believe everything they said about witches. She said I could be a witch too, when I am older. Maybe that is why Daddy didn't like her much."

So, the mother didn't die in childbirth as the witch had assumed. It was the men who finally got to her. The witch nodded sagely.

"Will you help me then?" the girl pleaded, "I will do anything."

Whoever the girl's mother was, she certainly hadn't done a good job in teaching her the rules of magic. Everything has its price, so it is always better to bargain.

The witch relented. "Yes, my dear girl. I shall certainly help you. But for that I need you to be very brave. Can you be that for me?"

It wasn't much of a request. The witch had learned the hard way that children were always braver than adults.

Myra nodded confidently, so the witch laid out the quest: "Your brother has been captured by the Winter King. To free him, you must free the heart of Winter from its crystal casket that lies at the bottom of the frozen lake. You need three things: an enchanted bearskin to brave the icy breath of Winter, a blade from the Summer Court warm enough to carve a hole into the lake, and the tip of a silver antler-head to unlock the casket that conceals Winter's heart. Only then will the King awake, and you can ask him to return what was never his."

"Where will I find these three things?"

The witch smiled. It always pleased her when folks got straight to the point and didn't waste precious time asking silly questions. It was another reason why she preferred children and ached for her lost Josef buried beneath layers of snow. "There is a cave a little way off where dwells the Great Black Bear. You must ask him to lend you his skin for a while."

"What about the antler-head or the blade?"

Myra's impatience reminded the witch of her younger self: how hopeful and reckless she'd once been. But unlike the witch, Myra wouldn't have to do this quest alone.

The witch hobbled to her knitting table. Taking out a map, she said, "The silver antlered stags roam this very forest and must be hunted down. And as for the blade, a trip to the Summer Court might be in order. But one thing at a time, girl! You must go talk to the bear first while I make some arrangements."

She pointed the cave's location on the map. Myra looked forlornly at the bearskin rug on the floor and the bear cubs on the quilt the witch had been knitting and the constellation of Ursa Major that hung as a painting on the wall. The witch pursed her lips. "No child, it isn't going to be that easy."

"What if he eats me?"

Finally, a practical girl who was afraid of being eaten by wild animals and not lonely witches. The witch took out a small dagger from her pocket that glinted in the firelight and began polishing it further.

"Oh," she said offhandedly, shooing the girl who made a move to grab it, "That's just a risk you have to take. Now off you go! I have work to do."

The forest was thick with snow and mist. The witch hadn't provided her with any woolens, and Myra regretted not taking the bearskin rug with her. Perhaps braving the freezing cold was part of a secret test to gauge the depth of her love for her brother.

At length, filled with trepidation, Myra tip-toed into the cave defenseless but determined. The tunnel was lined with torches, with runes scrawled along the walls. Then, at the far end, she saw the Great Black Bear waiting for her, separated by a row of metal rods, and she heaved a sigh of relief.

The Bear growled in disappointment, throwing himself at the cage to no avail.

Myra took a few steps back. "Hello," she said uncertainly, "I need your help."

The Bear fixed his gaze on her. "And I need yours as well."

This felt easier than she'd thought. "Then we have an understanding. I need you to lend me your enchanted bearskin for a while, and afterwards I'll come to free you."

"Oh, I know you won't."

"I promise I will."

"Then give me your heart. I'll keep it safe until you return."

Myra was stumped as she looked around helplessly, noticing a pile of small bones in the corner. The witch hadn't prepared her for this. Taking a deep breath, she edged towards the cage, her hand curling along the rusty metal bars.

"Please, you have to understand. My brother has been taken by the Winter King. I'm doing all this to free him."

The Bear crept closer, until his paws brushed over the girl's cold fingers. Myra felt a wave of warmth rush over her. The Bear looked at her sadly, as if struggling to say something.

"Please," Myra begged. The paw folded snugly over her small palm.

"If you truly love your brother, then give me your heart. I promise I will keep it safe until you return to retrieve it."

"What if I free you and you eat us up?"

"What if your brother dies before that?"

The Bear was being evasive and Myra was running out of time. There was a silver-antlered stag to be hunted and an enchanted blade to be found.

So, she nodded slowly. The Bear reached through the bars and clawed her heart from her chest and dropped it inside a glass jar that she hadn't noticed was lying on the side. It was all over in a minute and there was no pain or if there was, the shock of it was too much for Myra to scream.

Then the Bear stood up, took off his hide and passed it through the bars, and Myra wrapped it around herself before she bled too much. Shuddering, she turned and fled, acutely aware that there was no sound except for the roar of the wind, but she could feel the tick-tock of her beating heart, like a clock on a faraway wall, getting fainter by the second.

Emerging from the tunnel, she was back in the snowy woods, but the cold wasn't so terrifying anymore. She could see better in the dark, run faster and somehow still breathe the icy air. Snowflakes danced off her hair and skin, and she barely felt them.

Myra spied the witch hunched over near the stump of a gnarled oak and something moving in the shadows, and she ran towards it.

The witch heard Myra's footsteps and turned to face her with a satisfied smile.

The girl saw the silver-antlered stag slain behind the witch and gasped. The dark droplets of blood shimmered with a silver sheen.

"You…you killed it?" she asked, incredulous.

"You didn't strike me as quite the hunter, young one. Be grateful that I made your job easier."

Myra looked aghast. Gingerly, she stepped toward the fallen animal. It was quite dead, with sad eyes frozen in fear. The arrow had pierced its side, and a pool of blood congealed around the body.

In a matter-of-fact tone, the witch pressed her dagger in the girl's hands. "Just the tip of the antler," she reminded.

Killing the stag hadn't been a difficult task. After all, the witch had lived in the woods for many years and had to hunt game to survive when hotheaded young men didn't come traipsing her way. She'd also aided a fair share of maidens in their perilous quests because she'd been a young girl herself once, and no one had helped her then.

The witch had done Myra a kindness, but she doubted if the girl would be grateful. She seemed intensely sad about the dead animal, with tears trailing down her cheeks and mixing with the blood, as if her Daddy never slaughtered chickens or goats on their farm.

The witch wanted to laugh and ask her to hurry, but she didn't want to seem too cruel.

The girl clutched the dagger with trembling fingers and slowly cut off a part of the antler. Looking horrified at what she'd just done, she slowly lifted the antler-head to the witch, as though making an offering to a deity.

"No, no" the witch sighed. "Keep it with you. You have to swim to the Lake and get that pretty casket. I'm just helping you along."

Myra blinked, clearly disbelieving her. People always wanted someone else to do their dirty work but were so suspicious of help when it was unexpected or unasked for. But perhaps with good reason, she thought, as Myra got up and brushed off the snow from her new cloak.

"We have to travel to the Summer Court for the blade," she announced.

The witch registered the "we"- the girl was already thinking of them as a team- and shook her head. "You're already holding it."

The girl looked at the dagger in her hands. Runes were carved along the handle, and a blue-silver jewel glimmered at the hilt. She pressed the tip of her finger to the sharp side of the blade and immediately flinched. The faintest tendrils of smoke and heat exuded from the silver edge.

"Oh my god," she exclaimed. "How did you get this? Did…did you go to the Summer Court?"

"I did, a long time ago."

The nobles at the Summer Court had been no less cruel than the Winter King, and the witch remembered it well. She'd pleaded, then lied, then sought the help of an Autumn fairy who cloaked her with an invisibility spell lasting only for an hour of dusk to find a way into that enchanted glade, steal a blade from a drunk courtier, and run back before the guards noticed anything amiss. Later, the members of the Court exacted their revenge by banishing her from Summer entirely. Her cabin in the woods was enfolded in an aura of ice, and she could never step out into the forest except in winter, relying on the wild animals and foolish men to do her bidding.

And yet, for the briefest moment, the witch felt glad for sparing Myra all that pain.

"Will you lead the way to the lake?" asked the girl, her voice full of wonder and admiration.

The witch nodded, but her expression fell. Perhaps she'd been hoping that the girl would ask her why she too sought the blade in the first place. It would've been nice if the girl or someone asked her about Josef and all the sacrifices and mistakes and terrible choices she'd made out of sheer desperation. But Myra was busy looking out for her dreamy-eyed brother, and the witch didn't blame her as they trudged on through the snow.

Perhaps it was better this way.

The witch knew the way to the lake of course. She'd visited it countless times on her own or with someone else. It was where she'd lost Josef and failed to bring him back. She led the way through the woods, following a serpentine path past brambles and enormous tree roots and underneath branches that swayed and rustled in the wind. With the bearskin around her, the girl didn't get tired or as out-of-breath as the old witch.

Finally, when they reached the lake, the girl paused at the bank. "Why are you helping me?"

A shadow passed over the witch's eyes. "Because I was like you once. I had a son, Josef, and the Winter King took him. So, I tried to bring him back in whatever way I could. But alas…I wasn't worthy enough."

With fearful eyes, Myra asked, "Do you think I'm worthy?"

The witch smiled again. "There's only one way to find out, isn't there?"

Myra nodded and cut a hole in the thin ice. The witch watched her dive into the murky depths with a determined look in her eyes. She didn't have much time to wonder if the girl drowned because after a few minutes, Myra swam back up, holding a half-open casket in her wet hands.

The witch eagerly pulled her to the bank. Dropping the dagger, Myra slid out of her bearskin and knelt to properly unlock the casket. The jagged glittering heart of Winter cast a bluish glow all around. Transfixed by the light, Myra did not notice the witch bend down behind her. She held Winter's heart in her hands, calling out to him to return her brother when the witch stabbed her from the back, twisting the blade.

There was only the faintest of gasps from Myra, but whether it was the pain or the shock of betrayal, the witch never got to know for finally the pale silvery shadow of the Winter King stood before them.

"I bring you a sacrifice!" the witch rasped, kicking at Myra, "Give me back what was mine!"

Myra tumbled forward, but the witch was shocked to see the girl try to stand up and speak. Perhaps the wound hadn't been deep enough. "Give me back my brother!" Myra cried through chattering teeth.

The Winter King beheld them both with a bemused expression. "I have not taken your brother," he said to the girl, shoving her aside as he faced the witch. "You finally offer yourself?"

The witch looked momentarily confused before her face crumpled in horror. She'd already said the words, and the Winter King was carrying a bundle in his arms.

"No!" she screamed at the girl. "This must be a trick!"

"Yours is the only heart that beats. Only you-"

"HOW DID YOU DO IT?" the witch screamed after Myra.

Myra slowly pulled out the dagger. "I don't understand. The Great Black Bear…Wait, the Winter King never stole my brother. It was you all along!"

The witch didn't mind the look of vile loathing the girl shot at her. She was used to it from all the years of stealing children. "I did what I had to do to save my own!" she spat.

Myra's expression grew more pained as she put the pieces of the puzzle together. "You lied to me! You took Kay and turned him to a bear! You put him under a spell, so he couldn't reveal himself to me! And then you sent me because without his power or mine, the Winter King would never awake-"

The witch cut her off. "How did you hide your heart you little snake?"

It was Myra's turn to smile. "It was easy. I gave it away to someone to keep it safe, someone I trusted." And with that she shut the casket and threw it into the lake. The Winter King vanished as though he was never there. The bundle dropped from his arms as the ground beneath the witch shattered and thorns erupted, binding her and pulling her down.

Over the years, she'd led astray so many souls, offered up so many sacrifices in the hope of being reunited with her son again. In her last moments, the witch understood her mistake. She hadn't underestimated Myra, but her little brother.

A life for a life. That was the price, and the Winter King never bargained.

"Please," the witch cried, choking up. "Take care…of Josef."

Myra ran and picked up the bundle before the thorns could take it too, and then in the distance she saw the Great Black Bear bounding towards her with a jar in his jaws, and then she saw that it wasn't a bear at all but her little brother, free at last from the witch's spell.

"Kay! I missed you so much!" she said, enfolding him, as the bundle between them gave a cry and a lurch, and Myra's heart skipped a beat.

They peered into the bundle and saw a small child staring at them. Wrapping Josef in her arms, Myra said, "There's a town on the other side of this forest where things might be better. Perhaps there we can build a life together, with a new brother."

Kay gazed upon the child with delight. "A new brother!" he exclaimed, talking gaily about all the games they'd play as the girl and boy slowly made their way through the woods.

The snow fell thickly, leaving no footprints.

-End-

Frigid Lullaby
By
Alexis Hansen

We weren't supposed to cry outside. Papa said the tears could turn to ice and the monsters might hear, so I smothered my sob when I tripped and the snow rushed up to meet my face. It filled my nose and boots, devouring my mitten and crumbling beneath me as I tried to stand, trapping me in its stinging embrace.

Warm arms lifted me into the air and cradled me close. "Papa." My lips trembled as I wrapped my limbs around him. I wanted to disappear into his fur coat, safe and untouchable.

"Hush, Yana," he said, gentle but strained. He was crying.

We weren't supposed to wander off at night when we could get lost or lured away. The mountains were filled with perils, from the predators to the icy lakes and rocky crevices that couldn't be seen until it was too late. Winter was deadlier still, with its freezing temperatures and blinding storms.

Even worse were the nightmarish things that came every year with the frost.

And yet, Papa continued trudging through the unbroken snow. His strong legs carved a path between darkened trees, every step bringing us uphill. His breath grew ragged, but he didn't set me down.

I wanted to go back home. We should be snuggled under the blankets and listening to the whole town sing joyful songs. The music would lift everyone's spirits during the darkest day of the season and serve as a request to the Whitherling to leave this land and take the chill with him. Papa would join in, playing his flute to put me to sleep so I could dream of days when the sun would shine again. We *shouldn't* be out here because we were never supposed to go out on the Winter Solstice.

Why was Papa breaking all of the rules?

"It'll be alright," he whispered into my hair. I believed him.

Eventually, his movements stopped. He held me so tight it hurt, but I didn't care. I just wanted this to be over.

"Please…" his voice broke on the word. "Take me instead."

A rustle sounded, and the cold crept into my heart when I realized someone else was there with us. Was it one of the monsters? Could it be the Bearer of Winter himself, the Whitherling?

I didn't look. Maybe if I didn't look, it would go away. Papa was strong. He would protect me.

"He doesn't want you. He wants her." It didn't sound like a monster. It sounded like a girl.

Papa choked, and I could feel him shaking through the thick coat. "Why?"

"You have requested a great favor," came the reply. "This is his price. If you don't want his gift, then leave."

Papa didn't move.

"Of course, you may take your daughter, but your people will die. Perhaps she, too, will fall to the disease."

He fell to his knees, jostling me. Papa was always strong. He could fight the monster and make it go away. So why wasn't he doing anything?

I lifted my face from his chest and peered out at the monster. A gasp escaped my throat.

She looked older than me, not yet an adult, but her hair was white like an old woman's. Grandmama had hair like that, only hers was thin and frail. The monster was dressed in nothing more than a thin dress that looked as delicate as the frost beneath her bare feet.

She stepped closer. Close enough to see that her eyes shone red.

I shrank back into Papa's coat.

Papa squeezed me. "Why won't he take me instead? Please, I'll do anything!"

There was a pause. Then, "Ten winters. If you do not seek us out for ten winters, she will return, and he will come for you instead."

I heard Papa's sharp intake of breath. A moment passed before he could speak again. "The famine?"

"He will lift the famine, and the winters will be kind to you. The sickness will disperse, and your people will be healthy again." The monster's laughter sounded like music, happy and lighthearted in a place where neither belonged. "Are the lives of hundreds of people worth your precious daughter?"

Papa gazed at me with more fear, love, and sadness than I had ever seen on his face before.

"Ten winters?" he breathed.

"Ten winters," came the affirmation.

He hugged me tight, shoulders shaking with sobs. I clung to him, scared and confused. I didn't understand what was happening. He was supposed to protect me. He wasn't supposed to let go.

But he loosened his grip and pulled away, taking with him the only shred of safety and comfort I had left. I stiffened, trying to hold on tighter.

"Papa," I said, growing more panicked as he stood. "Papa, don't go."

His gloved fingers pried my hands away, but, from the look on his face, he may as well have been tearing his own heart out of his chest.

"Ten winters, my Yana," he repeated numbly, like it was the only thing holding him together. "Then you will come home."

Papa turned away from me and began the long march back to the village. He didn't look back.

"Papa!"

I tried to follow, stumbling through the tracks he left. Despite them, the snow was deep and uneven. My mittenless hand that had been pink from the cold was now turning blue. Papa's legs were so much bigger and stronger than mine. I couldn't catch up.

Tears streamed freely down my face now, and I no longer tried to muffle the sounds, crying out to Papa again and again. He was leaving me. He was leaving me, and the monster was going to get me.

"Papa!"

I didn't want to look behind me. Didn't want to see how close the monster was. I fought to get across the frozen ground. All I had to do was follow the tracks, and I would eventually get home. We'd walked a long time to get here, but I could do it. I had to.

My boot caught on a lump, and I tumbled. The snow wrapped me in its cold embrace yet again, and a small part of me was reminded of the cocoon of my bed. My legs wouldn't move. Gasps and shivers jerked my body, and my fingers and toes hurt so much. My tears had run dry—or maybe they'd turned to ice, just like Papa said they would.

Papa wasn't coming back.

My eyes darted around my surroundings. I'd made it to a clearing, fields of undisturbed snow stretching out all around me before giving way to the skeletons of trees. Stars glistened above me, the only witness to my despair. The monster was gone.

Maybe she left. Maybe I got lucky. Or maybe she was waiting for something.

I don't know how long I laid like that before the sound of crunching snow finally approached me. I squeezed my eyes shut, heart thudding in my chest.

Go away. Please go away.

There was no noise for a long time, and I eventually peeked to see if she left.

Large, black boots filled my vision. I smiled. He came back. Papa was here to lift me again and take me home. He would take away the cold that consumed me, and everything would be okay again.

But that didn't happen. More tears sprang to my eyes as I realized the boots were too large to be Papa's. The being who wore them leaned over me, and I could feel his gaze like a heavy weight though I couldn't see his face. I didn't know if he had one.

Even while stooped, he was taller than anyone I'd ever seen, yet he wasn't intimidating. He was shrouded in black, and the material looked silkier than a running stream, softer than the evening mist. I knew instinctively that he wasn't human, but he wasn't like the girl either. She had been as harsh as her surroundings, cold inside and out. He was still and tranquil like the empty night sky.

He extended a black-veiled hand toward me.

I wasn't afraid. His presence was more soothing than Papa's had ever been, and I knew—though I didn't know *how* I knew—that he could take away the cold.

I reached up and wrapped my bare fingers around his. They were so numb I couldn't feel his touch.

He didn't hold me or surround me with warmth and comfort like Papa would. He didn't do anything more than wipe the tears from my cheeks. The material covering his hands was even softer than I'd imagined. At his touch, my shivers abated. The snow didn't sting anymore. Instead, it felt fluffy and cozy in a way I'd never noticed before; a heavy blanket that spread a comforting hush over the land.

I wasn't tired or cold anymore.

The hunched man straightened and withdrew, drifting across the field. His movements carried a slow and gentle quality to them, like snowflakes meandering lazily downward.

He paused, looking back at me. Waiting for me.

I looked in the direction Papa had gone. His deep tracks lie ahead of me, marking the path home.

I turned away and followed the Whitherling into the forest.

Ten winters passed before I followed the path back to my hometown. It was once again the Winter Solstice, when the spirits of ice and darkness roamed free, and Whitherling was at his strongest. The last day before he would grow weakened and eventually travel south. The same day Papa had taken me into the mountains and was promised that I would return to him.

The town looked just as I remembered it. Every home was bursting at the seams with golden firelight to keep away the frost like it was an undesirable pest, chimneys oozing smoke and heat. Music and laughter drifted through the frozen air, shattering the silence I'd known in the mountains.

A torch flared above the town gate like a beacon. The brazier that held it was elaborately crafted to keep the flames fed for hours and protected from the elements. Every year, the best fuel was set aside for the torch so it could burn throughout the solstice.

It was an offering for the Whitherling to release his wintry grasp. As if he had any use for fire.

As a child, I'd looked to the flames with awe, praying that the Whitherling would hear our plight. Hoping that the light wouldn't go out. It never did. Back then, it had always seemed so steadfast and unyielding.

Now I saw it for what it was: a feeble candle in the face of the frozen sea that surrounded it. It was nothing more than an arrogant demand from those who had no right to issue such orders to the Winterbearer.

I passed beneath the flames and padded through empty streets. Families stayed inside tonight, taking comfort in the knowledge that winter was half over. Despite the years, the path was familiar to me.

Nostalgia dragged me in like a hawk snagging its prey, guiding my feet and haunting my thoughts with memories of smiles and hugs. Grandmama's wrinkled face, sneaking me candy that made my fingers sticky. Trying to catch snowflakes with our tongues. Nights spent by the fireplace listening to fantastic tales of both truth and fiction.

I shook the vestiges from my mind. I thought I was better prepared than this. My fingernails dug into my palms while I took a moment to compose myself. The sky was clear tonight; the deep black pierced by stars. I always found comfort in the empty void.

Papa's cabin was visible from here, standing on a hill near the outskirts of the village. It was the only home not lit from within, but I could see it clearly: half-sheltered by a grove of trees, their branches hanging heavy with snow and curled over the roof like claws.

I felt oddly light as I approached the place I used to call home and saw Papa sitting outside on the front step. He was alone, slumped against the door, nothing more than a bundle of furs and ugly remorse. The only indication that he was alive was the breath that misted in front of him. He knew what his fate held today, and he waited for it with patience.

No. It was me he waited for. After ten long years, he was here, still waiting for me.

Still unseen and unheard, I watched the man I'd looked up to. The years hadn't been kind to him. His hair had grayed, face turned gaunt despite the plentiful bounties I knew the town had enjoyed. His shoulders that once cut an imposing figure now held the weight of the years. Of his own regret.

"It won't be long now," he muttered, voice so much more brittle than in my memories. "I pray that you are safe, my daughter."

I held my silence no longer. "Did you keep your promise?"

He startled, standing stiffly once he caught sight of me. His frosted beard obscured a distrustful frown. "I did," he said. "Ten years, and I didn't seek her out once."

He spoke the truth. I wouldn't be here if he didn't.

"Then he has kept his."

Papa didn't need to ask who I was referring to. He took a step forward, fist clenched. "So, return her to me. Honor your part of the deal and take me instead."

He didn't recognize me. How could he? I had only seen seven winters the last time he saw me and was expecting a woman to return to him. Not a child who looked no older than the one he abandoned.

My thin dress fluttered around my bare feet as I stepped closer so he could see me clearer, and I looked up at him with a sweet smile. "Don't you recognize me, Papa?"

He paled, eyes widening as he took in my waves of white hair and eyes like blood-stained snow, trying to see his daughter beneath them. The desire to discover a lie was clear in his expression.

I saw the moment he could no longer deny that it was me standing in front of him. Despair aged his face in seconds.

What would he do, I wondered, now that he knew I was no longer his child, but a daughter of the frost?

Papa unclasped his coat, shedding it from his shoulders and placing it over mine. He knelt in front of me, cheeks wet with tears, and a thin smile crossed his face, strained but genuine at the same time. Then I was engulfed in his arms.

It was warm. Warmer than anything I had ever felt since that night.

He pulled away enough to see my face, loathe to let me go a second time. "I'm sorry," he said. "I missed you so much."

Something wet slid down my cheek, startling me from my daze. Papa lifted a hand to brush the tears away—tears I had forgotten I could shed—but once his fingers touched my skin, he jerked away as though burned.

I wiped the tears myself, watching the liquid turn to ice on my ice-cold palms. "Was it worth it?" I asked.

"Worth it?" he repeated numbly, looking towards the town, expression lost. "They all lived because I gave you up to the Whitherling. Hundreds of people…for the price of one. My own daughter." His eyes squeezed shut. "I would have readily given my own life to he who prevails over death and winter, had he accepted it. But he didn't want my life. He wanted yours."

"No," I corrected, grasping the sleeve of the arm that still held me. Frost formed on the fabric beneath my touch. "He wanted your sacrifice."

My hand slid up to meet his, and he gasped in pain when skin met skin.

"But what about my sacrifice? Do you remember that day, Papa? Do you remember how long I screamed for you as you walked away?"

Small bursts of mist escaped his mouth, and the pain I caused his body was nothing compared to pain my words caused his heart.

"This isn't the first time I've returned, you know. The first few winters, I ventured from the mountains, watching you enjoy your seasons of plenty that came about at my expense."

My gaze held his. I let go of him, and he clutched his arm to his chest while mine fell limp at my side. The energy that gripped me, the anger, the sadness, all of it…I let it go, and it drifted away into nothing.

Papa didn't try to deny his guilt. "He takes more than he gives," he said through gritted teeth. "You have returned but not before he took everything from you."

"He *gave* me everything. It was you who took it away in the first place." Though we were only feet apart, it felt as though a great distance lie between us. "But it's okay. I don't hate you. Do you know why I stopped coming back?"

He said nothing.

I leaned over him, but the movement did nothing to bridge that distance.

Good.

"I realized you weren't important."

Papa's mouth was set in a hard line. He couldn't look at me anymore. "Will the curse lift from you? Once he takes me in your stead?"

A shadow darted across the field, unseen by Papa.

I smiled. "There is no curse. I came back, as was promised to you. And now that I've fulfilled my part in your deal, I can leave again. And he can take back what is his."

A second shadow joined the first, and this time Papa noticed it as well. He squared his shoulders.

"Now he comes for me."

But instead of heading in our direction, the figures descended the hill, pulled in by the lights that shone like lures, each one indicating a home full of life. A third and fourth followed suit, then more, leaping from the safety of the trees and the shadows and into the light. They dashed across rooftops and slipped in through windows.

White hair flowed behind them, and though we couldn't see their eyes, both of us knew that each pair gleamed red like mine.

They were all like me.

Papa faced me in horror, apprehension chasing away the tenderness that had been in his frame only a moment ago. "What is this?" he demanded. "The Whitherling was only meant to come for me!"

"He takes more than he gives," I threw Papa's words back at him. "You should have paid closer attention to the details. You were given ten winters. All of you. And now, everyone who would have succumbed to sickness and famine are to be returned to him."

Papa was paler than the snow. At that moment, he looked no better than a corpse. "No," he whispered.

An icy gale rose with the arrival of my brothers and sisters. With glee, I watched them dance across the town, reaping the Winterbearer's harvest.

The stories said that winter followed wherever the Whitherling walked, and that his icy talons would take the lives of those who weren't careful.

They weren't wrong. We were his talons and his teeth. He was the stillness, so we were the wind. He would never seek vengeance or cruelty, so we would do it for him. We were his children and would give him everything and more, now and forever.

It was the least we could do to repay his great favor of holding us so we wouldn't die alone on frozen nights.

The torch above the town's gate flickered, the fire barely clinging to life. Then with a puff, it went dark. Beyond it, I could see the Whitherling. Standing. Watching. Then he turned and lumbered back into the forest.

Papa clutched my arm, ignoring the cold boring into his palms. "Please," he begged. "At least spare the children."

I looked at him curiously.

"You didn't."

I pulled away, and he reached for me like a lost child—like I had reached for him when he left me.

"Don't worry," I said in a mockery of reassurance. "We'll save you for last."

I joined my kin. A deep freeze would settle over the snow-swept land tonight.

-End-

May You Have Only Boys
By
Ashe Thurman

The longest night of her twentieth year, when the winter had just started to grow long, stretching its claws against the cold, freezing ground. She had always known what would happen. They all have always known what would happen. Her family. Her friends. The hundreds who had, over the years, walked the same path as her. In the dead of night, a knock would come on the door of the family farmhouse. A tumble-down thing snuggled gently between the road leading out of town and their acres and acres of grain fields and goats and apple trees and blackberry bushes that bite your fingers with tiny thorns when you try to pick them.

The knock arrives, and she hears it from where she's been waiting in the parlor. Instinctively, she presses her hand to a letter tucked in her breast pocket, then pulls it away, not wanting to accidentally reveal the thing she has secreted into her vest. She thinks, in that moment, the farm itself will be the thing she misses most. The sour taste of not-quite-right apples plucked from the lowest branch. The way the brambles caught on her skirt, tugging her, as if daring her off the well-trodden path and into the dark woods that lined the fields. The scent of the air as the seasons changed and shifted from one into the other. She takes one last breath of the winter air shaped by the corners of the parlor. Commits it to memory. A slight bite of chill covered by the scent of wood embers and smoke mixed with the heady spice of a rich soup broth that had spent the evening idling on the kitchen fire.

"Fiora. It's time." Her mother approaches from the kitchen, worrying the hem of her apron and refusing to look her in the eyes. Fiora nods and stands. When she steps, she stumbles against the train of her skirt. Her father appears at her elbow, pressing the palm of his hand to the underside of her arm ever so slightly. Another step, and she moves out of the halo of his presence, pulling away from his hand. The oldest of her younger brothers waits on one side of the door, the oldest of her younger sisters on the other. In the rooms above, another batch of younger siblings have been barred from seeing this take place. The oldest of these are at the windows, though. She's certain of this. They'll be watching her as she goes.

Sister, like Mother, won't look at her, and her hands clutch at her own skirts. Brother moves to open the door, and Fiora raises her hand to stop him. From here, she must do this alone. She's doing this for all of them, all who are under this roof. For the farm. For the goats. For the bramble bushes. Other women before her have taken this burden—the weight of the whole town, the whole countryside—proclaiming loudly as they went that they demanded remembrance for their sacrifice. And perhaps that was the least recompense they deserved. Fiora didn't have the mind to think so broadly, though, her shoulders too slim to carry something so heavy so far. But for a house. For a family. For a blackberry bush. She could give herself for those things.

The knob feels cold under her fist and catches as she tries to pull the door open. A little more force, and it shudders back. The night beyond the doorway glows dimly with lanterns. Escorts. The light bounces gently off a thin sheet of snow, barely a day old, able to withstand an afternoon that had failed to creep above the hard cold of winter daylight. She steps through the door and feels fingers of snow reach up and over the brim of her slippers immediately. They aren't made to withstand a journey such as this. They're not made to last more than a single journey to begin with. She pulls the train of her gown through the threshold so that it twines around her ankles. The door closes behind her, and all that's left is the light of the lanterns and the deep dark night that stretches out in front of her.

As she begins to walk along the road, her escorts moving alongside, she doesn't turn back. Refuses to. Despondent eyes will appear in the windows, and if she has to face them, she won't be able to do this. She stops herself from pressing her hands to the letter in her vest, again. Now, more than ever, she must keep it to herself, despite the strength she draws from it. Despite the way it feels like it burns in her pocket.

"This doesn't feel right, somehow." One of the escorts whispers to the other, but his voice isn't exactly quiet. It travels to Fiora easily, landing against her ears as she tries to focus on the path ahead of her, to keep her feet moving as they need to. "Does she even understand what's going on?"

"The tribunal said it's fine," the other escort replies, her own voice lacking tact. "That she knows well enough. And the gods made her this way, so if she's not an adequate sacrifice, well that's up to them now innit."

She lets them talk around and over and through her. She's accustomed to it. She's lived her life listening to the things others thought she was unable to understand. Were she more malicious...

Mother's voice rings in her head as a memory from another winter just like this one, not so long ago. She feels herself sitting at the top of the stairs, unseen, unnoticed. Her stocking feet pressed into the wood, gripping the edge of the step with her toes.

"They can't expect her to go," Mother cried. "They can't want a... a simple girl... like her..."

"The oldest daughter," Father said shortly. "The oldest daughter in each family. That's how it's always been. That's how it has to be."

"They gave an exception for the Murphys. When their oldest was taken by typhoid when she was small."

"Would you prefer, that? That Fiora died to a fever? That she didn't even get this long?" Father raged, flinging himself across the small room, kicking a chair for want of a better target. "Would you rather they take Arlene instead? Or that we had drowned all our daughters in the river like the Byrnes?" There wasn't an answer for such a thing, of course.

"May you have only boys," she whispered to herself, pressing the old, hand-me-down blessing into the wood under her feet, hoping there really was some kind of magic in intention. That no one else who entered this house would ever have to suffer through this conversation again.

Finally, the cold actually touches her skin, her cloak and gown saturated with it now, as they approach the edge of the woods. The lanterns extinguish, and the three of them move into the trees. The snow is thicker here, and it rises all the way up her ankles. It becomes even more difficult to walk as the train gathers more snow and becomes heavy. She pulls the sleeves down toward her wrists unconsciously.

Like the rest of the gown and cloak, they're black. Black as pitch. As tar. As the space where the moon should be when it's in shadow. Her skin beneath it is almost as dark, but it shimmers lilac when it catches a glint of bright starlight in just the right way. She pulls her sleeve down a little out of habit. She imagines what she must look like, traveling though the dark, a moving void in space itself. A part of the winter night that surrounds her.

The thought catches for just a moment. Were she to run, now, to flee into the woods, would her escorts be able to see her? Even with their brightest lanterns, she could hide so easily against the darkness, slip between the trees and down into the hollows formed by their lurking roots. She chances a touch to her vest letter under her cloak.

No. She knows what must be done. The letter has told her.

A clearing appears, bright against the darkness of the forest; the now knee-deep snow reflecting the light of the whole universe above it. Fiora's never seen this place before, so deep in the heart of the woods. There's a way about it, though; a whisper that persists and rattles through the trees. A gentle, rambling, murmur of familiarity. She reminds herself again that she has never been to this place, but she cannot quite bring herself to believe it. Her escorts stop at the edge of the trees, and she moves into the circle of snow alone. Then she understands. She understands why she thinks she knows this place despite all evidence to the contrary.

Pine needles and holly bushes, the scent of a mid-winter festival. Tanner kissed her on the lips, their mouths and senses dripping with ill-gotten mead. It was their last night together. Tanner was twenty, afterall. It had been a year of lasts. Of finals. Of never agains.

"What if I just didn't go?" Tanner said. Her voice was like warm, soft bread, fresh from the oven, yeasty and sweet.

"You have to," replied Fiora, "it's how it's always been."

"Who says?" Tanner asked and Fiora couldn't answer. Tanner's hands found their way under Fiora's skirt to ankles then shins then knees she was delightfully familiar with.

"You enter the circle, then the fairies come, but who's to say what happens then? What must happen then?"

"The witchwoman-"

"The witchwoman doesn't know!" Tanner declared, pulling her body closer to Fiora's, her toast and butter words catching on the hook of her ear. "The witchwoman cannot speak in the presence of the fairies! She can't even lay her eyes upon them. She's not permitted!"

"How do you know all this?" Fiora drew a strand of hair away from Tanner's eyes to better see how they had widened in excitement.

"The witchwoman likes to drink. And with a nudge, she'll tell you many things."

Tanner kissed her again, and there was no more talk of the witchwoman. Or of much really.

Fiora presses against the letter in her vest pocket again. A year of lasts. Then a year of horrible firsts. Then a letter. A letter left in the old spot in the log. She still didn't understand it. Not quite. Not yet.

The witchwoman appears on the other side of the clearing, emerging like liquid from the darkness of the trees, indigo cloak covering her from neck to foot, shimmering with captured starlight as she moves. Fiora walks forward to the middle of the clearing. It's strange now, without the escorts. She's still not alone, though. They're not alone. She can feel another presence in the trees. But those eyes. Those many eyes on her. They're not comforting.

The witchwoman meets her in the middle of the clearing, pulls her hands from her cloak, and demands in motions that Fiora do the same. From a pouch upon her belt, the witchwoman draws a loose, feathery powder. From her fingers, it falls like soot. As it strikes Fiora's palms, it shifts to a bright crimson. Most of it sticks, but the rest cascades to the snow below, leaving bloody pinpricks in the otherwise pristine sheet of white. The witchwoman grabs Fiora's wrist and lifts it toward the ever-more darkening sky.

She doesn't speak, but she holds it there as if to show the mark. To show the branding. The proof of Fiora's suitability.

The witchwoman cannot speak in the presence of the fairies. She's not permitted.

The woods seem to shiver and shake in anticipation. Thirsty. Hungry. Yearning. Fiora presses her eyes closed quickly, just a moment. Enough to gather her courage. To gird her heart. She stops herself from reaching for the letter for what must be the hundredth time, now. She opens her eyes. The witchwoman pulls her hand back down, letting her palm flower open again. From another pouch, a stone appears, glowing blue and green from a light that lives within it. The witchwoman places it in Fiora's hand then forces her fingers to curl over it. The witchwoman moves Fiora's hand, turning her wrist so that the inside of her fist presses against the place where her own hear resides. With crooked fingers, she insists the importance of the stone with what little language she can use. The witchwoman holds her own fist to her own chest and shakes it once before holding it firm again. Fiora understands. She nods. She shakes her own hand and makes it clear she will not drop it.

Gnarled hands press the top of her shoulders. The witchwoman leans in, presses her forehead to Fiora's, then steps back again. The witchwoman moves around behind Fiora, and she keeps herself from following the figure with her eyes. A hand presses her back and pushes her forward. The first step is a stumble, then she recovers, and she begins to walk forward through the snow. Only ten steps, and something else appears on the other side of the clearing, causing her to pause again.

Like the witchwoman, they seem to materialize from nothing out of the darkness of the trees. They're more like smoke, however, taking form as they drop from the air. Their cloaks are white and drag along the ground. Their faces hide under deep, folding hoods. Woven from starlight itself, say the stories. With thread spun from the reflection of light off a sharp knife. With a needle carved from a honeybee sting.

But Fiora can see them clearly from here.

They're wool and felt, undyed. Still tinged with yellow as though pulled raw straight from the back of the ewe that gave it. Against the gray-whiteness of the snow, it's obvious. How did this never appear in the stories? Perhaps because the only ones to see them never return to report. Even the witchwoman...

Fiora turns her head to find her, to see if she's alone in this spectacle.

"Do not look back."

Fiora snaps her head forward again. It's impossible to know from which form the voice emerged. Or whether it was either of them at all. It could have been from the forest itself.

"Only look forward, child." This is a different voice, and it emerges from the figure on the right. The hood rattles as they speak. The voice is like thick, heavy syrup, dripping sweet and sticky through the thin night air.

The speaking figure moves forward through the snow,

leaving their companion at the edge of the clearing. As they approach, their height grows and expands until, as they stand before her, Fiora must tilt her head up to meet their eye. But she doesn't. She keeps her eyes forward, locked on a silver beetle-shaped broach that catches the figure's cloak closed at their chest. A long, thin hand comes to rest on her shoulder. Gray, dull skin. Like ash. Like slate. And just as cold. She can feel it seeping through her cloak. Another hand touches her face, curling a finger under her chin, taps it a few times, then falls to their side.

"Will you come with us child?"

Fiora holds her breath. This was the moment. The moment the letter spoke of. The moment she had put all her trust in. Was she permitted to speak? Even so, would the words she was meant to utter be accepted? Or would she be struck down?

She might die...or worse...She might live, stripped of the mission for which her whole life had been portioned.

Both seemed equally terrifying.

"No. I will not." Despite her best efforts, her voice cracks hideously around the edges.

"Say again, child?" The voice is not angry. It stays its course. Monotone to the point of unnerving. "Will you come with us?"

Fiora steels herself harder, this time. She captures her breath in the bottom of her lungs where it can expand and fill her with purpose and presence.

"No. I will not come with you. I do not... consent... to be taken. I will not go with you." She stops her tongue. Succinct. Be succinct. Do not give them room to misread your intention or form their own from your words. That's what the letter says.

The clearing grows quiet. Still.

The figure...laughs. A soft, gentle chortle that gurgles up under their nose and spills out from between their lips.

"Alright. May I have the stone back, then, please?" That long, thin hand moves in front of them, into the small space their bodies form, and opens palm upward. Fiora is lost in her thoughts, stalled by the ease with which her request was accepted. It couldn't be this easy, could it? "Or you can keep it, if you'd like. You'll find it doesn't do you much good, though."

Fiora finally opens her hand, pulling it back from her chest to see the stone within it. It no longer glows. It is a hard, dark lump of smooth, inert rock. She drops it unceremoniously into the open palm. She lets out a breath she didn't realize she was holding. The thin hand clutches around the rock and spirits it away. A hand returns to the side of Fiora's face, a thumb pressing gently to the edge of her cheekbone. The figure dips their huge frame down. They drop a kiss on the top of Fiora's forehead. They pull away. She chances half a glance upward. The bottom edge of a face peeks from under the hood. It has a smile, crooked on the edges. Behind the smile, sharp teeth that just ever so slightly flash as the mouth presses into a smooth line again. Then the figure is standing, their hand pulling away.

"Be well, child. Be well and go. May you have only that which you desire." They step back. They turn, move off toward the woods.

"But where do I go? What do I do? What happens now?" Fiora says. Why does she say it? She doesn't know. She doesn't understand her own thoughts. Yet the figures keep moving away, silently folding back into the line of dark trees.

The clearing is silent.

Fiora drops to her knees.

She shrugs off her horrible cloak, letting it fall to the snow behind her.

Her hands reach under her vest, searching for a piece of now-wrinkled parchment. Shaking fingers try to unfold it without tearing. It doesn't quite work, and a slight rip appears on the very edge. Fiora blinks back tears that are forming in the hollows of her eyes.

She tries to read the letter through them. The words blur. But she knows them already. Has memorized the hasty halt and scratch of their creator.

Do not go with them. Do as I say.

"I've done as you said," Fiora whispers, biting her bottom lip. "I've done as you said, now what?"

"Fiora!? Fiora did it work?" A voice like bread and

butter, yeasty and sweet, rattles through the pine needles and holly bushes.

-End-

Cardinal Moon
By
Katie Groom

The frigid air burst through the door with a force that nearly blew the herbs off of the ceiling in the kitchen. Just as fast as it ran through the entire pub, it ended - but the door wasn't shut. It was his large, muscular 6'4" frame that blocked the icy winter air for a moment - but only a moment. As he stepped through the threshold, the wind followed him, bringing snow with it. It was probably going to be the last snow of the winter season. While there was still a hard frost each night, the snow had mostly melted over the past few days.

"Hugh, shut the goddamned door already, for fuck's sake!" Hendrick Appleton came across as an old curmudgeon, but after wearing him down, he could be a great ally in a pub fight. Hugh slammed the wooden door shut, knocking snow to the ground from the roof and sign outside. He took maybe three large steps and slapped

Hendrick's shoulder as he sat down. "Sorry I'm late, old man." Hendrick motioned for the barmaid to bring some ale over — a refill for himself and one to start off Hugh. "What held ye up?" Hugh shrugged. He grabbed an extra piece of fabric from his pocket specifically for pulling his long hair back into a ponytail. He had let it down to keep his ears warm as he walked to the pub.

"Aye, a few drinks from now, you'll tell me." Hendrick rose his eyebrow and took a drink.

Hugh put the cup to his lips and downed the ale in one large gulp. "Maybe."

"What's her name?"

"Blythe."

Hugh nodded towards the barmaid and pointed at his cup. "Blythe, eh? Sounds expensive." Hugh chuckled. "Doesn't matter. Won't be seeing her again. I don't have enough status for it to be a good match." The barmaid came over to get his mug. She leaned forward to reach it over the bar, letting her curls brush against his hand and also showcasing her low-cut shirt and everything that came with it. Hugh wasn't sure if she wanted a tip or for him to take her home at the end of the night.

"Why?" Hendrick asked. "You're what now, 60 years old?" He let out a chuckle.

"I'm 36," Hugh laughed. "And what of it?"

"Yer getting up there. You'll be needing a young woman to take care of you and to bear some wee ones to pass on your family name..."

Hugh cut him off. "Thanks, grandsire."

Hendrick elbowed him in the ribs. "I've best be going. The missus is sure to be worrying."

"It's cold out there," Hugh warned. "And the wind is like ice."

"It seems ye do care. Yer nothing but a big, cuddly kitten." Hendrick stood up — more like stumbled to his feet — and then put on his coat. He patted Hugh on the shoulder. "Until tomorrow." Hugh turned around to request another drink, but the barmaid was not behind the bar. He looked around and saw her at a table, delivering the drinks to a table. Well, she had already delivered them and was trying to get back to work, but she couldn't. Her forearm was gripped tightly by one of the patrons. With his free hand, the man ran his fingers over the laces of her corset. "Ye'll come home with me, whether it pleases ye or no."

She yanked her arm free and stepped back. "I will do nothing of the sort, William McPherson." She turned on her heels and started off towards the bar, but not before William could grab the skirt of her dress and lift it and all of the petticoats along with it. Before he could take the opportunity to further assault the barmaid, Hugh was there, with his hand around William's forearm. "The lady declined your advances, McPherson."

Failing to yank his arm free, William spat at Hugh's feet. "Stay out of this, Davies. It's none of your concern."

Hugh squeezed harder. "She. Said. No."

Suddenly, there was a crashing that sounded like glass shattering and Hugh's hand went immediately to his left cheek. It felt like a constant sting, and when he removed his hand, it was covered in blood. Hugh didn't have time to think about it because he was being drug outside just as the decorative knight statue on the east wall came crashing to the floor as one of McPherson's friends grabbed the sword it held. As they got outside, blood was dripping from Hugh's face, staining the snow a dark red. He felt something hit him, and, through his right eye, he saw a sword laying at his feet. He looked over at McPherson, who had a sword at the ready. *Shit. I have no idea how to wield a sword.* Hugh bent over to pick up his weapon. Not even knowing the proper stance, Hugh knew that he had no chance to win this battle, and even if he did, McPherson had three friends as backup. Hugh's only friend - Hendrick - was probably in a drunken dreamland already. The snow was falling heavily, and Hugh could not see out of his left eye. Even attempting to open it caused a burning sensation all the way down his face, so it was just best to use his one good eye. His opponent moved towards Hugh and started to spar with him. Hugh was able to successfully block a few attacks but eventually landed on his back in the snow. McPherson had the tip of the sword at Hugh's throat. "I would tell you to stay out of my affairs in the future, but you're not going to have a future."

McPherson pulled back the sword and then, full force, plunged it just below Hugh's left collarbone. Hugh would have screamed, but he didn't have the will nor the energy. The last thing he saw before closing his eyes was McPherson and his friends all leaning on the sword, pushing it further into the frozen ground below him.

Hugh never felt such pain in his entire life. He knew he was going to die, right there, laying on the ground in front of the Ye Olde Raven Inn & Pub as heavy snow covered him. His face burned. His chest and shoulder — hell, his entire left side of his body burned. He tried to open his eyes, but everything was blurry. Hugh knew he hadn't drunk enough for things to be spinning as much as they were. He felt like he was spinning in a different direction than the Earth. Hugh closed his eyes tightly and decided to let the Lord do with him as He would. He reflected momentarily on his life, knowing that he probably wasn't good enough to get into Heaven. He hoped that perhaps his act of valor that lead him to this moment was enough to keep him out of an eternity of damnation.

His breathing began to shake and become shallow, and then he started to choke. *This is it.* Or maybe since he had rested, he could try to get up. Hugh attempted to sit up, but the blade shoved into the ground was intended to keep him from getting up and acquiring help. Hugh reached his right hand over to the sword and tried to pull it out, but all that did was slice his hand along the blade. He felt his breath rattle, and the choking intensified. He closed his eyes and did his best to relax. His heart stopped. Hugh rested. His body laid on the ground as the snow continued to fall and cover him. The moon continued across the sky behind the clouds.

Suddenly, Hugh felt as if his body was on fire. Internally, he was screaming. *So, Hell it is, then, I suppose.* Everything burned. It wasn't just the leftover pain from the fight that he was feeling in the afterlife. It was something more. It was punishment. After what felt like hours of being lit on fire, Hugh's eyes snapped open. He was laying on the ground where McPherson had left him. *Purgatory?* He slowly directed his eyes to the sword that was still strategically holding him to the ground. The snow had stopped, and the clouds were gone. The light of the moon reflected poorly in the dull blade.

Fuck it. Hugh willed both of his hands to the guards of the sword and pushed as hard as he could. The blade released from the ground - and from him - with ease, and Hugh was able to sit up. He chose to do it slowly. He put his right hand to his wound. While his shirt was covered in blood, the wound was nearly healed already. He disregarded this oddity, acknowledging to himself that he didn't know how the afterlife worked. Grabbing the sword, he used it as leverage to pull himself to a standing position. He looked down at where he had died, making note that his body was no longer laying there. *The afterlife is odd.* Stumbling a little,

Hugh made his way to the outskirts of town. He knew of an abandoned shack he could hide out at. Sunrise was approaching, and he didn't know what the rules were in Purgatory, but he knew that he felt exhausted and, oddly enough, still feverish. He wanted to rest.

It took him what felt like a millennia to get to the shack, and, as soon as he got inside, he collapsed into a pile of old fabric and hay, falling asleep. When he awoke, Hugh wasn't sure how much time had passed. It could have been hours, or it could have been days, but he did feel rested. He still felt feverish, but it wasn't as painful as before. He did one of those big stretches — one of those ones that require closed eyes and a groan or other noise to be fully effective. When he opened his eyes, he gasped because his shoes were broken open to let his toes through, as they had grown exponentially during his death — not to mention they had grown quite hairy. This caused him to look at his hands and legs — all huge and having acquired quite a bit of hair.

Frantically, he looked around for something reflective, and he found and old plate. He wiped it off as best as he could with his torn sleeve. He gasped when he saw what was looking back at him. "You must have been sleeping for months," Hugh said to himself, noticing how much facial hair he had grown. He reached his free hand to his face and traced the scar from below his left eye down to his jaw. That's when he noticed his fingernails were long and sharp.

And then, he squinted to look at himself better. Instead of his usual green eyes, they were yellow. Out of shock and fear, he threw the plate to the other side of the room with enough force that it stuck in the wood that made up the walls of the shack.

After sitting very still for several minutes, Hugh decided to look outside. He could tell that not a lot of time could have passed during his rest, as there was still snow laying on the ground, though it was melting. He noticed drops of water from the icicles hanging from the roof. And, strangely, he recognized some of the townspeople in the distance. He rubbed his eyes and looked again — he felt that it was unnatural that he was able to see that far with such clarity. Hugh was starving, but he knew that his appearance would frighten the life out of everyone he knew — if they could see him — so he decided to suffer through it and wait until nightfall before he left the confines of the shack. He did, however, decide to grab one of the icicles off of the roof to get himself hydrated. As he grabbed one of the smaller icicles, it melted right in his hand, releasing steam into the air. He tried for a thicker one, and, while it did have the same effect, some was left over. He chewed on the ice as he pondered how one could have a fever so intense that it turned ice into steam and still be alive — if that's what he was.

As Hugh sat in silence, waiting for nightfall, he pondered his state of being. Was he dead? A ghost? In Purgatory?

Alive and just gone completely mad? Was this a fever dream? Or was he some sort of monster? He thought of ways to test a couple of these theories, but nothing that didn't have the potential to terrorize the entire town. That was when he decided that he had to leave and put his theories to the test elsewhere.

At nightfall, Hugh slowly opened the door to the shack to be extra certain that no one would see him. He was surprised to realize that he could see extremely well at night, almost as clear as if it were nearing dawn. He also noticed that he his hearing had become somewhat enhanced since his death — or whatever this was. He could hear small animals, and he shook his head a little when he realized that he had the ability to identify what they were, just from the noise they were creating. He quickly decided to head south. He was hoping that he would perhaps be able to find a store he could break into to get better clothes and maybe steal some food from a pub or tavern. Since it was nighttime and Hugh could see so well, he decided to start off at a jogging pace. However, while his body felt like it was jogging, his pace was faster than his quickest running pace. He was, in fact, going faster than any horse had carried him. He decided to push it and see how fast he could really go and for how long. He broke off into a sprint. Smiling from the fun of it all, Hugh let out a howl — which he had intended to be more of a "woo hoo!" — however, it came out more like a wolf's howl. "What an exhilarating dream!"

After a few hours, he found himself just north of London and exhausted. He found a church that appeared to be abandoned, and he approached it cautiously. Honestly, Hugh wasn't sure if he would be able to enter the church, as it was possible that he was damned. He entered slowly and found a corner to fall asleep against. He surrendered to his exhaustion before he could even make an effort get himself comfortable. He awoke to a gentle tapping on the bottom of his foot. "Hey, you alive?"

He slowly opened his eyes. "Not sure." Looking up, he was shocked to see the man who woke him wasn't afraid of him. Then he looked at his hands and feet, and, while his clothes were still torn to bits, his body had returned to somewhat normal. "I just had the craziest dream..."

"Do you know where you are?"

"Well, I thought I was near Westminster, but, perhaps, I just had the most incredible dream..." Hugh was still looking at his hands.

"Would you mind if my wife — she's a healer — would take a look at you? We could get you some clean clothes. Maybe help you find some answers." Cautiously, Hugh agreed. Then he requested, "Is there by chance any food or ale?"

The wife, who was a tiny woman — perhaps not even five feet tall and, on a day after a big feast, maybe 110 pounds, had a voice that sounded like starlight. "Of course. Please let me examine you first, though," she politely ordered as she entered the room, with a small pile of clean clothes in her arms. She sat them down on a pew and then left and quickly returned with a bowl of water and some cloths. Hugh nodded and moved to the pew with the clothes. Her examination didn't take as long as he had anticipated. and she told him to get changed and meet them in another room for a meal. Hugh made quick work of cleaning up; he was starving. The man, who apologized for not introducing himself earlier, was named Alvin, and his wife was Edith but preferred to be called Edie.

As they ate, things were awkward and tense, until Edie spoke up. "Hugh, if you don't mind, I would like the opportunity to be very direct with you."

"Edie…" Alvin tried to stop her, but she put her hand up, defying his wishes.

"It appears that over the last two days, you've gone through quite the trauma."

"That's putting it mildly." Hugh put down his bread and gave Edie his undivided attention.

"The world you live in, Hugh, is not as simple as you think. There are monsters out there that people cannot understand…"

"Edie, I don't think…"

"Alvin," she replied, with a bit of a staccato in her voice. "It is his choice if he wants to believe what I have to say or not." Hugh sat up a little straighter. "Edie. Alvin. I should be dead right now. Maybe I am, or maybe it's something else. But I'm not a complete simpleton. Something... unnatural... is going on here. If you have an explanation, I would like to hear it." Alvin nodded slowly at Edie.

She continued, "My best guess is that you believe that you should be dead, and when you woke up, you thought you were on fire. You perhaps think you were having a nightmare because you didn't look quite like yourself..."

"That's an understatement," Hugh scoffed.

"We saw you when you came in here, and we watched you change while you were sleeping," she continued. She took a deep breath. "I am not only a healer, but I'm also what is called a Warlock or, more commonly, a Witch." She continued, "Alvin here is a werewolf, as are you."

Hugh looked back and forth between the both of them. "So, I'm going to howl at the moon and turn into a giant wolf. That's not what I think happened here..."

"Those legends are exaggerated," Alvin quickly interjected. "The shifting ability is passed down from parent to child, and it shows up only when a shifter is violently killed, otherwise it never manifests."

"You saw me. I didn't look like a wolf..."

"It's just a general term," Edie explained. "There are a lot of monsters out there, Hugh. And you just happen to be one of them."

"You won't change with the moon," Alvin explained. "It's more like when you feel threatened or overly angered. You'll return to your normal form when you recover from the exhaustion of the change; clothing is handed to you; or when your soul mate calls your name."

Hugh was skeptical, but not enough to get up and leave. "Interesting..."

"I can teach you how to harness your power. I've taught others," Alvin offered. Hugh stood up from the table and looked out one of the windows, pondering his options — and if he truly believed in this werewolf thing. He watched as a deer and its newborn enjoy some grass. He noticed how he could see each blade of grass with precision and hear their breathing as if it were right in his ear. If he was going to be able to survive without going completely mad due to overstimulation from noticing every little sound, he would need to learn how to manage his new abilities. He turned back to Alvin and Edie. "Tell me everything."

-End-

Prisms
By
Elyse Russell

Ren tried the door handle then and felt a lurch as it turned easily in her grip.

Baby, you gotta lock your doors, she thought.

Ren paused in the doorway, half-terrified that it would smell like death in the apartment. It had been days since they last spoke. She closed the door behind her and advanced to the living room. She didn't bother to take her boots off, and she left wet spots on the ugly peach-colored carpeting. There were still clumps of snow on her feet. She headed straight back to the bedroom.

The door creaked loudly on its hinges as she stepped past it. It was chilly in the room; the window was wide open. The prisms that Miri kept hanging by the window were tinkling against the glass pane and cast faint spinning rainbows against the carpet.

Ren only had to scan the room for a moment before she found Miri laying on the floor, halfway into the bathroom.

"Oh God, oh God, oh God. Oh, no. Please be okay. Miri! Miri?!"

Ren knelt down next to Miri, whose eyes were wide open. At first, Ren was sure that Miri was dead. Miri had a history of depression. But then she blinked, and her chest rose and fell as she breathed through her mouth.

Ren pushed Miri's shiny, black hair back from her face and leaned in closer. She put her fingers on Miri's wrist and felt a steady pulse.

"Miri, honey, why are you on the floor? What happened?

Miri didn't reply, nor did she give any indication that she was aware of Ren's presence at all. Her eyes remained blank and dull. She blinked again and took another breath through her mouth. Ren laid her hand over Miri's forehead, then cupped her cheek.

"Sweetie, it's me. It's Ren. Come on, come back to me."

Still, Miri did not respond. Ren felt panic rising in her chest and tamped it down with great effort.

Oh, what do I do? Ren wondered. *Do I call 911?*

Ren looked up and into the bathroom. A bottle of pills sat on the edge of the sink, but it was full. Ren realized the water was still running from the tap. She got up to turn it off, mumbling inanely to herself about a high water bill. She checked the prescription label on the pill bottle.

Anxiety meds. She had seen Miri take those before. But this bottle had been recently filled. She checked around and peeked into the trash, but she found no empty bottles anywhere. She grabbed a washcloth from a stack next to the shower and wet it down with cool water.

Returning to Miri's side, Ren knelt down and pressed the washcloth gently to Miri's forehead, and then the back of her neck. She set the cloth on the floor and moved to lift Miri, sliding one arm under her knees and the other under her thin little shoulders.

Ren was a big woman, both up-and-down and side-to-side, so she easily lifted the very petite, featherweight Miri and carried her to the bed. Laying Miri down gently, she checked Miri all over for injuries. Then she stood and reached into her coat pocket to pull out her phone.

After scrolling through her contacts for a moment, Ren found the number for Miri's mother and dialed it. After three rings, there was an answer.

"Hello, Mrs. Howard? It's Ren. Yeah. I know it's been a while, look I…No, listen, I'm worried about Miri. I just came to visit her at her apartment and found her on the floor. She doesn't seem to be injured, but she isn't responding to me. It's like she's looking right through me.

What do ya mean, this happens all the time?! I've never seen her like this, and we've been dating for five months!

Oh, she hasn't told you…I thought she did…she told me she came out to you…well, it isn't important whether

I'm her friend or her girlfriend, right now I just want to make sure she's...

Look, drop the lesbian thing for a moment, and tell me what you mean about this happening all the time! What is going on? I mean, I know she struggles with anxiety, but... gosh, it's like she's had a stroke or something!

Mrs. Howard. What aren't you telling me?

Look, you're a nice lady and all, but what you're saying... it sounds like crazy talk here.

I mean, yeah, of course I'm going to stay with her. How long is the drive? Almost an hour! Sheesh! Are you sure I shouldn't just call an ambulance, Mrs. Howard? I mean, what if it's a tumor or something?

Well, okay. You're her mom; I guess you would know. I'll wait and see if she comes around. But if it takes longer than twenty minutes, I swear I'm going to call 911...

How come you didn't tell me about this before? I've been to your house loads of times, and this never came up. How come *she* never told me, for crying out loud!? I mean...

Okay. I guess. I'll see you in an hour, then. Of course, I'll take care of her, what kind of person do you think I am?

No, no, don't answer that. Nope, not listening. Just get here as fast as you can, please."

Ren hung up the phone and looked down at Miri, still very uncertain and frightened. She let out a shuddering breath and ran her hand over her face. *Keep it together, Ren.*

"Well Miri," she said, "Your mom said this has happened

before. Like, a lot. And that you always come around in less than thirty minutes. A heads-up would have been nice, babe. Just sayin'…

She also said something about a curse. I mean, I always thought your mom was a bit weird, no offense, but I didn't know that she was off her rocker. Is that why you never told her about us, or even just about yourself?"

Ren let out a nervous chuckle.

"She said something about an ancient family curse or something. What is that all about? Curses! Curses aren't real."

Ren looked around the room nervously and was reminded that the window was open when she saw her breath in the air. She shivered and muttered inanely again, this time about the heating bill. She went over to close it and then stopped in her tracks.

There were two massive, long-fingered handprints on the windowsill. They certainly didn't look like human handprints. And they were solid black, like the…whatever it was…had been covered in ink.

"What the hell?"

It was rare for Ren to swear. She was a church-going girl and didn't like to anger the Lord with vulgar talk.

Ren looked out the window and down at the traffic below. Cold wind swirled up at her face, carrying bits of snow to drift like ashes past her shoulder and onto the carpet behind her. There, the flakes quickly melted and disappeared. Ren's hand briefly touched one of the handprints, and she jerked with a yelp, bumping her head on the window. She withdrew into the room, rubbing at the back of her head. When she touched it, it felt like… like something could see her…something so *cold*…

She slammed the window shut and locked it, then closed the blinds as quickly as she could, which made the rainbows disappear. The prisms crashed loudly against the glass as they were jostled by the blinds.

When Ren turned around, Miri was sitting up.

Ren jumped and put her hand over her heart. Then she rushed to sit next to Miri to embrace her. She pulled back to look at her face, and cupped her cheeks in her hands.

"Miri? Miri?"

Miri blinked, but her eyes didn't focus on Ren. They were still vacant and glassy.

"Miri, you're really scaring me."

Ren sighed.

"Your mom will be here soon."

Ren held Miri closely and stroked her hair as though she were a small child. After a few moments, Ren felt like she needed to do…something. Anything. Just to not think about…

She helped Miri to lay back down. She covered her girlfriend in the powder-blue blanket that she, herself, had knitted. Miri loved the color blue, so Ren had made her the blanket, just because. Not for Valentine's or birthday or anything, but just because she wanted see Miri to be wrapped up in something from *her*.

Unbuttoning her coat, Ren got up and left the bedroom. She threw her coat over the back of a chair at the tiny kitchen table. Then she went to put tea on.

She fished through the cupboards to find a kettle. Miri had an odd, mismatched assortment of glasses and cups. One of them said "World's Greatest Dad," another was shaped like a cat, and one had pinup girls on it. Interesting range. Ren had never heard Miri talk about her father, actually, other than to say that he wasn't around.

Ren set the kettle on the stove and started the water heating, then went to anxiously check on Miri. Underneath the matted carpet, the old wooden floorboards creaked beneath her feet. One couldn't move anywhere in the house stealthily. The people in the apartment above sounded like a herd of buffalo when they simply walked from one room to another. They were away on vacation at that moment, though, so all was still, apart from the noise that Ren made.

Ren sat next to Miri again. Her heart leapt when she saw Miri actually move her eyes to focus on her. She leaned forward quickly to cup Miri's face in her hands.

"Sweetie! Are you back? Talk to me! Tell me you're okay!"

Miri did not respond. She stared at Ren for a few moments, and then her gaze shifted to focus intently over

Ren's shoulder. A shiver ran up Ren's spine, and she turned around slowly to see what had caught her girlfriend's attention in the still, silent apartment.

The heating system kicked on with a jarring system of clunks that startled Ren nearly out of her skin.

But there was nothing there.

Ren turned back to Miri.

"What…what are you looking at? What are you seeing, Miri?"

Miri looked back at Ren, who breathed a short sigh of relief. She stroked her thumb over Miri's soft, pale cheek. She always touched Miri delicately, being very aware of her large, rough hands. They were calloused from spending hours and hours gardening. Ren had always liked plants more than people. She had her own garden at home. In the summer she worked at a greenhouse, and she worked year-round and full-time at a local flower shop.

The kettle started to scream on the stove, startling Ren away from her drifting thoughts.

"I'll be right back, okay?" Ren assured Miri "I'm making you some mint tea."

As Ren was pouring the water into the cups and adding the tea packets to steep, she heard a strange clicking sound. Eyebrows furrowed, she looked around the room. There was nothing there.

She saw it as she was carrying the tray with the teacups back to Miri's room. It was crawling across the ceiling, and the clicking sound was coming from its talons.

It was pure white, but not a shining white like the coat of a polar bear. This was a rotted, deathly white. The white of something that had never seen the sun. It had a long neck that snaked out ahead of its bony body, with a humanoid head at the end of it. Its body, too, was vaguely like a person's, except with longer limbs and raised vertebrae all down the spine. Hair hung in limp patches from the scalp, and when the thing turned to look directly at Ren, she saw that its eye sockets were hollow.

The tray with the teacups seemed to fall in slow motion from Ren's grip, the amber liquid spilling out in glittering droplets. When it hit the floor, it made a thump and several clinks. The cups rolled out onto the thick carpeting and the tea soaked into the fibers. The thing smiled, baring several rows of tiny, razor-sharp teeth.

But what Ren noticed automatically were its hands. The fingers were hideously long, just like the black handprints on the windowsill.

The creature looked away from Ren, as though dismissing her. It clearly didn't consider her a threat. Then it continued on its away across the ceiling, heading right for Miri's room.

Oh, hell no, Ren thought. *Don't you dare touch my girl.*

Without thinking about it, Ren grabbed the baseball bat near the front door (that she'd insisted on putting there) and went after the threat. When she got to Miri's room, the monster was directly over the small form on the bed.

"HEY! I DON'T THINK SO!" Ren shouted.

The pale creature's face swiveled in her direction on that long neck, and then it hissed. Miri was laying back on the bed and just staring at the terror blankly. She wouldn't fight it, so Ren would do so in her stead.

"GET YOUR UGLY ASS OVER HERE!"

The monster growled this time, low and deep, and then flipped and landed on the ground right in front of Ren. It raised up on its hind legs, standing almost like a human, and swayed its neck back and forth while twitching its long fingers.

Once it was on Ren's level, she could see that it was actually shorter and smaller than herself. It was also very, very skinny.

Miri made a small sound like a whimper from the bed behind the creature, and it whirled around to face its intended victim. Before it could take another step, though, Ren swung the bat. Hard.

It connected with the back of the thing's neck with a sickening crunch, causing it to collapse to the floor. Ren was raising the bat above her head to bring it down on the monster again when it rolled over and lunged for her with impossible speed.

Ren felt as though hundreds of tiny, thin needles had sunk into her neck. The creature had bitten into her shoulder, and its grip was very, very strong. Ren gave a roar of rage and pain and wrapped those big, rough hands of hers around the monster's skinny neck.

The two of them fell to the floor and thrashed about, knocking over a chair and a coatrack in the process. They wrestled each other for several minutes that seemed to last forever. Ren squeezed with all of her strength.

Finally, she strangled the monster enough that it unlatched itself from her shoulder. The second it did so, she flung it across the room. It crashed against the bureau and fled to the window in a blur of motion. It had yanked the window open and fled outside before Ren could react. The blinds were left in tatters.

She scrambled to her feet and ran to stick her head out the window. She looked up and down but saw nothing. A cold blast of wind drove Ren back inside. She closed and locked the window, then backed up, panting.

The handprints were gone. The pain was gone. Ren reached up to touch her shoulder where the thing had bitten her, but there was nothing there. No holes punctured in her shirt with tiny teeth. No blood. Nothing.

"Ren?"

Ren whirled around at the small, quivering voice. Miri was sitting up in bed again, looking directly at her, and she was *back*. Ren rushed over and wrapped the smaller woman in her arms, kissing her all over her face. Then she pulled back and put her hands on Miri's shoulders.

"Are you alright now?"

Miri nodded and looked like she just wanted to snuggle back into Ren's arms, but Ren had too many questions.

"What was that thing? And why haven't you ever told me about it? How often does this happen?"

She was firing the questions off too quickly for Miri to actually answer them. Ren knew that, but all of the anxiety from the last forty minutes just came pouring out of her. She was interrupted, however, by the sound of the doorbell.

Both women jumped.

"Oh," Ren mumbled. "That's probably your mother."

She stood up and started to leave the room. Behind her, she heard Miri speak with an edge of annoyance to her voice, despite everything.

"You called my *mother?* What are you, nuts, Ren?"

Miri sat quietly, listening to Ren and her mother talking in the living room.

"So you saw it, then?" came her mother's voice.

"I don't know what I saw!" Ren responded. "But it's gone now. It just…vanished."

"It always does."

Miri stopped focusing on the voices and looked over toward the window. Her blinds were askew, and some sunlight was filtering through and hitting the prisms.

Little rainbows danced across the wall and the floor, and Miri knew that Ren had saved her life.

-End-

Visage
By
Joe Haward

The world falls still, a tangible hush that reduces the volume, allowing space for the silence *behind* silence to reverberate within my ears. The trees outside my window are dressed in white; a resplendent glow that signals their intent to dance according to the sounds of nature's symphony. Even beneath the ashen clouds, there is a radiant pale blue hidden within the air, emanating off the snow that dusts the ground with its ephemeral presence.

I tilt my head slightly, longing to see the world from another angle, tenacious in my inexhaustible pursuit of freedom. A life beyond the window beckons me, calling me by name: a whisper upon the air that floats with the fragility of ash in the wind. But reality assaults such delicate dreams; the beauty they possess diminishing with every passing second. On countless sunrises, I have released my screams of frustration; cries dulled against the glass that taunts me - the view a spectacle of all that I cannot have - living up to its name of window pane.

Snow is falling steadily, delicate symmetrical patterns striking my bedroom window and collapsing in upon themselves; intricate beauty obliterated as they touch the glass, their final resting place ordered by events beyond their control.

I close my eyes and picture traversing the edge of a blackhole. The place where eternity and space melt and converge. Time bending beyond its own laws and capacity. I imagine stepping through the fusion of my reality and past, creating a new moment and existence where my body is released from its incapacitated state. Perhaps everything can be made new?

Fresh pain jolts my eyes open. Razor blades sliding up my legs: my illness reminding me that such fantasies belong within the abyss of suffering it has created. My whimpering breath catches in the cold air; white clouds that hover for a moment, sycophantic ghosts praising winter's grip. Frost is beginning to track its way along the ceiling, creeping slowly with spindly legs, trapping every drop of moisture within its icy web. I glance at the door, imagining the hallway beyond leading to the stairs that reach down into the basement where the boiler sits. I'm not sure when it stopped working. I see the cardboard boxes sprawled around it like desperate worshippers once upon a time sucking in its warmth with vampiric necessity, now fragile in winter's bite. With a light touch, I open one of the boxes. My hands glide over the contents, exploring the details of every object. I bring a photo out, the colors faded under time's paratrophic restlessness. I see myself, dancing: head thrown back in joyful surrender, laughter traversing the canyon of forgetfulness, uniting us once again in this moment.

I am twenty years old, my body alive to every possibility. There is a cool breeze taking the edge off the sweltering summer evening, turning the sweat on my face into refreshing droplets. The smell of cigarettes and beer hit the back of my throat, warming my senses, inviting effervescent discontent. My body moves in fluidic harmony with the music, melodic vibrations coursing their way through me; taking over, limbs lost in my own paradisiacal delight.

A tear traces its way down the faint lines on my face as memories from nearly twenty years ago flood in. Lies drip their way through my consciousness as I swear never to cry again about all that has been taken from me.

Familiar scratches echo faintly in the background, charting a course along the far wall, but I'm too cold and too tired to pay it the attention it desperately craves.

Piercing shrieks, and then shouts of excitement echo up and down the street outside as children throw snowballs and pull each other on sleds along the road. I close my eyes once again and listen to the activity, savouring the warmth of their adventure. What else can I do but listen with rapturous attention to their freedom? To delight in their own delight? Who am I, or, more accurately, *what* am I, if I imagined a truck, the driver careless and overtired, losing control and plowing into that winter wonderland outside my window? What if the snow was baptised in red, the lives of the families who belong to those children reborn through tragedy? Perhaps, I think with self-loathing and inner disgust, each wail of misery beyond my window will lessen my own suffering, their pain absorbing my own?

I'm twenty-five. My mother's blood decorates the kitchen floor; its smooth, bright surface offering a mirrored sheen. I examine my face upon the surface's reflection; my features bathed in crimson, swallowing the last scrap of my euphoria within its bloodied abyss. I stopped by to tell her that I'd passed my exams. She stares at me through lifeless eyes; a glassy shine that anticipates the window of my bedroom many years later, an eternal prison not of our own making. My father has fled the scene. I'll never find out where he went. The police tell me that a blow to the head of that force would've killed her instantly.

She didn't suffer, the officer tells me three or four times.

I want to ask if they've ever been hit over the head with an iron. How do they know that my mother didn't suffer? What about the years of abuse she endured and you ignored? Was that not suffering?

I smile and say thank you before leaving.

I wake again, fevered dreams refusing my body the opportunity to rest. I need to use the bathroom. Grasping the walking stick next to my bed, I manage to push myself up into a sitting position, my breath ragged and unsteady from such minimal activity. Slowly, with pain shooting up and down my body, I swing my legs out of bed, my feet touching the carpet for the first time in twenty-four hours. I gently wiggle my toes, the softness beneath them a welcome sensation, even as my bladder burns for release.

I inch myself forwards, the walking stick my guide, navigating the way through treacherous and seemingly unscalable terrain. Sliding off the bed, my knees crash into the floor, pain radiating everywhere, yet I refuse to surrender. I crawl towards the bedroom door, shuffling through dust and cat hair; the distinctive musty smell disturbed by my movements, settling on my tongue.

I wonder where the cat is? It has been months since I've seen it.

Traversing the hallway, I make it into the bathroom, my muscles burning, each movement a crescendo of agony; my body the conductor in this orchestra of misery. Resting my head on the toilet seat, I gulp air into my lungs; sights and smells of little consequence in this desperate state of gasping. Eventually I manage to pull myself up, sitting on the toilet with such inner triumph that I accept my own adulation.

The white glow from outside bathes the bathroom window like a spectre gliding through, making itself at home. I fall asleep, exhaustion my ever-present guide like Virgil at Inferno's gates, ushering me into its circles regardless of my will or desire.

I wake to the sound of laughter. A trickle of delight that floats across the air. Rubbing my eyes, I look around, recapturing my bearings as I exit my dream's layered world, and see that night has descended, darkness penetrating every corner of the bathroom.

The laughter continues, a child's voice—or perhaps two tonight—the faintest of sounds bisecting the path I had earlier crawled.

If only such laughter came from children still playing in the street, their delight ringing out into my weary soul. But alas, my tormentors have returned.

I'm not even sure what the time is.

Repeating the same arduous process of getting to the bathroom, I make my way through the shadows and dust, dragging my human remains towards the bedroom. My stomach churns with hunger whilst the scratching down my throat intensifies, like swallowing ash and sand together. But I will have to wait for home care tomorrow morning before I can eat again. Phantom tastes and smells haunt my senses, my body's longing for sustenance ferocious in its desire. Desires that send me home.

I'm six months old, unable to understand why my mother's eye is swollen and purple; the complexity of the shapes that make a path in her iris hidden from me behind the explosive rubble violence has left behind. Her face, almost a mystery to me, is stoic in defiance:

something even my young eyes unconsciously see. She draws me to her breast, the sweetness and warmth of her tender care feeding my body and soul. Her screams — baked into the very fabric of the house — muted within the humanness of this moment. Even then, before I understand how to have a thought, something shifts deep within; a recognition of my father's appetite to take my mother's humanity away. But no matter how hard he tries, she holds onto her somebodiness: our empathic connectedness uniting us beyond his terror, continually reminding us of one another's humanity.

Back in the bedroom, as I collapse into bed, the laughter stops. Muffled beneath whispers that implore the other to hush. I will not call out, asking who hides — a penumbra of menace stalking beneath obsidian shapes. I'm too tired for such games. Perhaps they might let me rest for a change? But something moves upon the window, taunting me with their ability to come and go with such ease. It appears that tonight I will be summoned once again. I quickly fall asleep, traversing the freedom that slumbered landscapes offer me.

A familiar pressure upon my chest wakes me, the sheets damp as my body shakes with intimate terror. The darkness of the room presses in all around, the air becoming thin as fear propels me further up dread's mountain; the path precarious, crumbling beneath my feet. One slip, and I will fall to my death.

If only it would let me die.

But it will not be so careless as to allow my suffering

to end with such ease.

The entirety of my being is bound beneath its power and control. The midnight of despair descends upon me, coalescing into form and substance, settling across my body like a spider preparing its meal. Night itself grows darker, swallowing the intensity of my fright and smothering me in its stench.

I search for solace, casting my mind away from this moment, excavating my memories that I might bury myself within them: covered in the dust of joy and regret, either one preferable to what hangs over me at this moment in time.

I'm thirty-three, walking home as the sun bleeds into the horizon, stretching up to usher in a new day. Its furious heat, even at this early hour, mocks me; its impenetrable glory ever more impressive in light of my own insignificance. But on this morning, I smile at its derision, the magnificence of being loved creating incandescent vivacity that causes the sun to nod in mutual respect.

The night before, lovers kissed — a tenderness of touch still resplendent with power. We spoke with fluidity and vulnerability, each attentive to the other; walls of ignorance broke down, bathing each of us in the capacity to be heard.

Promises were shared, the excitement of potentiality humming all around as utopian ideals drifted upon the air with fragranced convictions. But the scent of such aromatic vows would fade faster than either of us could have imagined.

By the time I have walked home, I know that something is wrong. Horizon's song rising like a melodic masterpiece suddenly choked in the back of my throat as all sensation on the right side of my face is lost. Pain crawls into the fibres of face, leg, and arm muscles, ripping them apart and making its home. Collapsing on the lawn outside the front of my home, this will be the last time I smell fresh grass; its scent, the coolness it leaves on my tongue, denied to me from now on.

Seven days later, discharged from the hospital, I lay entombed; my linen sarcophagus a blasphemous insult to the majesty of Ramesses. Whilst he rests in the Valley of the Kings, I am a tormented traveler in the pit of chronic despair.

During the first few weeks, people come and go, offering support and a helping hand. Dinner is cooked. The house is cleaned. A lover's hand holds cold flannels on my fevered head. As weeks bleed into months, enthusiastic care evaporates within the desert of my perennial pain. Friendships sink. That lover's touch turns resentful.

I am alone.

My mind snaps back, torment's pressure dictating every thought and sound; my memories infected with its malignant toxins. Each time this intruder calls, I fight, resisting its demands and manipulation. But again, as with every one of its visitations, the final walls of resistance crumble.

I'm twenty-seven, waiting for a friend in our favourite bar. The second drink warms my throat, deep flavours that dance off my pallet, relaxing my body. Sustained laughter forces its presence within the entirety of the space, unwelcome in its cruelty and derision. Like a siren's signal, it urges me to look across, find its source, embrace its contempt. I glance, a moment, nothing more. The predators have cornered their prey.

What the fuck are you looking at?

Paki.

Terrorist.

You don't belong here.

Go back to your own country.

Do you even understand what we're saying?

I make my exit, vulnerability no longer a strength I can use to withstand the damage their attacks produce.

The world descends into further darkness, neither memory nor reality offering sanctuary or shelter. Winter suspends my breath above my head – frozen screams captured in the air, withheld from a world that no longer remembers people like me.

I can feel the blood rushing through my veins, searching the extremities of my body. Every beat of my heart thunders – the roar of panic an alarm that will prove meaningless.

The cloud of unknowing settles upon me, who I am determined by the force of its presence, hovering with intent over this chaos. For the briefest of quixotic flashes, I fantasize that it will act with mercy, allowing me to pull and stitch back together an identity that has been torn from me. Such fantasies soon evaporate as my skin pulls tight.

Each time is slightly different, but the pain always

resembles the feeling of knives sliding up and down, as though I am being cut out of paper, an invisible dotted line around the edge of my body.

I feel my skin being pulled back, separated from muscle and connective tissue.

I'm being peeled like an orange.

The pain is excruciating, white lights bursting behind my eyes, pain detonating inside my head – yet unconsciousness dances away from me, agony screaming throughout my entire being.

Disorientated and delusional, I fade in and out of reality and dream, momentarily sitting with my mother as we read stories together: her gentle voice teaching me new words, smiling with pride and joy as I grow in confidence. Then we are outside my bedroom window, peering through the glass as I'm flayed, shaking our heads at the demonic exhibition. We walk away whilst I scream at them, pleading for rescue, for the liberation of emancipators. My screams fade into the ether of the night as mother and I build a snowman together. The snow crunches beneath our boots, sticking to our gloved hands as a snowball turns into a white boulder. Taking off her scarf, mother wraps it round the snowman's neck, his coal eyes giving us a wink of gratitude.

Looking up into the inky sky, a single snowflake falls onto my face, its uniqueness now bound to my own; both unparagoned in beauty, singular phenomena transposed into a collective.

I look at my mother as I begin to melt, tears frozen to the corners of her eyes, a breathless goodbye whispered as I shrink into oblivion. I glance towards my bedroom window, my own dulled screams still reverberating from the inside, hitting the glass, stuck and sliding down, converging into my own abyss. Every fibre of my being wills the void to consume and welcome me into its eternal rest, yet I return to my bed, hell's hand excoriating me.

Voices susurrate, rancid vibrations soaking their acidic deceptions deep into the recesses of my brain. High pitched giggles bounce off the window and walls – faint and indistinct at first, as though outside, buried in the snow, then deafening and overwhelming, intrusive and imperious. Something scratches at the window whilst scuttling noises move across the ceiling, misophonic sounds building in volume, maniacal energy, my mind and body burning in agony. The crescendo builds, and the world descends into darkness.

I'm woken by my carer, terror's signature written into their expression. Bleary-eyed and confused, I look down, trying to bring into focus the reason why their face is filled with awe and dread. My bed sheets are damp, the stench of diaphoretic fear filling the confines of the bedroom. A winter breeze whips around the room, the backdoor left open; my carer's desperate attempt to rid the house of the malodor that threatens to cling to skin and clothes alike. As my eyes adjust to the light, I realise the true nature of my condition.

Crimson stains push past every color on my bed, and it is then that I notice the strong metallic taste in my mouth. Lacerations cover my naked body; razor strokes of hate from diabolical artists, sight, sound, and shock their chosen medium. The *self* and *other* their canvas.

The final stages of full immersion into my illness are occurring, who I was no longer holding meaning as to who I have become. In the eyes of all who have known me, and, indeed, all who will subsequently meet me, I am this *becoming*, absorbed into this final, defining form. I consider exposing the darkness that haunts me, dissolving it with the light of empathy's power, begging my carer to listen and understand what this terror is that remakes me into its image. However, to those who cannot see Erebus's chasm, those falling are considered insane.

I can hear my carer speak, yet sound and understanding have dulled; serious voices that now lay beyond me, muffled as I stand outside my bedroom window, looking in.

Police and paramedics arrive, and I know that I will leave this place, bound and confined to a new room. Only this time I may not even have a window.

-End-

Pan
By
Elyse Russell

Sorry I'm late. Mind if I lay my coat on this chair? Freezing out there, huh? We're supposed to get more snow later.

I'm here for that interview you asked for. I don't care if you record this. Sounds fun, actually. I will warn you that I'm quite profane, though. Hope that's ok. You could edit it out later, I suppose.

What's my name? Well… I suppose you could call me Pan. I'm surprised you found me. Normally, I pass quite well as a human. I was so curious when you handed me your business card. So ominous! So, I looked you up on the internet and saw that you two yahoos like to debunk supernatural shit in your column for this two-bit newspaper, am I right? If that's your job, though, why did you come up to me? If you think none of that is real?

Oh, you're Sensitives. So, you've been looking for

something real. May I ask how you knew that I wasn't human? Oh. Yeah, teleportation would be a bit of a giveaway. Oops. Most people don't notice, though. That's why I called and agreed to this interview. Always looking to spice things up. So here we are! And I come prepared.

You sure you want to do this now? You aren't hungry? Oh, you're having a pizza delivered. No, thank you.

Oh, I'm always hungry. But a pizza isn't going to cut it for me, I'm afraid. You wouldn't want to see me eat, anyway. It would really fuck you up. When is it getting here? Well, that gives me some time. I brought something to help you to better understand this story I'm going to tell you.

This, my friends, is something no human has ever seen before. It is a miraculous little device called a Mind Scope. When you wear this on your face, you can view the experiences of different individuals. This remote allows you to switch from being to being. We'll wait a moment to start it up. I don't want the pizza guy to wonder what the hell we're up to in here.

Ah! Speak of the devil, there he is. No, I'll wait. Take care of it.

Go ahead and dig in.

Anyhow, after I've explained the basics, we will give this a whirl. Don't look at me like I'm nuts: just pay attention. I have something to hook it up to the computer so that the person not wearing it can see, too. It will be like a movie. You can take turns with the controller if you want. I see you're skeptical. Just give me the benefit of the doubt, here.

What am I? Well, that's my little secret. I'm here to spill the secrets of others. I'm a bit of a hypocrite, truth be told. I'm just doing this for kicks. I'm bored as fuck. You would be too, after thousands of years. Now, where should I start?

What if I told you that every monster ever imagined is actually real?

I'm not talking about some philosophical bullshit about how humans are the real monsters. Mankind is mankind's worst enemy. Everyone knows that. You watch a documentary of chimps tearing other chimps' babies apart, and you see *yourselves*.

What if I told you that every benevolent being ever imagined was *also* real? No, I'm not talking about saints or humanitarians or heroes or Beyonce. Stop trying to make everything about yourselves, you selfish little shits. Typical human outlook.

I apologize. I shouldn't have insulted you. Of course you are narrow-minded: all of your kind are. Maybe what I have to tell you will broaden your horizons.

Seriously, though. Guardian angels? Real. Vampires? Unfortunately, real. Little grey men? You bet your sweet ass. Cyclopes? Actually, no, not those. That was just humans being morons. They found some mammoth skulls and thought, *hey look! A giant man with one eye socket!*

Humans are always looking for their own image

everywhere. Ever notice how most aliens in your television shows are humanoids? Give it a couple hair feathers or some forehead ridges or blue skin and look: an alien!

Don't get me wrong. I love sci-fi shows. They entertain the hell out of me. But seriously, you really think that evolution would work like that across the entire damn universe? Everybody with a form almost exactly like yours? That would be some seriously improbable convergent evolution, right there. Like I said: selfish.

But I digress.

Where was I? Ah, yes. Dragons? Yep. Bigfoot?

Well, I guess. But Bigfoot is a chump. Don't tell him I said that, or he'll take a shit on my lawn, and his shits are *massive.*

Anyway, my point is: it's all real. It's around you, invisible to the majority. Every now and then, some Sensitive will see something. But people have no idea what the fuck they're looking at when they *do* see this shit, so their minds fill in the blanks to try and make it make more sense. You think a unicorn really looks like a horse with a horn on its head? Wrong. Some dipshit just saw one and equated it to the thing closest to that shape within their experience. They're not damn *horses.* They're white, yes, and they usually have legs and manes, but the similarities end there. And the horn? Yeah. That's its dick.

They are beautiful, though. And the dicks are quite sparkly, as dicks go.

Ghosts? Sure, lots of things can *seem* like ghosts, but they aren't the returning spirits of dead humans. You're convinced that thing in your attic is granny? Well damn, kid, granny's got way better shit to do in heaven. Why would she hang around this hellhole to haunt your scrawny, myopic ass?

Sorry, I'm working on the politeness thing.

Yes, heaven is real. God, too. Or whatever you want to call it. The Creator. And yes, it is an it. God is so far above the constructs of sex and gender that it's laughable. It isn't a "he." Nor is it a "she." It just *is*. It *is* God. P's and V's don't matter all that much. And P's aren't any better than V's, despite what a lot of men think. It was some dude that decided to call God "he" and "the Father" because he sure as shit wasn't going to admit that any woman was better than him, even if she was God.

You're an atheist? Whatever blows your skirt up. I'm not here to preach at you.

What do you mean bUt ScIeNcE? There is no God versus science. God IS science, motherfucker! Where the hell else would all this crap come from?

Of course, evolution is real. Why the fuck would God create an ever-changing planet and put creatures on it that couldn't adapt over time?

You guys are polar opposites. An atheist and a creationist.

We're getting off-topic. I'm not here to debate theology and religion and whether or not evolution is a thing.

Because it totally is. Don't narrow your eyes at me.

I'm here to tell you about what you're missing all around you. These beings pull at your minds, influence your actions, save your lives, and, sometimes, prey upon you.

Ok, I see you need some proof.

Who wants to try the Mind Scope first? What about you, sCiEnCe? Ok, I'll strap it on your melon. I'll hook up the cord…voila!

Pick up the controller. Turn that knob and push that button forward. Go on, don't be a chicken-shit.

There! You're the first human to give one of these a whirl. You lucky bug.

We have our first view. Perspective on the ground. Let's get the thought sensor on and hooked to the speakers…

Ok, sit back and relax. It's like a fucked-up movie.

The sidewalk is filthy here. Cigarette stubs, gum wads, candy wrappers, yellow snow, beer bottles…is that a condom? Yuck.

I don't even know what the hell THAT is.

Humans.

When your prey is this disgusting, you don't feel too bad about eating them.

Speaking of which…back to the hunt.

I love cities. All-you-can-eat, finger-lickin' good. To think, some of my kind are scared of the cities. Too much risk, they say.

Hacks. Pussies. More for me.

Let's take a whiff. Fast food, gasoline, exhaust. Underneath: armpit, piss, and fart.

Need a target. Let's see…too lumpy. Too lean. Too…sticky. Interesting. Moving on. Too sinewy. Bad diet, yuck. Ever hear of greens, dude? Too…wait.

There.

Female. A bit skinny, but… ohh, she took a kid's vitamin this morning. Huh. Must be a mom. Who cares. Let's go in closer… hmmm…

Sweet thighs: look at that! I just wanna…

What was that? I thought I saw…nah. That would be impossible. One of THOSE hasn't been seen around here in centuries. Where was I? Ah, yes. Lovely thighs. Let's follow and wait until she's alone…

Oh, shit! Let go! No, bastard, you don't get to eat ME. I'M the predator! No, get…

Oh, haha. He bit it. My friends, you just experienced the world from the point of view of a Thing.

What are Things? Nasty buggers. They're responsible for more than half of human disappearances worldwide.

I know you didn't get to see it, since we were looking out through its eyes, so I will describe it as best I can.

Things look like fleshy gray blankets with legs like water striders. Hard to visualize, I know. They can expand their folds of skin to swallow a human whole.

What ate it? Well, I think it was a Hound. If you use the knob on your remote, we can toggle over to the being closest to the dead Thing, which will be whatever is currently eating it. There we go. Ooo, deep voice.

These Things never taste nice. Serves him right, though. He should have sensed me coming. It isn't as though we Hounds are difficult to spot. How do you not notice a great, black, hairy beast headed straight for you? Then again, Things only think with their stomachs. Now, back to the job. Follow and protect, follow and protect, follow and protect.

My charge is going into a coffee shop. The smells tend to irritate my sensitive nose. Part of the job. Follow and protect, follow and protect, follow and protect.

Rider. I hate those. It's on person right next to my charge… better not look at her. Fingers wrapped all the way around that man's spine. Poor guy: he's drained to almost nothing. The greedy parasite is gorging itself. Looks ready to pop. It's fixing its creepy eyes on my charge now… oh, no you don't! You put that blue tongue back in your nasty mouth. Follow and protect, follow and protect, follow and protect.

A menacing growl should teach him to keep his eyes away from her. That's right, Rider. Follow and protect, follow and protect, follow and protect.

Don't stare at me with those goggly eyes of yours. Gonna bury your face in the back of your unknowing host's neck, huh? Seeking protection from that which you are slowly killing. Classy. The poor slob has no idea what's hanging on his back. It's too bad there aren't any Angels around, or that Rider would be toast. I'd deal with it myself, but it's against the rules of my contract. Follow and protect, follow and protect, follow and protect.

She's got her mocha now. Time to move on, thank the Creator. I must follow and protect, follow and protect, follow and protect.

I'll be burping up Thing all morning. But this woman is going to be the mother of some great scientist. I must follow and protect, follow and protect, follow and protect.

Ok, that's enough. If I hear "follow and protect" one more time…

That was a Hound. Strangely, they're the reason some people believe in guardian angels, and, paradoxically, werewolves. If you squint, I guess they sort of look like wolves. If you ignore all the extra legs, horns, and saber teeth.

They are usually hired by higher powers to protect people that have a big role to play in fate, or, in this case, the mother of someone who will do something important. Not bad blokes, by any means. I mean, they kept Alexander Fleming safe so he could discover penicillin, right? That has saved countless lives.

They're just a bit one-note to listen to. Not as bad as that Rider we saw, though. Let's give that bastard a listen. Toggle over…

Is…gone? Bad Hound. Hate Hounds. My host. Not yours. My feed. Mine mine. Move on. We go. Dark day. Snow soon. Hate snow. Hate world. Hold tight. My host. Mine mine. Feed feed. You suck. I suck. World suck. Happy thought! Mine mine. Yes more. You sad. Should be. World suck. Go home. No talk. No help. No hope. Host dying? Die soon? Need new. Host falling! Hold tight. Wait no. Bad smell. Know smell. What is? Is Angel! No no! Mine mine! Go away! Can't have! I bite! Mine…

You get the idea. He's toast, anyway, just like that Hound wanted. The Hound can't kill something unless it's harming his charge. He's bound by contract. I bet he called in reinforcements on the sly, though. I told you Hounds weren't bad blokes.

Okay, Riders: they are parasitical beings that hang like backpacks on humans and wrap their fingers around the spine. From there, they can absorb and feed on every good thought their host has. They also feed on misery, so they send messages up to the brain through the spine to drive their hosts' spirits down as far as possible.

Ugly motherfuckers, aren't they? They all pretty much look like that. They all have those useless hind legs that just hang like limp dicks. And the big, humped backs, and all those rolls of pink and red skin…yuck. It's the eyes that really freak me out, though. They're so big and dull. It's because nothing is ever reflected in them. Dead eyes. Their hosts' eyes can start to look dead after a while, too.

What are they? Well, they're what you would call depression, I suppose. Being depressed is never anyone's fault. How can they fight something they can't see?

Riders are actually responsible for the phrase "monkey on your back." Someone saw one once, and thought it was a monkey with mange.

Let's find out what offed it.

The poor, dear man. This Rider was attached for far too long. Oh, she's going to pull out the spine. I can't bear to watch it. I know the Rider must be exterminated, but I can't help it: I love all beings.

Okay, she threw the Rider's body away. Now I can approach and do my work. Oh, my. Why has no one taken care of you, Christopher? Why has no one noticed your depression? It is written in every line of your face.

That's right, come back to us. Shhhh, it will be alright. Here, have some hope. Breathe it all in. Wake up, sweetheart, and feel something other than sorrow for once. That's the spirit! There's more to life than you've been able to see from the Rider's clutches.

Ok, I'm going to lend you some strength, now. Enough to stand. You'll freeze, laying here like this. Easy, now. Don't fall. I can't catch you. You've really been through the ringer, haven't you? It's in the past now. Take a step forward. I will be right back, Angel Angela. Let me get this lamb to someone who can help him.

I'll steer you in the right direction. Just go where I lead you. Follow your instincts; your instincts will follow me.

I can see the hospital. You can't walk that far, can you? Especially not in this cold, with that threadbare coat. I'm going to get some help.

Where is a person that would help a stranger? Oh, there! That dear fellow can help.

Hello, Ayaan. What a perfectly apt name. God's gift. How lovely. You used to be a paramedic! I need your help, please. Look up!

I need you to notice the man over there, leaning against the wall. Yes!

Look at you, going over to help him all on your own! What a lovely soul. I do believe you can take it from here. I thank you with all my heart.

That was refreshing. We got to see an Angel. No, they don't look like humans with wings on their backs. I mean, they do have the wings. But the bodies seem to be made of light. Angels flit all about Earth, saving people. They can't be everywhere at once, of course. There's only a few of them, but they work tirelessly. They are usually the reason that "miracles" happen.

The being whose eyes we were seeing through was what your kind would call a fairy. We call them Patchers. She looks a bit more like a praying mantis than a human, though. A praying mantis with hands and hair and bird wings, maybe. Ok, I don't know how better to describe her. Sue me.

Each Angel has a Patcher partner. The Angel dispenses justice on the evil, and the Patcher helps to mend the harm in its wake.

No, I don't have anything snarky to say about Angels or Patchers. They're just good blokes all around.

Ok, let's try just a few more.

Where did they go, oh where did they go, oh!

Hee hee he'll never find them, oh no, no, no!

Where's the keys, oh where's the keys, oh?

You'll never know, no, never know, oh!

And…we're already done with that one! That was an Imp. Relatively harmless, but they delight in messing with people. That one appears to have hidden some poor idiot's keys. They always sing off-key.

What do they look like? Fugly. Kinda like Elf on the Shelf, but with a much bigger ass and ten times the creep factor. Remember these skanky turd bags the next time you can't find something.

NEXT.

Oh, boy. This makes me nervous.

Oh, my goodness.

Oh boyohboyohboyohboy.

Ok, umm…deep breaths…

In. Out. In. Out. In out in out inoutinoutinoutinout

AHHHH I CAN'T DO IT ANYMORE SOMEBODY HELP ME IT'S NOT WORKING WHERE'S A HUMAN? TAKE IT AWAY I'M DYING THERE'S A PERSON OH BOY OH BOY HELP HELP

Ahhhhhhhhh. Much better. Innnnnnn. Ouuuuuuut.

Sorry, dude. It's a doozy. But, hey! Better you than me, right?

Let's stop that one before I have a heart attack. That was a little Panic Bug. They look like a cracked-out squirrel bumped uglies with a cockroach. They get all worked up every four hours or so, and they can't get rid of the feeling until they touch a human. Then the human absorbs all of the anxiety, and the Panic Bug is fine again and can go on about its business. The human is fucked up for a little bit, though.

Ok, one more. I'm getting hungry.
uuuhhhhhhmmmmmmuuuuuhhhhhmmmmuuuuhhhhm-mmmmnooommmmmmmnooommmmmmmaaaahhhhh-hyuuuuuummmmnooooommmmmmmmmnommmmmmmmnom-mmmmm

I need a shower. That was a Blob. They like to eat people's grossest thoughts that fall out and soak through the ground. That's why it was a black screen- they live underground. It was probably licking the underside of a sidewalk or something. Not a whole heck of a lot going on in their heads. Although, honestly, I don't know if they have heads…huh. They're usually just giant grey or black chunks of jello. I saw one that was baby-shit green, once. Lord only knows what HE was eating.

There's all sorts of beings out there like that. Some are bad, and some are good. Some can touch a person on the shoulder and give them a boost of confidence to get through something difficult. Some will make you think you heard something when you didn't. Some can delay you if they know that you could be headed to an accident and thus save your life.

All of these creatures can influence human behavior.

This was fun, guys. Let's never do it again.

It's too bad we couldn't catch a unicorn tonight. Those guys are entertaining. And horny. Soooo horny. Pun absolutely intended. Anyways, any questions?

Well, this is going to sound cliche, right? It's said over and over again. But maybe you'll listen if I say it.

Here it is: BE KIND. Stop fucking tearing each other's babies apart. Be forgiving. You never know who has a monkey on their back.

-End-

The Worst of Behaviors
By
Hector Duarte, Jr.

"Why did we come here?" Lucciano asked. They were still in the car, parked by a sign welcoming visitors to Camp Blanding, Florida. Almost exactly where Mom had parked that last Christmas.

"I don't know." The trip hadn't seemed senseless to Luccia when she had planned in, packed the car, or at any point during the more than five hours drive north.

Lucciano hadn't said a word the whole time, as usual. Not until they were parked in front of the sign, with all the driving and silence behind them.

There was nothing here for them anymore. Hadn't been since that last Christmas.

The last time she could, vaguely, remember them being kids. Before Lucciano's pill-popping had reached critical mass. Pill popping was inaccurate. By the end, he'd taken to crushing the pills into fine powder and tooting them; instant high begets instant fall.

Luccia had taken him in, pretending he had a terminal illness. Her brother was sick. What else to do but take care of family?

For Luccia Artola, guilt was a massive motivator.

Luccia didn't apologize for the five-hour trip. Lucciano didn't make her feel she had to. Her brother had many defects, but one of his admirable traits was that he hadn't yet started to let his addiction affect their relationship.

In her attempt to revert back to when they were still kids, she attempted to pull mom's magic trick out of its hat. "Want to go to Disney World?"

Lucciano shrugged and looked over at her. "You don't have any plans?"

"Nope."

He shrugged. "Sure. Sounds like fun." No fist in the air like Superman; no hollering or giggling. A shoulder shrug was the most he'd give.

When she pulled up to The Peabody Hotel, Lucciano looked up, way up to the height where he thought they had stayed, and smiled. He knew that the last Christmas with Mom had been the best one ever for either of them. "Yeah, this makes sense," he said.

She'd booked the same room. The hotel had been renovated and changed names but its core, the structure that took them back to that last time with Mami, remained.

That's what she needed. She knew her brother needed it too.

The hotel still did its kitschy nightly show, having a procession of ducklings come out of the main elevator and waddle through the lobby. It was hugely popular with families and small kids.

As the ducklings passed, Lucciano smiled like he had on that last Christmas, when mom had finally confronted dad about his cheating. Six-year-old Lucciano had become so nervous, he'd thrown up all over dad's military-issue boots.

Now, Luccia apologized for having taken him to Camp Blanding. "You're right. There was no point going there."

"I didn't feel anything," Lucciano said, looking at the ducklings, not at Luccia.

"What?"

"That's the point of the trip. I always feel something when I think of Camp Blanding. But not today. Not anymore. I was meant to come here to know I don't feel anything anymore."

After the procession, they hung out by the pool, watching the glow reflected from the water glide across each other's faces.

"That place really fucked us up. Dad really fucked us up," Lucciano said.

Luccia didn't know what to say.

"Me." He corrected himself. "It really fucked me up."

"I'm sorry." Luccia said.

Lucciano leaned over and grabbed her forearm. "For

what, hermanita? You're not the one who needs to be sorry. He's God knows where. He should be apologizing."

Luccia was suddenly sobbing, like she was the age she'd been the last time her father turned his back on her, facing the monolith of a fucking military base that had swallowed his entire being as he slowly walked back inside, out of their lives forever. "I'm sorry Dad didn't treat you like he did me."

Lucciano sat up and threw his feet over the side of the beach chair. He patted his sister's thigh twice and said, "Again, none of this is your fault. He's the asshole who left us without explanations."

They chatted until hotel security kindly reminded them the pool was closed for the night.

The next day, Lucciano asked if they could skip the park. He wanted to be a lazy ass. Luccia was drained too. They agreed to stay in, order room service, and binge ION Television. After three different *Law and Order* episodes, bookended by *Criminal Minds*, it was duck-procession time.

Lucciano was a quarter of the way done with a philly-cheese steak sandwich as long as a submarine, and almost as expensive. With a mouthful of bread, meat, and cheese, he mumbled for her to go on ahead, he'd catch up.

It was a Friday. Most families were out at the parks, staking out prime spots for the end-of-night fireworks displays. Luccia was able to nab a primo duck-watching spot right by the elevator. She didn't have to widen her elbows to ensure comfortable standing room. As the ducks passed, Lucciano still hadn't shown up. She took some pictures and video to show him.

When she returned to the room she saw: he'd hanged himself. For what? So many things. Some likely her fault, others not. One thing was certain. Lucciano wanted his sister to find him. He'd left a note by the bathroom sink.

Haven't used in the last five days. Wanted you to know I didn't do this under the influence of anything. I am lucid, clear, and conscientious. I don't want to be here anymore. Don't cry, don't question. This is the best thing I could have done for myself, for anyone. Te amo, hermanita. Nos vemos en el otro lado.

Luccia clutched the note, pulled up a chair in the middle of the room, and sat there watching her brother hang from the wardrobe closet; just the two of them for close to an hour before she called it in.

Using the blunt honesty she'd always admired in her brother, she told hotel security she'd come up from watching the ducks and found her brother, Lucciano Rodrigo Artola, wrapped around his brown cowhide-leather belt.

"Why'd you wait so long before telling us?" The female house dick asked, scrawled furiously in her blue dollar-store memo pad. She sucked her lips and nodded whenever Luccia finished a sentence.

"He wanted me to find him. I wanted to be alone with him. I'll never see him again."

The furrows on house dick's forehead deepened. "I'm going to need you to hang around until I get cops in here. You understand why, right?"

"Of course. I booked this room through the weekend."

"Ma'am. This is a crime scene."

Luccia shrugged.

"You're not going to be able to stay in this room."

"But I'm booked through the weekend."

"The concierge will find you other accommodations, I'm sure."

There was no need. By midnight, the investigation was over and the cops were clear, just like Luccia had been as soon as she'd walked in and found him. She didn't need a note, but it was like Lucciano to leave one.

The hotel insisted on refunding the rest of her stay. Luccia resisted. The concierge insisted on hotel credit, at least. Luccia agreed, knowing she'd want to return to the site of her brother's death.

Christmas 2020

"What are you doing?" Edwin was staring as Luccia pressed hands against the bathroom mirror.

She couldn't say how long she'd been there. Probably just a few seconds, right? Or he would have said something earlier. Gone was the humidity from the scalding water, the fog all over the mirror, her brother's handprints. "I," she began, knowing the rest of what she wanted to say would be absurd and ridiculous. She went with absurd and ridiculous anyway. "You ever play the Bloody Mary game?"

Edwin scoffed. "Yeah, when I was, like, eight. Why was the water running so hot?"

Luccia shrugged. "Let's go see the ducks."

"Go by yourself. You're gonna drag me to this stupid ass park, I need some sleep. Oh, and we have to stop and get beer at some point tomorrow." Edwin walked to the toilet, unzipped, and pissed. He hocked up a big loogie and spat it into the fizzing yellow puddle.

Luccia stood, mesmerized by her brother's message. So entranced, she didn't realize she'd been staring at Edwin.

"Wish you'd stare at it like that more often," Edwin said.

Luccia giggled. Not at Edwin's attempt at a quip.

The park itself just wasn't the same without Lucciano. She missed the little-boy wonder he had always carried with him, like he'd been seeing everything for the first time. In the last five years of his life, she'd credited that quality to the drugs. Now she knew it'd always been there, and the drugs had numbed it.

Edwin needed beer to keep him at bay. He constantly rolled his eyes at the fantasy of the park, and by lunch, with eighty dollars of beer swishing in his stomach, he was ready to go. His eyes were glassy as he yawned like a sleepy cat, louder and louder, to remind Luccia he was over it.

She didn't acquiesce until her feet felt like compressed hot dogs about to blow from the pressure. By the time they hit the central square, she was ready to call it but there was one more ride to hit. Lucciano's favorite: The haunted mansion.

Edwin breathed a sigh of relief at the upcoming end, noting he could not bear one more line and his wallet was nearly empty. He wanted to keep his buzz going, but not at ten dollars a pop.

They were in the first part of the ride: the haunted elevator. Edwin's breath filled the entire space with a musty beer smell. Luccia was ready to head back and sit alone by the hotel pool. She had tried to honor her brother's memory, and she genuinely hoped Lucciano appreciated the effort, but she could no longer put up with the man-child at her side rolling his eyes at every childlike facet of the park despite acting so much more immature than its target audience.

The elevator suddenly went pitch black. People screamed for dramatic effect. Edwin scoffed, blowing a beer belch over their heads. It disgusted her and some of the others.

When the lights snapped back on, Edwin jumped back and pointed at the corner of the elevator's faux ceiling. It was only there a split second, but Luccia saw what he saw. There was Lucciano, pointing right down at him from inside one of the ride's fake portraits. With a smile, her brother motioned slashing across his throat with a long, thin, bony thumb.

She'd recognized him anywhere.

Edwin squeezed her forearm as people snickered at him, as they filed out to the second part of the ride.

"Did you see that?" he asked.

Luccia played dumb and shook her head silently. Of course she'd seen Lucciano. And she was happily complicit.

"How could you not see it?" Edwin asked. His voice filled with annoyance that no one else was sharing in his experience.

Luccia shrugged. "I didn't see anything."

Lucciano made his second appearance on the last part of the ride. Right at the end, when holographic ghosts pop up next to, or in between, passengers. There was Lucciano— clear as day. All six feet of his hunched posture. She always made fun of him for standing as if a hanger were still inside his shirt—sitting between her and the drunken man-child.

Now, Lucciano had one arm around his sister, was smiling at Edwin and flipping him off.

Edwin pushed the safety bar away before the ride had come to a complete stop.

Someone whispered, "Asshole's too drunk for his own good."

All the way back to the hotel, Edwin asked how she didn't see that guy following them through the ride. Luccia played dumb as Edwin described her brother to a tee.

Edwin got back to the hotel room, popped open a beer, and fell face-up on the bed, snoring off the beer and anxiety churning through his system.

After the ducks had waddled through the hotel lobby, Luccia went to the pool. No one was out. She was all alone to watch as the reflection off the water glided across her face. In the water, she saw her brother smiling, exactly as he'd been the two other times she'd seen him today. Smiling right at her while scaring the shit out of her drunken asshole of a boyfriend—her companion for companionship's sake—was classic Lucciano.

"Ma'am, is everything all right?" It was the same private dick as two years back. She didn't—maybe didn't want to—recognize Luccia.

"Of course. Why do you ask?"

"I've called your name a few times now."

"I didn't hear you. What do you want?"

"To let you know the pool closes in ten minutes."

"So I still have time."

"For what?"

"To stay down here."

"Yes, but just a gentle reminder, if you're still down here when it closes, I will ask you to leave. Again."

"Thank you."

The house dick turned. When she got to the short entrance gate, Luccia called out. "Do you know where they keep the ducklings that file out through the lobby every night?"

"Yes. But I can't tell you."

"Why not?"

"For the ducks' safety."

"Okay. Thanks."

"Have a good night, ma'am."

"You, too. Thank you for the heads up."

A gust of cold wind whipped through, but the water did not ripple. Smooth as glass.

Knocking called her attention to the room's window ten floors up. No way she could have heard from so far off, but there it was again. Knock, knock, knock. The shade had been pulled wide open and the TV light flickered in the dark room.

No way for her to see inside, but she'd bet another five overpriced beers the room was lit by police procedural television. What she did see, clear as the pool's water, were Lucciano's hands slowly imprinting themselves on the fogging window glass.

Back upstairs, the TV was muted. The only sound bouncing between the four walls was Edwin's truck-loud snoring.

She could roll him on his side but then he'd be up the rest of the night, light sleeper that he was, bitching about why the hell had she had woken him. Hitting the power button on the remote did nothing. Shemar Moore's bare chest would not flicker off to a digital sliver. Edwin's klaxon snoring slowly faded to nothing as another sound took over.

Ducklings quacked inside the bathroom. They were in the bathtub, swimming in a circle atop scalding hot water that fogged the mirrors and suffocated the room with its thickness. Quack, quack, quack; a duckling merry-go-round.

Luccia sat on the sink's countertop and watched with a smile. A smile like the ones she'd stretched her face with whenever Mom told her they were going to Camp Blanding, whenever they'd first seen dad on their arrival. How Lucciano had smiled when Mom had railed against their father that last Christmas after he barfed all over PFC Artola's combat boots.

Luccia always knew how Lucciano would end up if she supported the worst of his behaviors. But at least it kept him around a few years longer.

"What the fuck is going on here?" Edwin asked, rubbing the sleep from his eyes.

Luccia giggled. "The ducks from the lobby. Look at them. They're in our bathtub. Chirp, chirp, chirp."

"What the fuck are you talking about? Ducks don't chirp."

"Seven ducks swimming in a circle. Look."

Edwin peered into the bathtub then turned to Luccia. "¿Estas loca o que? Nothing's. . ."

The shower's retractable clothesline slithered from its base and wrapped taut around Edwin's neck in three loops. Tighter and tighter until his tongue lolled out and his face went blue like the swimming pool water. Seven ducks quacked as Lucciano's distinctive hands imprinted themselves on the off-white shower tiles. Hands she could recognize in a line-up.

Luccia did not scream or move as Edwin faded to nothing; literally. In a few minutes, the ducks still chirped, but Edwin was completely gone, as if he'd never existed.

She smiled. Finally, they'd get to stay out the entire reservation. Luccia, Lucciano, the ducks, and Christmas.

-End-

Rena and The Focaccias or The Tragedy of Silent Stairs
By
Suraya

The last sweltering air carries a distinct aroma for seasoned bakers. In their mind's eye, the oven spring starts —the heat melts the salt and drains the oil-infused dough for the final time; gas escapes the gluten lattices through the delicate golden crust, but not before lifting the focaccia. In Rena's mind, a different image. She decided that Sayeed's coquetry from a few hours ago was a good distraction. Surprised by the undeniable closeness between them, rose-tinted vignettes from their first date – or first meeting to be more accurate – flickered on since the start of the graveyard shift. But his charm was not the reason for these replays. She could excuse the creaks from the floorboards above as wintery night sounds. Wood often contracts and squeaks for no reason, more so during one of the coldest weeks in January. On a different day, the atypical noises won't register in her focaccia-occupied mind. But she was alone and even the snow dust on Sayeed's curls did little to assuage her concerns about a message written in flour:

Ciao Renaa

Misspellings of her name occurred as often as its mispronunciations. But this time, it was not indignation that rose. This time, she was silent, and it was fear.

Emergency. can start shift @ 4? open bakery and normal batches. will pay 2x.

She's dreamt about the elusive double pay since September when she started at Uncle Johan's bakery. Is he trusting her more now? Having known her before she even knew her own name, Uncle Johan has always trusted her to do the right thing. But trusting her *baking abilities*, that was different. It seems that he now trusted her enough to open the store alone and do the normal batches – leavened focaccia doughs are stretched evenly on baking trays, slathered with superfluous amounts of secret olive oil emulsion, dimpled with deep repositories for the oil and then salted and baked. There was a beam on Rena's face when she caught her reflection on the darkened phone screen. She could use the money to pay for that culinary course on her wish list. But volunteering herself would mean pulling an all-nighter because she could not conceive the idea of rescheduling her first date with Sayeed. "Okay so a nice dinner, yada yada, go home, study for an hour, quick shower, quick nap, and then drive to work. Doable." she thought.

It was also a chance to practice driving in this cold weather at night instead of having mum or dad drop her off at work. She'd always known she was cooler and more independent than her pastel-coloured hijab and chamomile-shaped buttons let on. Hitting the road at 3:45am with Dua Lipa at a volume loud enough to belt out – but not loud enough to disturb neighbours recovering from overeating and maddening conversations – was another treat. The upside of Christmas-and-Epiphany celebrations was the additional seven days of winter break. The downside for people actually celebrating was the opportunity for families to make each other twice as miserable. Also, driving at 3:45am with ice on the road is a lot safer and easier now with new streetlamps outlining the five converging roads in her town – Rena's mum learnt that being persistent with the backing of anxious white women harping on the safety of children – *"think about the children"* – was the strategy she needed to get the town council to do anything. So now the roads lit brightly enough at night. The snow tires under the hooded pockets of their family car were the final layer of assurance she needed.

Floating in her glee, Rena never questioned why Uncle Johan had sent a text from an unknown number.

If watching the morning news at 5am was a habit, she would smile every time Alessandro Zucchini came on screen. To her, food-based last names were endearing. Names. Her mind jerked back to read '*Ciao Renaa*' once more. A cute love interest, heart-warming reports on Epiphany celebrations, and Alessandro Zucchini – none of these had worked as distractions. The message-in-flour (she went with this description) obscured the smooth silver surface of her workstation with fine flour dusted all across it the way tables look before a baker kneads dough. It was photographed and brushed away by Rena when she assumed it must have been Harianti's prank before the human-like noises started upstairs. She glanced back at the table behind her. But there was really no need with her phone's volume set to the maximum for an alert tone so obnoxious. The message-in-flour matched the playful demeanour of Harianti who had the final shift the day before and would have long endured a variety of butchering done to her name. Between them, there were few shared interests. These shared experiences helped them bond.

A thud. Right above her. She texted Harianti before starting on the first batch. By now, the second was slathered in uncle Johan's olive oil concoction, waiting to be dimpled by her fingertips. It made more sense that she was asleep than awake at this hour. The sun gleams in January, too shy to disrupt slumbering bodies warmed up under duvets and one another. Her mum might be up on her feet to ready for morning prayers, ambling past the guest room, shaking her head at her husband's still reverberant snoring. Maybe Harianti sets her alarm for the first prayer too? Maybe. Rena guides her thoughts elsewhere. Making focaccias became a life-affirming passion after she received an offer for the job. She fell in love with the science behind the salty delicate bread – the gluten forms when proteins, glutenin and gliadin, meet water and whisk to the rhythm of the gigantic industrial mixer. Sprinkles of yeasts, crystals of salt, and teardrops of lard add depth to their dance. All this had little to do with her social work and public policy master's degree which she promised her parents she would finish this semester, a semester earlier than her cohort. But the promise of halal focaccias and having a literal hand at them was far more magnetising. She has always loved them.

Sixteen years ago, she moved to Italy with her parents. She was eleven, and her neighbours were the Angelicos. She knew Cassandra better than Simone because she would help her rake the leaves on their front yard while he played video games all afternoon. Afterwards, Cassandra and Rena often took a respite from the heat with a cold glass of lemonade or iced tea accompanied by a spread of sweet or salty biscuits and, sometimes, focaccia. So much of her mastery over the language traces back to these Saturday conversations about Hollywood films, local politics, and

Italian food; all while munching down on the glistening flatbread. Months passed before curiosity brought her to that fateful Wikipedia page: like almost everyone else in the country, her Italian neighbour used *pork* lard in her focaccia recipe. Rena's parents never bought anything from the supermarket's Delicatessen, nor did they get snacks from the aisle everyone else got theirs. She assumed frugality. She never questioned the minuscule halal stamps on all their food. Hitherto, her confession to Cassandra haunts her – Mrs. Angelico stopped serving focaccias and all the biscuits. Instead she brought out the same strawberry wafers Rena ate at home. Nothing really changed between them, some Saturdays she would eye the grease-spotted paper bags she imagined held salted flat bread from the bakery to the Angelico's dwelling. Rena never asked her about them. Simone's acceptance into the University in Bologna became an impetus for the Angelicos to move and stay closer to him. Mrs. Angelico gifted her a book about Northern Italian home-cooking before bidding farewell. They stopped sending holiday cards two years ago.

The upstairs had been quiet for about two minutes. Rena grew convinced that the message was Harianti's innocuous revenge for switching shifts a while ago. No one was awake at this ungodly hour during the winter break unless they are paid overtime or lead a life with intense, punishing schedules in the name of 'success'. The thought of leaving her post for the safety of home occurred earlier, but it did not feel right to abandon the leavened dough to deflate. She also had no evidence that there was a real threat – the message was unnerving at best, not threatening or violent. The bakery was Uncle Johan's bread and butter – he was raising his daughter with its modest surpluses. Her parents' approval for solely his bakery also meant that it was the only place in town Rena could gain employment - the baker married her dad's cousin, bringing lots of halal focaccias to *kenduris* that didn't stop even after their divorce. In their books, and she imagined in many others, he was a good man. Rena withheld judgement until she completed her two-week probationary period. The man was a visionary in his own right, opening the first and only halal focaccia bakery in town after getting a small loan from members of the community. As his marriage disintegrated, his reputation and batches of bread swelled – the store attracted visitors from towns over, and some from the city. Rena was paid 16 Euros per hour, meals during and after her shift, and constantly met compassion when she had to leave a little earlier for lectures. They were right about him, but her phone's shrill alert tore her away from that conclusion.

She was mid-dimpling the last tray, so she hastened the process without compromising quality. Completing the work was more important than anything cheeky from Harianti or her service provider. Like a doctor ready for surgery, she held her hands high and at a good distance from her shoulders. She inched closer to her phone and tapped the screen with the tip of her nose. The bright light almost stunned her, but it was fine enough to read. "Harianti: Heyyya, nope. Uncle Jo closed shop last night, some emergency. I…," the preview ended. Rena tapped her nose again, now with urgency. It continued, "I wasn't at work…ARE YOU BEING HAUNTED? Hehehehehee." The god of all things going wrong was also awake at half-past five in the morning because at that moment, boxes toppled above her. If she swore, she would have sworn she heard scuffling.

Denying that she heard the tumbling coming from the attic would be reckless at this point. She looked at the dimpled focaccias minding themselves on their baking trays, each one parallel to the other like babies in a hospital's baby room. "Baby room? Surely that's not what you call it? Where—" another distinct movement, quieter and more careful like whoever was upstairs knew that their mistakes must have gained her attention. Rena wiped her hands and fingers to rid of the oil smeared over them. It was a fool's game because they came out of the fabric looking glorious and silky in the warm light of the room, useless for grabbing something as a weapon. She made do. The pan that heated up her snack earlier was now repurposed – any burgling hand could grab a rolling pin and turn it against her, but how was it going to grab a slippery, burning Teflon when she comes at them? Behind her, the baby focaccias cooed themselves to sleep.

About 45 degrees upwards – this was hardly the time for precise math – but the door to the attic was about 45 degrees up from where Rena was standing at the bottom of the stairs. If she opened the door and the intruder lunged at her, she would fall; she might break her neck; she might die; she might get maimed; but she would most certainly fall. Contrary to popular belief, not all wooden steps in old shophouses creek, thankfully. Back to the wall, her fingers stretched to make contact with the edge of the door handle, gentle enough to not make a sound while she pushed it down. With a sudden gust of energy, she pulled the door back as close to her as her generous breasts would allow (she had a love-hate relationship with them). Hidden in the triangular space between wall and door, the sliver of light coming in allowed Rena to observe any movement in or out of the attic. "Now what?" The adrenaline had abandoned her and there in the small pocket of the corridor, she noticed the back of her waistband was so wet that it became cold, chilling her spine.

Logic questioned her. Most people would not have contrived this situation for themselves if they feared an intruder had broken into their workplace. No employment is worth a life, so a logical self-loving person would have left the bakery, rushed home, and explained everything to Uncle Johan who, and Rena is above confident in this, would have not only understand her actions but *expected* her to behave as such. No such luck here – Rena wanted to assume the best and prove to herself that everything up until that point had either been a prank or a mere coincidence: an unnerving message traced out in flour and made out to her by name? A joke. Harianti claiming it's not her? Another joke! Sound of boxes falling in the attic above? Winter noises, right?

Almost ten minutes must have passed since Rena caught herself between a rock and a hard place: the wall and her imminent demise behind the door. Pan in her dominant hand, there was stiffness and tension as she glided against the wall and held her breath to crouch inside. Naïve tourists and café lovers hoping to delight in a rustic attic of a bakery in an old shop house would scowl at this sight. There was nothing to romanticise about a broken combi, a working combi, an assortment of metal machinery, equipment, baking tools, a dozen plastic carboys filled with home-made focaccia emulsion, unlabelled boxes, and other things her brain categorised as paraphernalia so that it was easier to process the mess. And of course, cobwebs and the spiders responsible for them. No intruder though. At least, not one she could spot with the illuminance of the street lamps (she made a note to thank her mother). As she scanned the room in her crouching position, the pan-holding hand was still at the ready to strike. She scanned again, moving 180 degrees leftwards: the strategic benefit of her position right next to the door. The boxes were in place. In fact, nothing seemed to have moved since she came up here with Harianti to grab more olive oil concoctions. Was there any sense in what she was doing? That question was punctuated when a sharp needle-sized pierced through her thick jeans and the flesh of her left thigh. Dropping the pan to her side, she started to relax, and she rubbed the wounded area. As the residual tension left her, she was no longer scared.

It was Notte, as in *buonanotte* or goodnight in Italian, but also Notte, as in The Cat, Sarah's cat. His red collar dotted with white pawprints and a green bell was gone – she had gotten it from her mother as a *Christmas* present much to Uncle Johan's dismay, but he'd tolerate just about anything for his sweet daughter. Notte's love on the other hand was conditional; he must have wiggled his tiny head out of the collar when no one was looking. Rena left the task of finding it to her boss. Notte had troubled her enough for one night. She carried the little cat in her arms and made a quick series of movements before closing the door behind her. Then, standing at the top of the stairs, she was once again a frightened 27-year-old woman, but now holding a cat. It was a small fright though; fear gave way to recognition. The eyes that were not there when she came up to the atti, belonged to a man she had known for a long time. She was very sure that he meant her no harm, and that the fierce, confused expression on his face was reasonable coming from a boss who found their employee with a cat instead of a completed set of focaccias.

Her heart sank when he spoke. "So you didn't need me to come in early today?" Rena queried. Uncle Johan was doubtful but given the hectic day he had, he supposed he might have. Fragile was a strange word to associate with him, but Rena knew it was the right one. Sarah was hospitalised with a high fever and had asked for her mum. It took too long to get in touch with her and, in the frenzy, a frantic uncle Johan got caught in the doorway. There was a red latex Band-Aid decorated with smiling green dinosaurs on his forehead. It would have been a stark accessory on a good day. "Nursery," Rena muttered as the divergent thought came to her but he was not listening. He said, "let's get these home to your parents, and I'll pay you for the hours today," as he carried the second and third tray of focaccias into the oven. He managed a smile to compliment her beautiful handwork, and she could tell it was genuine, if tired. He was especially grateful that Rena found Notte because he realised too late that he left a precocious adolescent cat in a bakery. She decided against telling him about the message-in-flour and the noises. It would only compound his bleakness.

With the kitchen cleared, the pair prepared to shutter the store for a week. Notte stayed behind to post by the glass window of the bottom-most oven; not to stand guard but for warmth and some light entertainment. He would have made a poor guard. When Rena was helping Uncle Johan close, Notte ignored the man who made no noise as he slipped out of the attic and climbed down the stairs. This was the tragedy of cats and silent stairs. It was a man that Rena knew but didn't notice when she was looking for him earlier. Out in the falling snow, spotted only by an apathetic cat, cloaked in icy white flakes, he escaped.

-End-

Jackie
By
Kasimma

Father Francis relished in the jangles of his voice. He talked about how Buhari was the worst person to happen to Nigeria. Even if I only believe a rumour after the government has denied it, I agreed with Father Francis that the president man knew he was unfit for the crown. Father Francis' facial muscles contracted as he spoke animatedly, counting the nation's failings on his fingers. I poured him another glass of Bailey's, my thoughts occupied with the final touches to my plan. For six months, I calculatedly worked my way into Father Francis. The first time he noticed me, which was actually three weeks later than he should have, was when I went to ask for forgiveness for my "impending suicide." His kind, fatherly voice reached me through the thick wood of the confessional. I glimpsed him through the gauzed hole, his head bent and eyes closed as he listened. He then asked me to come to his office where he began counselling me on how to draw nearer to God during travails. The counselling section ignited our close-knit friendship. He became a constant visitor to my house.

Father Francis tapped my lap as if to call my attention. His eyes shone as he spewed words about the Ghana Empire. This gist was better than the knackering rant over Buhari's incompetence.

"The Trans-Saharan slave trade, I guess, was as intense as the Trans-Atlantic slave trade, but with far lesser documentation," he said.

I decided to say something abstract to check if the "love-portion" I had dropped in his Bailey's had started kicking. "Those who looked up for rain should now look down for mud."

"Exactly!"

I smiled, satisfied.

"Look, bah," he said, tapping my lap, "if Africans don't tell her story, another person will tell it for her, and, then, God help her."

What's my own with stories? I almost laughed. Almost. Harmattan will lick the lips of a person who refuses to lick them themselves. If Africa like oh, let her not tell stories oh, or sing songs oh, or act movies oh, or what-is-my-blessed-own oh! E no concern me; I don't care. My concern was about to go down, and I could not wait. My breath scented of calmness irrespective of my pumping adrenaline. I was close. Very close.

Father Francis kept enjoying the sound of his voice. "See bah, Jack, even if all Nigerians become storytellers, we will still not be enough to tell the story of Nigeria. The land is vast, but there are no farmers."

His forefinger dragged sweat from one point of his forehead to the other, salting my rug with his filth. I mentally counted to twenty, channelling my anger to the nonentity I bumped into, during my afternoon walk, along Ahmadu Bello way, in front of a building that was formerly Lion Bank, later Diamond Bank, now Access Bank. A girl ran out of the bank's ash bar gate, clutching her stomach. She spurted forth a slimy mixture of beans. I jumped back, missing a puke bath by a hair's strand. The girl kept throwing up. I wanted to grab her by the neck, raise her face to mine, and slap her until her "yellow" face turned red or blue or even dead. Almost did. But I jumped over the thing and passed.

"Okay, imagine someone like Gowon. You know Gowon, right?"

I nodded. What a stupid question! Which Nigerian my age had not heard of Yakubu Gowon?

"Good. Tell me why Gowon has not written a very good book about the truth of what caused the Biafran war. Who shall we run to for the truth? Wait, I'm coming, let me go and urinate." He got up, dragging his feet. He entered my bedroom and shut the door.

A bat flies at night because it is aware of its ugliness.

I wondered how Father Francis was so oblivious of the pockmark of foolishness imbued on his fat, pot-bellied, stout form. He reminded me so much of Mama Tapgun, the black statue of a woman holding a baby on one hand and a pan to her head with the other hand. The statue stood on the roundabout in the middle of the Jos Terminus Market until one short-sighted governor pulled her down. The door creaked as it opened and Father Francis staggered out, zipping his trousers. He dropped on the sofa, emptied the contents of his tumbler, belched, and continued rapping.

"Okay, do you know that some history books said Awolowo refused to give the Igbos all the monies in their account when they fled. Sfssffsfihiwns…"

O ruo na omume! It was show time! I smiled; my interest piqued. His head dropped to the side, he jerked up, smiled to himself, rubbed his eyes.

"Awolowo should have written a book so that we can know his side of the sto…"

He dragged the "sto" so much that I was not sure if he wanted to say "story" or "stole." Whatever he wanted to say, I did not care, just sleep already! As if he heard my thoughts, he abandoned his head on the headrest and, finito! Ya ka re!

The best person you can send on an errand is yourself. Dragging Father Francis to the car proved difficult, but I had stored up enough strength for this task. I had not come to this city, which seemed content with talking to itself, for tourism. Jos. Terminus market. Apata suburb. Traders. Hawkers. Beggars. Madmen. Men in suit. Men, mad, in suit. The whole gamut of it — solitude in a deep, noisy, busy, mind-your-goddam-business — rankled the hell out of me. But my time here was now a billboard screaming, "Adios amigos!" I could not wait to leave this cold city: always "colding" for nothing. Winter always threatening to arrive but never staying. My father used to say that if a man chases away his woman, he would live alone. So if Jos froze everybody, it would be alone. Alone as I had been for twenty-two years, since Mercy took an overdose of her drugs. And, no, she did not kill herself. It was another hand that triggered the process: the hand that I'd soon snip.

Thunder cannot surprise one who was cooked for lightning. I wore my double gloves as per precaution. I did not expect the Nigerian Police to dust for fingerprints. Of course not! They were not that smart. But I wore the gloves anyway because I no fit shout. Father Francis lay in my backseat, snoring, puffing like a train. Without headlamps, I drove the short distance to the place I liked to call, "My crime scene." I did not go to the main road. I cannot be that idiotic. I stayed within the streets. Studying my area was the first thing I did when I returned to the city of my birth. Jos tasted of sweet, sour nostalgia. The BQ I rented at Liberty Boulevard was accessible from the back pedestrian gate. The compound was as big as those of the other houses around, which suited me well. When I settled in, I sought and found a crime scene. It was an abandoned warehouse, more like an old shipping container. That settled, I stalked the shit out of Father Francis for five weeks. I knew that after celebrating evening Mass every Friday, Father Francis dressed in joggers and jogged away. When he was out of Apata suburb, he would board a taxi and head to number three Dilimi Street.

Because the cloud does not darken for the fun of it, one day, I went to number three Dilimi Street and knocked on that door. A light-skinned woman answered. She gawped at me. As she deepened her looks, her forehead creased, her eyes thinned. I claimed that I was selling hair products. She looked at my chest, my beards, and cornrows as if doubting my maleness. Three children, the oldest would be maybe nine, came to the door. Shi ke nan, that's it. They all had Father Francis' dark complexion. The eldest had the same Mama Tapgun's nose with nostrils hospitable enough to house a stopper. Father Francis' round mouth that resembled those of a chronic porridge beans-and-yam eater was unmistakably chiselled into all their faces.

"May I come in?" I asked.

Her answer came out cold. "No."

Her heart seemed frozen. And, no, it was not Elsa's undoing. The woman gathered her children inside and banged her door.

Death comes visiting with its own bed and chair. I dragged Father Francis into my crime scene and locked us in. I flicked the switch. The dim, yellow, joke of a light bulb flickered on. The floor was an infant refuse dump. It seemed that heavy rain, or series of heavy rain, washed in the dirt. For me: the dirtier the better. My new, metal, armchair with grid backrest was right in the middle of the room where I had left it. I bought one that was big enough for his size, and I took it to a carpenter to cover its arms in leather. I got my concoction of Super Glue mixed with Araldite out of my backpack. I rolled him on his face and applied a good portion of my adhesive mixture on his trousers before I stuck his fat bum to the chair. He even relaxed well. I chuckled. The idiot! I hastened up because my love-portion, the Rohypnol, I added to his Bailey's might wear out soon. I applied a generous amount of the adhesive on his hands and stuck them to the leather chair. I wore him oven gloves which I secured firmly on his wrists with a rope. I stuck his feet to the cemented ground. Then I still used a strong rope to tie his ankles to the legs of the chair, because Local Man no fit shout. I passed one end of my rope through the grid, around his tummy, around the back of the chair. I continued like that until I had circled his stomach five times with the rope. I then knotted the rope tightly at the back of the chair. I also firmly secured his lap to the seat with a rope. This was unnecessary considering that his butt was stuck to the chair, but should A fail, B would keep him right how I wanted him: seated. Having bound him, I pulled down his lower lip and painted them with adhesive. I needed absolute noiselessness. I still had a duct tape oh, in case the adhesive failed. Satisfied, I unmasked, sat opposite him, placed my jotter on my lap, and waited.

A secret back-stabber shall also receive a secret reward. When Father Francis betrayed his friend, my father, in the secret of the night, and got away with it, he did not know that his own reward would come twenty-two years later, at night, about the same hour.

Father Francis woke up. It was a slow movement of the head and silent "umm." His eyes opened sluggishly. He blinked. I guessed his vision was blurred. He attempted to move his hands in vain. The frequency of his blinks intensified. I smiled. He struggled to move. It was a serious struggle from a weak body. He stopped when he noticed the rope around his stomach. Then he looked at me. His eyes narrowed, then widened. His lips tried to move but could not. I raised my palm. He stilled. I opened my jotter. First page, in a clear handwritten imitation of Times New Roman,

What is going on here?

He nodded briskly. I turned the page. It was difficult to achieve that with my gloves on, but I did anyway.

Abduction.

His eyes widened. He looked around him as if to take in the details of the place. I waited. When he looked at me, I turned the page.

Where am I?

He nodded like agama. I smiled and turned the page.

No need to know.

He pressed his eyes closed for a short while. He sighed. I turned the page.

Why am I here?

He nodded. I turned the page.

A patient dog eats the fattest bone. Calm down.

He looked at the ceiling that bore the map of a leaking roof. He looked at me, his head tilted to the right as though he was wondering who I was. I flipped the page.

Who are you? Where is Jack?

An eager nod from him; a page flip from me.

Na me be Jack. But shaa call me Jackie the gluer.

Onye ma mmadu n'egbu ya, someone who knows you can kill you. Father Francis' eyes got even wider. His face, powdered in confusion, pleased me. I was not going to tell him that I had been pretending to be a boy. I would not go into details of how I wore a plaster over my nipples every day to make my tiny breasts invisible. I did not have the time to tell him how I wore fake beards daily. If he had any sense, which I doubted, because it was his senselessness that condemned him to that chair, he would have wondered why I always wore baggy long-sleeved tops and a face cap whether it was sunny or not.

I flipped the page.

Alaye, say your last prayer.

When the anus farts, the head receives a knock. Father Francis' head was about to be knocked for a fart of twenty-two years ago. I guess his eyes could not get any wider. His lips shook as if he wanted to cry. Soon enough, tears dropped from his eyes. I almost laughed. Almost. Bros did not even have guts. Ordinary "Say your last prayer" and Oga wanted to cry Justin Timberlake a river. He did not need to talk for me to know he was pleading for mercy. But I could not give what I did not have. Mercy died with mercy. Because we were twins, I was not allowed to attend her burial. They bundled me to Olot where I then grew. They hoped that the distance would heal me from the trauma that took my sister. It did not. I mean, how could it?

Father Francis sobbed like a freshly widowed woman. If tears could stop evil, Mercy, and mercy, would still be here. I flipped the page.

Father Francis, have you asked Kyrie for eleison?

He shook like a Titanic survivor. I wished he would die with dignity. You don already know say you go die, die with your heads-up. How hard was that? He did not answer my question: could not. He looked up at the ceiling instead. Maybe he was praying. I bet that he was thinking of his woman and children at number three Dilimi Street. Well, too bad.

When poop is not cone-shaped, then there is diarrhoea. Father Francis shit on himself. The brown paste that dripped from his trousers to the ground had the disgust and smell of fear, anguish, hopelessness, everything, but regret: the one thing I hoped it would have. The stench was inhumane. It must have come from the spirit world. It was time to go. I dropped my jotter. His eyes turned to letter O, watching my steps. I walked behind him. His body stank of concentrated sweat. I held his temples and bent his head up. I looked him right into his pupils, which rolled here and there in fear. I wanted to see the recognition in his eyes. I did not. He did not remember? How dare he! I almost shouted. Almost. But I kept staring into his eyes. Then I saw realisation flush into his eyes. He must have finally seen in my eyes, the eight-year-old Mercy and Marcy. He must have remembered that night when my parents entrusted us to his care and how he violated us. The shock was still in his eyes when I dropped my adhesive into his right pupil. He "umm!" squeezing his eyes shut. I pressed the top of his left eye, not minding if his eyeball fell out, until he opened it. I gave his left eye a dose of my "eyewash." His "Umm!" was nonsense. I stuffed his nostrils with two balls of cotton wool and stepped back. Na there the shaking start. No, a fish out of water had nothing on him. He puffed his cheeks as though doing that would give him oxygen or let out carbon dioxide. I saw his head get bigger, or was I imagining that?

They that plant yam shall eat yam. Father Francis planted a whole field of abomination. He would have difficulty eating everything he sowed. As Father Francis struggle for life, I thought of Mercy and how she bled until our parents picked us up from the parish house the next morning. I thought of how we carried pans of blood away from under Mercy's bed every day. I thought of how she shrank into a skeleton in a garment of thin, dark flesh. I thought of how many nights I woke up to find her crying, dying of trauma and bleeding. She wanted to end it. She wanted to die. I wanted her to have peace, but I was not ready to live without her. Then one morning, someone with a strong grip yanked me out of bed and ran! I screamed, but my father kept running, shielding me from Mercy's corpse. Had I seen her corpse, it was believed that I too would die.

Father Francis got away with it until now.

The evil that men do dies with them. Father Francis had stopped shaking. His face looked distressed except that there was this smirk on his lips. I felt his neck for a pulse: none. I packed all my kaya, my properties, and left. I left his nose stuffed maka adịghị amama, just in case.

I locked the door, wondering why he died with a smirk. I almost ran back to punch him. Almost.

-End-

Copper Snow
By
Zoë Markham

Charlie's glass is empty again. He sets the well-thumbed photo album aside to pour himself a re-fill only to find that the bottle is equally empty. He blew the last of his cash on the cheap Scotch, and hadn't intended to dispose of it so quickly.

His stomach lurches. There's no food to be found in the squalid, abandoned flat he's claimed for the night.

The photo album lies face-down on the stained sofa beside him. Charlie's in two minds about picking it back up. Some days it's the one thing that gives him comfort; others it's the most painful thing he owns. Looking around the damp, top-floor flat within the empty high rise, ear-marked for demolition any day now, he decides he can't handle any more reminders of the past tonight. Closing the album and running a grimy thumb gently over the cover, he sets it on top of the hold-all that contains almost everything he owns. With a sigh, he pulls his thick, oversized patchwork coat around himself, lies back on the uncomfortable sofa, and closes his eyes, waiting for the drink to work its magic.

Charlie can't sleep without alcohol inside him anymore. A luxury he can rarely get his hands on now, he wants to make the most of it tonight.

As he slowly falls into the welcome darkness that's been eluding him for days, the snow continues to fall outside, thick and heavy. The unusual run of arctic weather is approaching its fourth day and showing no signs of stopping. Ice begins to form on the inside of the flat's single, cracked window, and Charlie shivers in his sleep.

The suit bag hanging from the thin, plastic curtain rail shudders as a freezing gust of wind hammers the glass. The ghost of Charlie's past dances excitedly as his body lies comatose. On the windowsill, surrounded by thick, black mould, a slim leather case sits beside a broken shard of mirror.

A lifetime in the business, man and boy. Family, school, work, and play; it was more than his job, it was his everything.

Until they took it away.

What did he ever do to them? What could he possibly have done to anyone to ever deserve that?

Charlie sleeps, and the room gets colder. The snow outside, thick and heavy, muffles every sound, and an unnatural silence blankets the estate. Deep within this silence, a harsh, manufactured laugh begins, echoing through the room; six false, recorded tones playing on a slight downward scale. On the sixth repetition of the sequence, Charlie rises from the sofa in one smooth move. His eyes open but unseeing. Neither awake, nor asleep, his movements are slow, but assured.

Taking the suit bag down from the window, he sheds his coat and dresses himself in the filthy, rotting clown outfit within. Once bright and brilliant, his former pride and joy; his badge of office, livelihood, and legacy. A Harlequin clown like generations of his family before him, the suit Charlie's limbs mechanically find their way into was once a dazzling white, with simple, striking black diamond decals. Now, torn in many places and soaked through with so much blood that no white, or even black, remains, it's an insult to everything the profession stood for. The thick, coppery smell of the fabric fills the frozen air around him. Charlies pauses for a moment, breathing it in. A brief but fierce flash of life sparks in his eyes, his movements gaining a little pace as he crosses to the window and opens the leather case to reveal an old, well-used set of stage makeup. Fingers finding their familiar way, he sets to work on the classic white, sad face, complete with one black teardrop. His application is assured, the thick white paste completely covering the accumulated filth on his skin and contrasting sharply with the deep, rusty brown of the outfit. Finally, he pulls the conical, formerly white hat – now a deep red too, but visibly less blood-soaked and rotten than the suit, with its three black pom-poms still recognisable – from the bottom of the bag. Placing it gently, reverently, on his head, the transformation is complete.

Charlie is no longer Charlie. No longer destitute. No longer destroyed.

Charlie is 'Zanno' once again – world famous, classically trained, international star of the circus. A household name in his heyday, the European King of the Clowns. Young ones queued for hours, dying to see him, wanting to be him; old ones queued beside them, looking on with approval. They understood: Zanno was tradition and history and sacrifice and hard work. Zanno was the circus, and the circus was Zanno.

He never wore blood back then, of course, nor did he go out in the dead of night in the middle of winter. But Zanno is different now. A Zanno for *today*. His job isn't to entertain, delight, amuse, or enthuse. His only role now is to pay back the considerable debt he owes the generation who killed his career.

He doesn't make them laugh anymore, but he can still make them cry.

Reaching into the holdall, he retrieves two items from within. Shrugging back into the large patchwork coat now, he places each item in its own pocket. Slipping his feet into the long, comical clown shoes that don't go with his style of outfit at all but are a concession to the now more recognisable style, catering to the lowest common denominator, he's ready.

Zanno leaves the flat in his blood-stained finery.

The lifts in the high-rise haven't worked in years, and the stairs aren't easy in these shoes, but he has plenty of practice behind him. He skims down fifteen flights with no sign of fatigue. The fitness earned over a lifetime of hard, physical training isn't lost easily. Three shows a day, seven days a week. Charlie may be broken and weak, but Zanno is as strong as an ox.

Through the main doors now, and out. The long shoes crunch satisfyingly on the fresh, powdery snow that sits on top of yesterday's iced-over slush and leave behind the most outrageous footprints.

Charlie sleeps, but for Zanno, the hunt is beginning, and he's wide awake.

The snow-covered estate, usually loud at all hours, looks deserted in the wintry night. Empty alleyways, unlit windows, car-free roads. No tyre tracks or footprints mark the fresh snowfall ahead of him; Zanno walks in a pure, untouched world. . . on the surface, at least. Underneath, he knows all too well, it's a very different story.

It takes longer tonight. He has to walk farther than he'd like before he finally finds one, but they all need to pay, and he won't stop, no matter how long it takes. Standing statue-still in the road, he stares in at the bright, un-shaded window. He appears completely absorbed in the boy, but his mind is busy, whirring into action, gathering in each piece of available information.

First-floor window. No other lights in the house. No car in the driveway. Obnoxious soundtrack playing loud enough to be heard in the empty street. A week night, he thinks, he is almost sure. The information floats to him, merges, churns, and prints out the conclusion: the boy is alone.

From where he stands in the street, Zanno can see the girls and the cars that fill the large, wall-mounted flat-screen. He can't quite make out the boy's features, but he can see his posture; the way he grasps the controller like it's a lifeline, how his whole body moves as he plays the game. It *has* him, completely. The boy is in the game, and the game has exactly what it wants.

And now there's something Zanno wants. The boy has to pay.

Easing open the side gate, he makes his way to the back door. He doesn't worry about the noise his shoes make in the snow, or the footprints they leave behind. He's focused on one thing and one thing only: taking back what he's owed.

Folding the end of one rust-coloured sleeve over his hand, he makes a fist and punches through one of the small, glass panels in the door. The volume level of the game keeps the boy upstairs ignorant. He snakes his hand through the broken pane and lets himself into the small galley kitchen. Standing for a moment, looking down at the snow he's tracked in with him onto the smart, laminate flooring, an oddly-familiar scent catches his nostrils, and his stomach cramps hard in response. Half a cold pizza sits in a box left on the sideboard. Without thinking, his hand darts out and he crams down one, then two of the greasy slices before the pain begins to ease. Picking up a third, he takes a bite and slowly chews on it as he walks through the living room, the last remnants of snow sinking into the deep carpet beneath his feet. He glances up at the stairs. Light spills down from the open door of the boy's room. This time, Zanno leaves his shoes at the bottom of the staircase, a comic getaway car waiting for his return.

Thirteen barefoot steps and Zanno reaches the landing. Only the boy's door is open. Gunfire, rap music, and other obscene sounds emanate from it. Zanno can stand quietly and look in without the boy noticing. He has eyes only for the screen, this product of the generation that stole his livelihood; that turned away from traditional, family-based entertainment and killed the industry that gave Zanno life. Consoles and darkened rooms, now. Indoors and alone. Eyes open but blind.

He can't be more than fourteen, fifteen at the most. Charlie's broken heart aches to see a child's delight spent on such an unthinking, unfeeling, impersonal piece of technology. A violent, virtual world he surely isn't even legally of age to enjoy. Gunshots ring out. Blood splatters the screen. Rage and delight pair and dance in the boy's eyes. Charlie wonders if anyone ever thought to take him to the Big Top. If his eyes ever sparkled with pure delight at the wonders contained within.

Zanno's heart fills with resentment and bile and loathing. Generations of skill and talent destroyed by the ignorant, lazy, image-obsessed youth of today. Reaching into the deep pocket of his coat, he pulls out a curved, wooden-handled machete. It gleams in the escaped half-light of the boy's room, and Zanno maliciously angles it to catch the light and reflect it back into the boy's eyes. Finally he's distracted from the game, and Zanno strikes; fast, well-practiced strokes from his fiendishly sharp blade remove the boy's heart in an instant.

Why, his own heart was ripped out of his chest many years ago. A new heart, surely, is the very least he's owed?

And he offered the boy more courtesy than he deserved. He was quick, and clinical. There was no fear, no suffering. His own decline had been torturous, drawn-out, painful, and uncertain as fewer and fewer families came to see the shows. His possessions and his savings evaporated slowly as he tried endlessly to come up with new means of attracting the crowds. Friends and colleagues gradually let go, fed to the wolves around him. Family holding on 'til the last, as loans were taken out and defaulted on. Expensive, irreplaceable, generations-old equipment repossessed by goons who stripped away all meaning in their frenzied search for value. An entire way of life relentlessly chipped away until nothing remained but the coarse dust of memories.

Had someone offered him a choice between that and a quick, sharp blade, he knows which option he would've picked.

Zanno wipes the machete clean with the edge of his coat. His feet are soaking in the boy's blood, and it feels warm and comforting after the icy chill outside. He re-pockets the machete and takes a second item from his other pocket. A small, orange bag with the word "Laughter" printed beneath the smiling face of a childishly drawn clown. He kneels by the side of the boy and carefully rolls the bag in his blood until it gleams. He then glances around for the TV remote, and finds the mute button. The silence is a blessed relief. How could anyone think with *that* going on in the background? It's no wonder children can't concentrate on anything anymore. Leaving the game spinning impotently in the drive of the console, he drops the bag on top of it. Artificial laughter cuts through the fresh silence, and Zanno wiggles his toes in the still-warm blood, savouring the feeling of a job well done.

It doesn't undo what's been done, but it's all he has.

Leaving bloody footprints in his wake, he finds his way back to the shoes. They see him cleanly through to the kitchen, where he pauses to eat the final slice of pizza, and to look for any food he can take back to the flat. A slab of cheddar and a packet of burger rolls join the machete inside his bloody, cavernous pocket, and he helps himself to the last of a six-pack of crisps, which he dips into as he makes his way home through the still-falling snow. His fingers are blood-covered, making the crisps warm and wet; giving them a sharp, coppery tang. His stomach growls in pleasure.

Still the only soul on the streets, as if they've been cleared just for him, he takes this as a sign. What he's doing is *right*. If it wasn't, how could it possibly be this easy? With fresh snow still falling, even his large footprints are soon swallowed up behind him. Everything is in his favour. The snow is for him alone.

He finishes the crisps, and this time smiles as he walks.

Turning the last corner towards the condemned tower block, however, Zanno hears the sound of a car engine idling, and his smile fades. There, just outside one of the garages in the supposedly abandoned block, an expensive saloon with blacked out windows sits, unmoving, as if weighing up the amount of snow on the road and considering its options. Should it reverse straight back into the garage? Or should it soldier on?

Zanno has to rapidly consider his own options in response, before realising he has no choice but to continue walking, right across the path of the vehicle. He will already have been seen by whoever's inside, and logically there's nowhere else for him to go. Dipping a hand into his pocket, he snakes a path through the pilfered food with his fingers, and clasps the handle of the machete in readiness. He doesn't look at the car. He stares straight ahead, powering through the snow, and is almost past when the distinctive *clunk* of the door handle stops him in his tracks. A burst of genuine laughter follows, accompanied by music that reminds him of the boy's game pouring from the stereo.

"Nice shoes, brah!"

He lets out a long, slow, exhale, watching tendrils of his breath swirl and play, warm and elegant in the freezing air. Not turning. Not yet.

"Hey! Mate! Where's the party, then? Fancy dress, year? It's dead down here tonight. And I've got goods to move, y'know?"

Goods? Zanno spins, and looks closely at the man. Dark clothes. Dark car. Heavy pockets. A glint in his hooded eyes that Charlie recognises even if Zanno can't quite place it.

"Jesus! What kind of nightmare outfit is that? Some kind of Stephen King shit?" The man laughs, again.

Zanno bristles.

"Not a talker, eh? Fair enough." He shrugs. "Just give me an address. Like I said, goods to move, man. In fact…" he reaches into a pocket, and pulls out a mass of pills and small wraps of powder, "…take your pick. Two for one. Just for you, Pennywise. Everything must go. They're blowing this place tomorrow."

Zanno takes a couple of slow steps towards him to get a better look. The man could have walked straight out of the boy's video game. The car, the drugs, offering the same shiny, superficial high. Charlie sees men like this around the estate – around every estate. Tempting the young ones, satisfying the old ones. Breaking everything in exactly the same way. Ruining it all.

"Seriously, *mate*." The man's tone changes, becoming as sharp and icy as the wind. "Where's. The. Party?"

Zanno sighs. He doesn't have a spare laugh bag with him, but that's OK. He brings out the machete before the bemused dealer has any idea what's happening, burying it deep inside his chest in one, swift move. He tumbles to the snow. The hot, fresh blood melted a warm, slushy nest around him. It only takes him moments to die – once again, more than is deserved. Zanno allows himself a brief pause to enjoy the beauty of the spent life painting the snow in an ever-slowing crawl, before anger at the deviation from his routine takes hold. Bending to haul the lifeless body to its feet, Zanno drags the inconvenient individual back to his car, and pushes him into the driver's seat through the still-open door. He doesn't want this particular heart. It's too rotten, too far gone. Corrupt. An insult to everything he stands for.

He takes a moment to think. It feels sloppy to leave things this way. Zanno had always been a responsible, diligent entertainer, and he sees no reason for this to be any different.

Reaching in, he releases the car's handbrake, before removing the machete, switching off the engine, and quietly shutting the door. It's not easy to move the car, initially, but once he gets some momentum going, he's able to push it back into the garage along the deep tracks in the snow it had already made coming out. Proving once again that the snow exists purely for him tonight. He smiles, cleaning the blade in the snow at his feet, before pulling the battered garage door down. His work is done. He turns and makes a slow, elegant bow, the crowd roaring its approval at tonight's specially extended show in his ears.

He makes it back to the flat with no more interruptions.

It feels icier inside than out, but still Zanno slowly and carefully removes his outfit and rehangs it in the crumpled suit bag. He takes a bag of baby wipes from his holdall and diligently removes his make-up along with the worst of the bloodstains from his hands. He places the cheddar and rolls on the windowsill. Tomorrow's breakfast. It's as cold there as any fridge. Laying the machete on the floor beside the sofa, he cocoons himself once more in the filthy, oversized coat, and lies down to sleep, satisfied.

Hours later, Charlie wakes, shivering violently in the cold with a sick, twisted, feeling in his gut and a coppery tang in his mouth. He struggles to sit up, looking around with bloodshot eyes. His first instinct is to wrench off the blood-soaked coat, but the frozen air of the flat takes his breath away, and he's forced to pull the foul smelling thing tighter around himself for warmth, retching at the stench.

Not again, please…not again…

He reaches for the holdall and checks on the deathly sharp blade, the last remaining souvenir of the family circus that had been in his blood for generations. It's still safely encased in its sheath. He pulls it out to be completely sure, the blade shining clean and unstained. Where then, had the blood come from? It never made any sense to him. He has lost count now of the number of times he's woken in this inexplicable state. Each time, he packs his bags and moves as far away as he can manage on foot and by hitching. There would be days, sometimes weeks, before it would happen again. Charlie doesn't know how, or why, but he knows it's time to leave.

It only takes seconds to gather his things. He leaves the food with the bloody thumbprints on the windowsill, convinced it has nothing to do with him. Hoisting the holdall over his shoulder and tucking the suit bag under his arm, he shuts the door on the flat and heads down the stairs. Through the front door and out into the snow. In weather like this, he knows he'll be walking a long, long time before he sees a car. Fresh snow begins to fall softly around him. Mocking him.

Sighing, he sets off, shivering, into the clean white of the morning.

Deep inside the holdall, the blade twitches and shines in the darkness, and by its side a brand new, bright orange laugh bag appears.

The blade remembers. The blade won't ever forget.

-End-

The Sound of Wolves
By
Gwen C. Katz

The howl rises above the screaming wind, its sound pained and hollow.

"*Volki,*" says the serf, or something that sounds like that. By way of explanation, he bares his white teeth and snaps at Ulrik.

"Wolves!" says Ulrik. He shudders.

The serf nods, though whether he understands, Ulrik can't say. His name is Grishka. At least, that's what the other serfs call him; Ulrik hasn't yet sorted out the tangle that is Russian names. Other than that, Ulrik knows nothing about him, and their acquaintance isn't likely to grow, for Grishka doesn't speak Swedish, and Ulrik doesn't know a word of Russian.

Or at least, he didn't. Now he knows one word: Wolves.

The two of them pull their blankets tighter around themselves and sink lower into the muddy ditch that will one day be a street, not that it would offer any protection if the beasts decided to attack. Their work crew had to claw out this ditch with their bare hands, which was hell on Ulrik's still-healing arm. If there are any shovels in this worksite, Ulrik hasn't seen them.

There are wolves in Sweden, of course, but Ulrik lives in an apartment in Stockholm and has never even seen a wolf. Or rather, that's where he lived once. Before the Army. Before the battle. Before he was captured and press-ganged into building a city for his enemies.

He rubs his arm. The bones have set wrong, leaving a kink in his forearm that blazes with pain when he bends it wrong.

The wind shrieks through the ditch, which, far from sheltering them, seems to funnel its full force directly onto the cluster of workers. There are no buildings here yet. Just ditches and the foundations of a lone fortress. The serfs haven't even had a chance to build shelters for themselves. A fat raindrop splatters against Ulrik's cheek as though God is spitting on him. It's raining. Of course it is.

As the downpour pelts them, Grishka looks up at the sky and shrugs, as if to say that he didn't expect any better.

And the worst part, thinks Ulrik, is that it's summer. It's going to get worse. It's going to get so much worse.

The architect half-walks, half-jogs down the street, trying to keep pace with the tsar's long-legged stride. On either side of them, cranes rise over pastel edifices. The temple spires of a modern religion.

"The workshops are over there," says the architect, nodding to his left. "That one is a woodcarver; the one next to it does sculpture."

"I've seen the first couple of pieces they've produced. Exemplary work. I'll stop in and have a look myself soon; I've always wanted to learn woodcarving," says the tsar. He is tall and broad-shouldered, with a handsome mustached face. Striding down the street in his blue silk sash and polished boots, he cuts an imposing figure.

"We've recruited only the finest artisans for the tsar's new capital," says the architect.

The young city is a bustle of activity. Carts full of bricks and beams make their way up and down the broad main street, their drivers shouting at pedestrians to get out of the way. Craftsmen perch on scaffolds, painting murals and installing molding.

Everyone stops and bows as the pair passes. The architect enjoys the attention, but he's careful not to get too comfortable. A tsar's favor can vanish as fast as the morning mist that hangs over the swampy harbor.

"The lampposts are almost finished," he says, pointing to a work crew digging post holes. "Think of the benefits:

Less crime, fewer accidents. Saint Petersburg will be the most advanced city in Europe."

The tsar's carriage is waiting for him on the street corner. The tsar turns and faces the architect. "I'm deeply impressed with all you've accomplished here. It's hard to believe that, a few years ago, this land was nothing but a mosquito-infested swamp. Now look at it!" He sweeps a hand over the domes and arches. "It's like a miracle. Christ said he would rebuild the temple in three days, but next to this, that's nothing. Yet there is more work to do. Come to see me tomorrow. We'll begin discussing the gardens."

His doorman helps him into the carriage, and they drive off, the bas-relief eagle on the carriage gleaming in the evening light.

It's not late, but it's October, and the sun sets early at this time of year. The architect pulls his hat down over his ears. He's still not used to the Russian cold. On days like this, he misses France.

The lamplighters are out, walking down the street on stilts like strange insects. I did this, thinks the architect as one of them pauses to light the oil lamp above him. I made this happen.

The lamplighter moves on. and the architect starts in surprise.

In the alley across the street stands a figure. And it's looking at him.

It's autumn, and a boy is dying of the flux.

He was pale and weak that morning, but he could stand, so the soldiers forced him to march out to the worksite with everyone else. Today, they're dragging logs off a horse-drawn sledge and using a makeshift pulley and weights to drive them into the ground. Or they're trying to, anyway. The swampy earth is already half-frozen. Pain stabs through Ulrik's injured arm, and, as he drags the rope, he seems to sink deeper into the muck than the log does. Aside from the thud of the weights and the huff of the horses, who are as miserable and half-starved as the humans, everything is quiet. No wolves today, at least.

Conversation is limited to the occasional "Pass me that fucking rope" or "The fucking runners are stuck in the fucking mud again." Ulrik is beginning to pick up a little Russian; mostly profanity. Russians seem to have a swearword for everything and can hold protracted conversations using nothing else, which, considering the circumstances, seems entirely reasonable to Ulrik.

"I wonder what the city will be like," says Ulrik, piecing together the words he knows as he and Grishka pull the rope. "Will it be beautiful?"

"Why do you give a fuck?" says Grishka. "It's not like we'll live to see it."

"We might," says Ulrik mildly.

Grishka laughs. "As what? A couple of half-dead

skeletons? Or worse?"

"What's worse?" asks Ulrik.

Grishka puts down the rope and turns to Ulrik. "When a man is truly beyond everything—beyond life, beyond hope, beyond caring about anyone or anything—he becomes something *else*. Something not even human. When that happens, I don't know who deserves more pity—him or the poor bastard who sees him next."

He takes up the rope and drags it as if he's trying to strangle someone. His teeth are set, his eyes bloodshot from lack of rest. He scares Ulrik, but it's not as though Ulrik can ask to be transferred to another work crew. Might as well ask for a pony and a feather bed.

They're an hour into their shift when the boy collapses.

A soldier shouts "Get up, you lazy motherfucker" and kicks him in the stomach a few times, but the boy only whimpers, so the soldier points to Ulrik and Grishka and says, "You two cocksuckers, get this lazy son of a bitch out of here."

Ulrik grabs his hands and Grishka grabs his feet, grumbling about getting the worse end of the deal. Ulrik winces as he accidentally torques his bad arm. They carry the boy to the cluster of sod huts that they've finally put together at the edge of the worksite. They lay him on his blanket. He's fourteen, maybe fifteen, with crooked teeth and eyes set too low and too close together.

Too weak to make it to the latrine trench, the boy

gradually shits his life away over the course of the day. Ulrik lingers as long as he dares, telling himself he isn't just glad for a momentary break from work.

"At least it isn't smallpox," grunts Grishka. The disease tore through the camp a month ago, claiming more serfs than Ulrik could count. He still has peeling scabs on his cheeks and neck. "And can't you take him off that blanket? I want it when he's dead and it's getting all nasty."

"He can hear you," says Ulrik.

"So?"

Around then, a soldier comes through and yells at them to get back to work.

When they return that night, the boy is still with them, but barely. Flies are crawling across his face, settling on his eyelashes, biting the corners of his mouth. Ulrik is glad for the autumn cold dampening the smell.

The boy looks up at them and wets his dry lips.

"Fuck," he says. "This can't be all there is."

"Sure it can," grunts Grishka.

Ulrik wants to take the boy's hand, but he can't overcome his revulsion. So, the boy lies there, his legs streaked with shit, until his eyes go glassy.

As they throw him into one of the ditches, Ulrik realizes he never asked the boy's name.

After

The figure follows the architect for weeks, gliding

across empty courtyards, peering out from behind half-open doors. Sometimes he flees it; sometimes he tries to confront it. But whatever he does, the specter slips away, leaving him wondering if his mind is beginning to crumble.

He throws himself into his work. A palace rises on the banks of the Neva, all colonnaded porches and golden capitals. It is a masterpiece worthy of the world's greatest kings. The tsar says as much. Yet, as the architect stands before it, all he sees is a dark silhouette reflected in one of the gleaming windows.

Then there is a dispute over sewer work. He finds the foreman and the workers standing around the sewer's mouth, shouting at each other.

"What's going on here?" asks the architect.

"They won't go in," says the foreman.

"Put off by a little smell?" asks the architect, though he certainly isn't planning to lead by example.

"It's not that and you know it," snaps one of the workers. "You know what's down there."

He does. He hasn't seen it himself, but he's been told of the piles of bones that lie beneath the streets and houses, not neatly stacked like the Paris catacombs, but lying in haphazard tangles where the bodies were thrown.

"Come now, what are you afraid of? Ghosts?" he says in his most placating tone. "I assure you; the dead are all resting peacefully."

But even as he speaks, something flickers in the dark sewer tunnel.

He turns to drink, hoping to banish the vision. Happily, the tsar keeps the city well stocked with wine and cognac; the architect thinks vodka tastes like horse piss. But even when he blacks out in his room, he awakes to find the shadowy specter still hovering nearby. His work suffers. Midway through presenting his garden plan to the tsar, he gets confused and forgets what he's saying, and the tsar ends up rejecting the whole thing outright.

As the architect trudges home that night, he spies the specter standing in a doorway. Though it's in shadow, he can see a white slash of a smile spread across its face.

Before

"There's not a single piece of fucking cabbage in my fucking soup. It's just warm water. How do you like that?" says Grishka.

Ulrik hunches over his own bowl, letting his hands absorb its warmth. It's been snowing now for two weeks straight.

"You've got a great big leaf in there. Give it to me," says Griska.

Ulrik says, "Fuck you. It's the only leaf I've got."

Grishka gives him a look almost like respect. "We've made a proper Russian out of you at last. Won't stop me from breaking your other arm, though. Hand it over."

The look in Grishka's eyes tells Ulrik that he's not joking, and he bitterly hands over his bowl, which is more than half full. Living out here has taught him to eat like an animal, but he's still not fast enough.

Grishka lifts the bowl to his mouth and drinks, his throat working. He sets it down with a satisfied sigh and begins picking his teeth with a twig. Grishka has perfect teeth; Ulrik doesn't understand how. "What I wouldn't give for some real food, though! Do you remember meat?"

"Barely," says Ulrik. He isn't even joking. The time before he was captured is fading from his mind. What did he do back in Stockholm? What did he like? What kind of person was he?

Books. He used to like books. He wonders if he'll ever read a book again.

A howl cuts through the night air. Grishka scowls at the doorway, though nothing is visible past the ragged hanging blanket except falling snow. "Ugh, those fuckers are back."

Ulrik tries to curl up small. He still fears the wolves. He says, "Maybe they'll stay in the woods."

Grishka laughs. "Not likely, when there are so many delicious hot meat pies all piled up in this hut."

Another howl. Ulrik huddles. The sod hut barely dampens the wind. He feels the cold even more sharply with his empty stomach gnawing at him, and the break in his arm still aches. Even indoors, his fingers are gray and numb. At this rate he's not sure the wolves will get the chance to finish him off.

The next howl is closer. Grishka jumps to his feet, his eyes wild. "What, do you want me? Then come and get me! Quit hiding out there!"

Another howl.

"Fine!" shouts Grishka, pulling aside the blanket and striding out into the woods. "I'll come to you!"

"Wait, Grishka! Are you crazy?" says Ulrik, running after him.

Away from the camp's scattered candles and oil lamps, the night is lit only by a wan wash of light where the moon shines through a thin patch in the clouds. Ulrik stumbles over rocks and twigs as he tries to keep up. Branches scrape his face. But Grishka runs like a hunting dog that's caught a scent.

They emerge in a clearing. There is the wolf. It stands with its legs tense, its lips drawn back to reveal long, curved teeth. It's black, lean, grizzled around the muzzle with gray. An old wolf. Who knows how many of their number it's already devoured.

Grishka paces around the edge of the clearing, circling the wolf with his arms held out. "Well?" he roars. "Are you coming for me or not?"

The wolf lunges, swift and silent as a knife thrust. As it falls on Grishka, he grabs its jaws with his thick hands and forces them open. Wrenching the wolf's head, he twists its neck back at an unnatural angle. The wolf whimpers.

Grishka lowers his head and buries his teeth in the beast's shaggy neck. Blood leaks out, staining its fur. Grishka raises his head over the now-still wolf, its raw red flesh hanging in gobbets from his white teeth, its dark blood streaming down his chin.

He looks at Ulrik.

After

The architect wakes with a start in the middle of the night. Sweat sticks his nightgown to his chest. The specter is gone. Nothing in the windows. Nothing in the corners. With trembling fingers, he lights a lantern. When he holds it up, it casts wild shadows around the room. But still there is no sign of a human figure.

No. It's not gone. It's out there somewhere, waiting for him. He can feel it, an amorphous malevolence seeping through his skin to gnaw on his bones. It will keep stalking him, slowly draining the life out of him from a distance, until he gives it what it wants.

He dresses and runs out into the snowy street, the lantern in his hand.

The night is freezing. He's forgotten his felt boots in his haste. Cold stabs through his shoe leather. Soon his toes are numb. Amid the finery he helped build, it's easy to forget that this is still a frozen wasteland.

The click-clack of nails on paving stones rings out

through the still air. A wolf. They still venture into the city at night. He spies it just behind him, creeping out from the shadow of an unfinished building. He quickens his pace. Another wolf emerges from an alley in front of him. He turns and flees.

Now he is running down Nevsky Avenue, and wolves are pouring out of every gap and side street, a whole pack of them, their tongues hanging out, slaver dripping from their jaws. They always remain just behind him, not quite close enough to snap at his heels. He braces himself, waiting for them to fall on him, but they never do.

They're not hunting him. They're herding him.

He knows where they're driving him even before he sees the sewer's black entrance looming before him. Piles of bricks and pipes are scattered around the dark maw. The work is still not finished. The wolves close in, in front of him, behind him, on every side, until there's nowhere to go but down.

As he enters the sewer, the stench of humanity's underside greets him: not just piss and excrement but vomit and menstrual blood and the rotting carcasses of animals. His stomach revolts. He forces himself to keep walking through the sludge. Soft pants tell him that the wolves are still behind him.

A hundred meters down the tunnel, the brickwork has broken down, and the effluviant soaks straight into the silty dirt. There are the bones, hundreds of them, thousands of them, stained and broken. His lantern illuminates ribs and vertebrae and shards he cannot identify, dislodged from the earth by the stagnant puddle of human waste. He accidentally treads on a long bone, one of the thin ones from the lower arm. There's a lump in the middle of it where it broke and then healed. He staggers back with a shudder.

Ahead of him, the specter emerges from the darkness.

In the lantern light, it's not a silhouette anymore. It's a man. He's gaunt and stooped from work, the worn remains of his clothing plastered to his skin with sweat and mud until it may as well be part of his body. Reddish-black residue stains his lips, his neck, the front of his clothes, layer upon layer crusting his skin. When he opens his mouth to speak, his teeth are startlingly white.

"Do you know who I am?" he asks.

The architect shakes his head. His throat is too dry to speak.

"I think you do," says the man. "When you took this job, when you came to this city, you knew what you were building on. You knew whose sacrifice made your masterpiece possible."

The architect casts his eye over the floor, at the bones drifting in sewage.

"Do you know how we died?" asks the man. "Do you know in what numbers? Starvation and cold, exhaustion and disease. The unluckiest among us were devoured by wolves."

He steps forward and places his thick, callused hand around the architect's throat. The architect expects the touch to be cold, but it's hot as a fever. "Which fate shall you share? Shall you starve, the flesh melting from your bones even as you eat until your stomach swells? Shall the cold bite through you even as you huddle before your hearth? Or shall the wolves devour you here and now?"

He releases the architect, who staggers to his knees, suddenly weak. The architect's skin begins to itch all over. He scratches until he bleeds. Sores break out on his arms, his legs, his neck, red patches of skin blooming into constellations of welts that erupt into angry pus-seeping lesions. The architect collapses, fiery pain wracking his body. He struggles to breathe as the lesions overtake his face, covering his eyes, his ears, and the inside of his mouth until no one could tell that the mass of blood and sores was once human.

"You have your city," says the man, standing over the architect. The architect's diseased eyes can no longer see him, but the man's voice echoes in his swollen ears. "But it will pay for every dead serf who lies beneath these streets. I will make sure of it. By the end, they'll be begging for the wolves."

The man walks away into the darkness, wolves at his heels, leaving the twisted heap of flesh that was once the architect lying on a bed of bones.

-End-

The Storm
By
Kisstopher Musick

The booming sound of the thunder, accompanied by the bright flash of lightning that shook the building, made Susan grateful that the building had lightning rods. This was one of the worst thunderstorms of this winter, and she couldn't shake the cold. This feeling of being chilled to the bone was only made worse by her anxiety. She really wanted to smoke a cigarette. The doctors had been grim, "quit smoking or die". She had noticed the difficulty in her breathing years ago along with the hacking cough, but that wasn't what had motivated her to see her doctor. It was the migraines. She never would have imagined what would come next. The flurry of tests and series of surgeries to save her life. It was the worst year of her life, but at least she was nearly done with her treatment. She had found the treatment to be agonizing.

As she stood at her window, watching the storm rage,

she twirled her empty vape pen and contemplated her refection. She was not the woman she used to be, and she knew there was no chance that she would ever be her former self. She felt frail and weak; words she had never associated with herself. She pondered hearing those words for the first time, "lung cancer". She remembered thinking how fitting it was that there was a hailstorm for the first time ever to hit the city and all the chaos that filled that day. It was if the world was manifesting her internal state - very much like tonight. She smiled to herself and reflected on her love of winter. She always got big news and life changes in winter, and the unpredictability of that seemed to fit well with the unpredictability of winter and storms.

She was married on the beach in winter, and everyone had advised against it, but the day had been clear. The entre week leading up to her wedding was sunny and clear. The beach was dry, and the tide was low. It was a perfect day. She had met Jack two years before they were married, and that day, too, was unseasonably warm and sunny. Maybe this was why she felt like Jack brought the light into her darkness and made miracles happen. Susan often felt like it was the strength of Jack's will that had kept her going through the treatment process. Jack was an optimist full of hope and light, which was a nice contrast to Susan's pessimism. Just as Susan was contemplating how lucky she was to have Jack, he appeared as if by magic behind her: encircling her in his arms. She relaxed into his embrace.

"Are you enjoying the storm?", Jack asked.

Susan smiled and replied "You know I am. Don't ruin it with your sunshine."

They laughed at the old joke. Things were always easy between them even when Susan was not at ease. They had always felt comfortable with each other, and Jack somehow was always able to make things feel lighter even in the heaviest of times. Susan often wondered how Jack managed to have endless hope and optimism even when things were at their bleakest. She also wondered about how that fit with his streak of sadism. As the storm raged on, she wondered when Jack would suggest they order pizza. He had this perverse habit of ordering pizza on the stormiest of nights. Maybe it was unfair to call that sadistic. It was the joy he took from making the pizza delivery driver go out into the rain. He knew that, in their city, pizza was delivered on scooters, making the journey perilous. Jack had always argued that if it were truly dangerous, they would simply not offer pizza delivery. Susan doubted that and wondered if Jack really believed that.

Right in time with another flash of lightning Jack said, "I think I'm going to order pizza. Do you want your usual?"

Susan smiled at the familiarity and predictability and said, "yes".

As she watched the clouds roll and turn, she continued to think about Jack and ponder if he had a sadistic streak, and her mind became dark. Susan wondered if his optimism and hope provided cover for what was perhaps actually joyfulness in times of strife. Did he enjoy how tormented she felt throughout her treatment? She shook her head in an attempt to change her thought process, but her mind began to fill with flashes of Jack's smiling face and joyful eyes: there after every surgery and during each chemo treatment. In her mind, those smiles turned into a gruesome thing. Did Jack really think she could beat it or was he relishing in her fight and struggle?

When Jack went to order the pizza, her mind started to drift back through the years. Back to their first winter together, and the moment Jack said he knew he wanted to be with her. It was one of her darker moments. She remembered it as if it were yesterday: sitting in her car crying her eyes out because she didn't think she could face another day, her only solace had been the rain. When it rained, it always felt like the world was acknowledging her pain and even more so on that day. On that day over 20 years ago, the rain drops where thick and swollen as if filled with her grief, and her tears had been as equally thick and swollen as they ran down her face.

Jack held her and swore to never let go., all the while smiling with eyes brimming of hope and just a hint of joy. Why hadn't she noticed the hint of joy before now? Why was she only just seeing it? Susan was so lost in her thoughts that she jumped at the sound of the doorbell and had to suppress a scream. Had she really been standing there lost in her thoughts for 30 minutes? She felt sick thinking about the pizza now, as her stomach was soured by her changing opinion of Jack.

"Pizza's here. You should have seen how soaked the delivery guy was, but our pizza is still hot. I was sure to give him a good tip for his misery." Jack said as he walked to the kitchen table with the pizza.

As Susan turned, she couldn't help but see Jack's smile and joy as sadistic enjoyment and celebration of the poor pizza delivery man's suffering. As she silently walked to the table, her mind was filled with images of Jack ghoulishly smiling with delight as those around him suffered. She was full of disgust as she sat down across from him and could feel her resentment turning into hatred and a desire to slap that self-satisfied, sadistic smile from his face.

As soon as Jack looked up and saw her face, he knew things were about to take a turn. He saw the familiar hatred and braced himself for the oncoming barrage. Almost as if on cue, Susan scowled as she asked, "Are you really that pleased with yourself over tormenting that poor pizza delivery man?"

Jack sighed and locked himself into his patient place, hoping this was going to be quick. He needed tonight to be a good night. He knew speaking would only prolong things and make them worse.

"Look at yourself, grinning from ear to ear filled with delight over how much suffering you were able to cause some poor, unfortunate person tasked with bringing you pizza that I don't think you even want." Susan continued almost yelling now, "You are such a sadistic, hateful, soulless person."

Some might have been shocked by how quickly Susan's mood had changed but not Jack. He knew when he met her that she had been diagnosed several years earlier with a seasonal affective disorder that made her moods have big and sudden shifts in winter. Jack often wondered why Susan thought of winter as her favorite time of year when almost everything bad in her life seemed to have taken place in winter.

Jack often sat with a blank face and let his mind wonder when Susan needed to vent. He knew it wasn't her fault and that, just like the one outside, the storm inside would pass. This time, his mind was looking back over the winters they had spent together. There was a tragedy for almost every winter that caused seismic shifts in their lives. There were five consecutive years of deaths that cut Susan and Jack to the bone. It began with the death of Susan's mother, then her father followed by her maternal grandmother then grandfather. Then the last death was the one that was worst of all. The loss of their child. The one neither of them had ever really recovered from. Jack marveled at the realization that even with all of this loss, Christmas was still her favorite holiday. Jack returned to the present right as Susan began to apologize.

"Jack I'm so sorry. I don't know what came over me. I know you're not a soulless sadist." She said as she began to cry.

Jack walked over to her and held her until the tears stopped, then offered to reheat their pizza while she put on some music. Jack smiled as he heard the Ella Fitzgerald Christmas album begin to play. He chuckled to himself, relieved that maybe tonight wasn't going to be such a bad night after all. After putting the pizza in the oven, he walked over to Susan and held her close, and they swayed in time to the music.

Susan breathed him in. She loved the way Jack smelled. For her, Jack smelled like home and safety. As Jack spun her around, she asked, "Can we go away this year?"

Jack tried not to stiffen. He tried to keep his smile in place as spoke the lie, "Sure, where do want to go?"

Susan's eyes brimmed with hope, "Spain?"

They had gone to Barcelona right before they knew Susan was sick and had talked about returning to visit Madrid. "Spain? Didn't we just go there? What about Pompeii or Austria?"

Susan rested her head on Jack's shoulder as they danced. "Hmmm. Pompeii might be nice."

Jack asked, "Do you remember when we first talked about seeing the world? You told me the first place you wanted to see was Pompeii, and somehow we've managed to go everywhere but Pompeii." Just then, the oven dinged and signaled that their pizza was ready. As Jack brought the pizza to the table, Susan rummaged through travel books looking for their books on Pompeii.

"Susan, come and eat. We can look through the travel books after dinner." Jack said.

Susan replied, "My mind will rest easier if I know where the books on Pompeii are." Susan kept looking until she found several books on Pompeii and brought them all to the table.

They each looked though travel books while happily eating their pizza. Jack showed her pictures of the architecture, and Susan showed him pictures of the dead.

"Do you remember what I want done with my body after I die?" Susan asked.

"Yes, my love, you would like to be cremated and turned into a coral reef.' Jack replied.

"Do you think that I could have my body flash scorched like the ones in Pompeii and then be turned into a coral reef? That would be beyond fabulous. I love the idea of me at the bottom of the sea look every bit of myself." Susan said.

Jacked smiled. He enjoyed these moments of vanity. These moments when Susan forgot that she was bald and frail. He knew to lean into these moments and felt his hope of the night being a good night grow. "What if we hired an artist to sculpt your ashes into a beautiful sculpture of you rather than covering you in molten ash?

Susan laughed and liked the thought of being sculpted into perfection rather than a lump of ash that vaguely resembled her. "I think I'd like that very much."

Just then, her favorite track of Christmas album began to play, and they continued to dance. They held each other close, and Susan whished this moment could last forever with the storm raging outside while she danced in Jack's embrace. Jack had always been a good dancer, and he marveled at how Susan felt in his arms as he, too, wished this moment could last forever just as the song came to an end.

Susan sighed and stepped away from Jack and turned to go get the dishes from the table before he gently pulled her back to him and whispered, "Not yet." They continued their dance. As he swayed with her in his arms, he remembered what it was like to hold her when her body wasn't so frail and the feeling of her hair on his check. He missed that. He missed her being healthy. As he swayed with her, he fought feelings of resentment. Why hadn't she quit smoking years ago? Why did she wait so long to see the doctor? There were so many whys, but Jack fought back his feelings of regret and despair and instead cherished the moment that they were having. This moment. Jack gently guided her towards the bedroom, and they lay down together snuggled in the way they did with her on his chest and his arm around her. They had slept that way for years.

Susan looked up at Jack and asked, "Can we talk about her?" The tears were briming in her eyes, and Jack felt his voice catch as he said, "Yes".

"Do you think she would have liked it here?" Susan asked. They had been living abroad since her death. They rarely talked about her because it was just too painful. Their daughter had died shortly after Susan's grandfather, and they could no longer bear to live in the house that was once filled with her laughter. It was just too cold and empty. The ache of her too great. Leaving America had rounded the corners of their grief, making it almost bearable.

"Yes, I think she would have." Jack said and believed his answer.

"What do you think she would have liked the most?", asked Susan.

"The rain" said Jack, "I think she would have liked the rain, and I would have liked watching the two of you dancing in the rain."

"Do you think she would have been happy?" asked Susan.

"Yes, I do. You were always so good with her. Sometimes I felt as though you could read her mind. The two of you were so close. I always liked that you were so close but never left me out of anything."

Susan rolled over to face Jack, and as he wiped away her tears she said, "You've always known how to say the most perfect thing. You've always known how to bring the lightness into my darkness."

Jack smiled, and she wondered how she could have

ever thought that his smile was anything other than kind. She could clearly see the light in eyes was love, not some demented pleasure. She knew that all he wanted was for her to feel loved and cared for. "Is it time" she asked? "Please let it be time: this moment feels like the time."

Jack sighed and asked. "Are you sure? Are you sure that it's time?"

Susan smiled and said "Yes, I think it's time."

Jack rose and opened the drawer of the nightstand where they kept her medicine and an unopened the pack of her favorite cigarettes. Jack handed her the pack.

"Will you join me", she asked.

Unable to refuse Jack said, "Yes. Do you want your drink as well?"

"Yes, I think I'd like both on the balcony in the rain" Susan answered. They had lounge chairs like the plastic ones usually set out by a pool on the balcony, which was half-covered and half drenched in rain. It was quite the show when there was thunder and lightening. They had spent many evenings out on the balcony. Susan eased into the lounge chair, opened the pack and cigarettes, pulled one out, brought it to her lips, placing it between them, lit the match she brought up to the cigarette, and pulled a long, deep drag. She felt the familiar catch in her lungs as smoked filled them. Each pull of her cigarette was better than the last. She wondered if she'd be able to smoke the entire pack.

Jack had always hated the smell of smoke and had usually avoided being around Susan when she was smoking and was glad when she had finally quit. All of this made tonight all the more bittersweet. He handed her a glass, and she began to sip from it as she smoked.

"I know how much you've missed this" Jack said as he watched her take deep pulls form her cigarette she looked more satisfied with each drag. "Was it worth it?" Jack asked. "All those years for all the years you've lost."

"Please don't. You promised." Susan said.

Jack couldn't help himself he had to know, "I have to know, was it worth it?"

Susan sighed, "Maybe if she had lived, I would've lived too."

"Don't" Jack pleaded. "I can't take the pain of it. Not tonight of all nights. You didn't stop even after she was born. I don't now if anything other than cancer would have stopped you, and I need to know. Was it worth it?"

Susan pondered for a moment before answering, "It's an impossible question. You've asked before, and I still don't know. So many other things have happened they all jumble together and make me feel as though this moment is where I was always destined to be."

Jack nudged her and took his place behind her on the lounge chair so that he could hold her in his arms as she drank and smoked. "I want you to know that I forgive you."

"Thank you" Susan replied. It was a relief to know

that he forgave her. She never meant to get cancer, and she never meant for the treatment to not work. She never meant to die so many years before him. She was thankful for the mercy of tonight.

Jack could tell the morphine was starting to take effect and wondered how much time they had left. "I love you and always will."

"Don't love me so much that you forget to live. I want you to have a full and rich life after I'm gone." Susan hoped he would.

Jack leaned over and kissed her as she slipped away. One last kiss before she was gone, and he was left alone on balcony. He finally understood why Susan had thought winter was her favorite time of year. The storm as it raged was a fitting reflection of his internal world as Susan died in in his arms.

-End-

The Bear and The Bee
By
André Santana

Out in the ocean, Haylem is not a man. He hopes to find purpose out there on the water, past the horizon. While this is difficult, nothing in his world is harder than the ice that strangles his boat and hoists the bow up into the air.

For the past several days, Haylem has woken up and dragged a spiked metal beam from the bow pulpit, his knees trembling as he slides down to the submerged stern of his boat. He stands, surveyor to the valleys, looking over his work before sliding the sharp metal across the stiff ocean in arching curves. And he writes:

Dear Andrew,

How many times can I say your name before it counts as sinning? Before the sky swallows me up and takes me back to Channel Cay Drive? I am holding your hand right now—in my mind—in the

Exhausted and tinged purple by the fading sky, Haylem collapses onto the ice, a reckless ball of panting. When he looks up, there is nothing to obscure his understanding that the universe is a thing for gods to hold in their hands and laugh about. And he is as much a part of the scenery as the stars and the ants.

When he returns to his boat, he rips up a new plank from the deck and smashes it under his foot until the painted strips resemble kindling. Holding the tips together with the care of a new father, he sets them ablaze using a dwindling collection of matches. Down at the stern, where the ice seems to curve right through his boat the way tsunamis swallow cities, he watches the fire burn and the smoke curl up until he remembers.

And he remembers well.

Andrew is sporting a faded green button-up when he pops out of his red wagon. He wears his eagerness just below his chin, his chest out in the open sun as he walks up to the type of home his parents would clean. Haylem answers the door; his face a national tour from shy to embarrassed to unsuccessfully nonchalant as he gestures for Andrew to finish his top buttons. He obliges just as Haylem's parents appear behind the cracked door: two walking paintings just begging to be bought up. They smile so brightly that Andrew has to step back. His poor car starts to whirl in anxious confusion, headlights blaring, the Florida sunlight melting from sepia to black as—

Haylem wakes up with a start, lifting his upper body off the ice. The fire is long gone, dissolved into ashes and embers which the wind has dutifully tried to carry away. He hears the rhythmic blaring cascading across the ice. He gets up, one sleeping leg at a time, and tries to find the source of the noise. Swinging his body in circles, he covers one ear, then the other, leaning out beyond himself. But everything is everything, and the noise dies away, taken in the tones of the wind.

The next morning, Haylem finds a sledgehammer. With his free hand, he pulls himself up alongside the stanchions until he is standing at the tip of the bow, looking out over the unbroken valley as the sun starts to rise. However, unbroken is not what he made the ice with his hands, and he carefully turns around to see his letter to Andrew stretching out across the ice. On the dawn of another cloudless morning, he swings his sledgehammer in a furious arc and strikes at the ice holding the underside of his boat.

With each strike, Haylem can feel his body slip away. As he balances at the precipice, bringing his shoulders up and down again and again, he can feel something detaching from his skin. This wetsuit of sorts peels off from his fingers, then further up his arm. He worries for a moment that it's simply his circulation until the wet slides off his shoulders and lower back. The lightness is so absolute that, with the right breeze, he might just be lifted away.

The weight slams back into him as if the sledgehammer has circled around and pounded him in the head when the sharp blare returns to the air. Surprised, the tool slips out of his fingers and down the jagged ice, almost taking him along. Haylem stands there momentarily, feeling every blood vessel pump as if it were brand new while the noise wails and wails across the ice. For a moment, he contemplates going the way of the sledgehammer. What better way to lose the ghost in you than to send it up to God in a jetpack? But he leans back to stand up straight and lets the noise shoot through his ears until the wind takes everything away again.

That day he does not write on the ice. Instead, he slips through the companionway into the cabin and scratches onto the wooden walls:

Dear Andrew,

Let's just walk along the beach again. This winter has stretched on longer than I can bear, and I cannot imagine anything more breathtaking than a summer of you. We were spoiled by the woodrats and cotton mice. It is so easy to lose yourself in nature while your devil's garden blooms. I am so sorry we didn't choose somewhere nicer. You deserve memories sweeter than bare knees and woodlands. But maybe that's where it starts? You pick an apple off the tree, and you glare down at it in your hands wishing that it was greener until you have wished for so long that the apple decomposes right in your hand. And now there is no apple left. There is only a stench wafting up from the fruit you remembered.

Haylem pauses to ask himself if he really remembers. If he really, truly remembers Andrew stepping into his home and putting on the show of a lifetime for his parents. High from the attention, Andrew stands up and yanks the tablecloth out from under the exorbitant dinner. Everyone freezes, looking around at the unmoving dinnerware, shocked that this little stunt has actually worked. Later, cuddled up in a wicker chair together, Andrew would admit to Haylem through unstoppable fits of laughter that he had never attempted anything like that before.

That is precisely how one stays warm through the winters. The thick fabric of moments like this, when rolled around each wrist and pulled into knots, makes blankets that burn the darkness away. Haylem basks in the fleeting darkness as the memories of Andrew softly splash over his face and calm his heart, sending him off to sleep. Another night of stars and the dust of too many forgotten moments tells him what is squeezed in the space between his body and the ice. He hears the softly chanted answer of what he is when he is not a man.

Amidst the search for purpose, Haylem had worried that not being a man meant being a child. Yet the truth is, some children must also become men. At seventeen,

Andrew had long been a man. The kind who would hook his fingers in through Haylem's curly hair and list out every moment when he had realized that he was in love. A tugged pinky to pull through a kink, and a story about an unsuspecting waiter at the beach grill pouring water all over another boy.

Maybe beautiful things are easier when they start in the middle. When Haylem looks down the scope of his life, he lands there often: the middle days, somewhere after a new love and somewhere just before a new life.

If Haylem had been a painter, he would have run the world's inkwells dry trying to capture the beauty of Andrew behind a lectern. There was a sun-stopping radiance in his eyes when he taught. Some animals escape a zoo and let fear guide them through the city, but Andrew unleashed sought only adventure. Between the end of his workdays and the start of Andrew's, Haylem would find himself propped against the doorframe of a university classroom watching the love of his life blossom through the concrete of an unexpected world.

Andrew always spoke with his hands, and the way he would reach out as if throwing clay mid-lecture, curving his palms through the air to reiterate the most important points—Haylem knew this as the founding principle of a magical world. If someone like Andrew could come into his life and stay, then anything was possible… anything except breaking through ice, apparently. Though… carving into it?

Andrew. I feel unwell when I say your name, and it's never been that way before. Every moment draped in honey is being rinsed away under the hard glare of the sun, and I'm starting to wonder how much you really loved me. But that's not quite fair because in forty years, you never made me question anything. You dawned resilience like a brilliant robe no matter how many times I tore through it with my bare teeth. Maybe I am both the bear and the bee. Maybe that gives me too much credit for the man you became.

But when I look closely, I see the scuff marks on the walls of our brand new home. You paint and lie to me; let me drag my heels through the hallways and bang my head into doors as if I'm perfect for this. Forty years, and you never asked to see a therapist. You just paint and lie and paint, as if curled up with me in that wicker chair — this was exactly what we asked of each other.

When he falls asleep that day, Haylem is working to build his own ocean. Time and space don't have clear answers, but they insist on putting the same slides beneath the microscope over and over. To inspect his own life this closely and not buckle under the weight of his observations, Haylem would have to be the kind of man who deserved to be trapped in the ocean like this. And he can't be that. Not yet. Not until the pitter-patter fades away, and he wakes up to something new.

The pitter-patter does not fade, but rather triples upon itself until a vibrant symphony has dominated this icy wasteland. A sea of tambourines shaking to the surface like meerkats, finally finding a way into the ears of Haylem who bolts upright covered in a concoction of tears and sweat. The sound of the rain greets him the way unwelcome guests do; with fists and unclean hands. He quickly opens the door and climbs up onto the companionway, soaked slick through to the bone as he stands and looks out over the ice, over his letter to Andrew.

Dear And

What people say about loved ones existing in your heart is true. But Haylem cannot help feeling like this letter to Andrew was the final string stretching across the ocean and leading back home. So delicate that it snaps under the weight of raindrops. He falls to his knees, desperately trying to read what's left behind.

Maybe I am both the bear and the bee.
Maybe I am both   and
Maybe I

As suddenly as it started, the pitter-patter softly fades away. Instead, the sky pours out armfuls of brilliant white snow that begin to pack the plane. Even the last *Maybe* gets hidden like family gems in the attic: a single white blanket tossed over to lure interest away. When Haylem falls, he falls backwards. And maybe this is for the best. After hitting your head like that, it is much harder to remember anything.

In this state, Haylem struggles to remember the first time one drink was too many. If your beautiful husband builds a bar in your beautiful home, you use it. If your powerful boss offers you a bottle to drink on company time, you drink it. Haylem does not come from a clan that lets things go half done. Moderation is a privilege for those who have nothing to prove, and he proved it every time he could see through the clear bottom of a bottle like a telescope.

Andrew hated this. Not because alcoholism was an unmanageable problem—there was no real sense of "I" in his vernacular and therefore no sense of personal inconvenience—but with each night came a new man. Haylem was not predictable. The second your parents die and leave you no money and no understanding of the heart to mourn them with, you will start searching for them.

This was almost inevitable. Most people might go digging in the hearts of others. They might reel in their children closely and light a candle and cry. But the problem with Haylem could simply boil down to one thing: having perhaps never truly lived, he only became a child when his parents died. Then, this child quite literally found his parents' names inscribed in the punt of every bottle of wine he finished.

The quietly failing business that shuttered upon their deaths left a pallet of unclaimed bottles on Haylem and Andrew's doorstep. And what started as a tradition of mourning became breakfast, became a quick working lunch, became a pre-fix dinner.

Andrew could skip over the challenging parts. His own childhood had taught him that not every surface of humanity was beautiful. When Haylem did ugly things, Andrew was masterful at breathing in the toxic fumes and breathing out his anger again. He could not, however, skip over the man Haylem became after his recovery.

The two of them had lost almost everything in the fires that Haylem set. Their relationships burned, their careers went up in smoke, until the only thing they had left was the husk of the daunting home they had stumbled into together on a late November afternoon years before. For weeks they would wake up just to sit on the linoleum and look across at each other, drawing cheap caricatures of the people they used to be onto the fogged-up glass leading out to the backyard.

But winter is a fickle thing.

As work came back, and as apologies were made, and as Andrew started to see the deep pit that scarred Haylem's heart in the wake of his parent's death, a new problem emerged. To Haylem, there was no longer a now. As he wrote to Andrew in a text, *I want my body to mean something. Don't you get that?*

When you remember pushing off the bottom of the sea and swimming straight up, holding your breath just long enough to breach the surface, it can be hard to remember that the air you just released from your lungs was what kept you alive on that long journey.

At the age of 54, Andrew finally added "I" to his vocabulary. All of these years spent together, and Haylem could not recognize him as the air he was, as the coastguard, as the ladder and lifeforce and savior. As the sturdy foundation or as the welcome mat, as the epinephrine, as the person to whom Haylem's body meant everything.

So when Haylem dipped into their savings and bought a boat, Andrew didn't have the chance to say no. The betrayal was clear, the victim was unambiguous. The crime tantamount to murdering the love between them. Yet, the only thing on Haylem's mind when he slid his husband's credit card across the counter was that he wanted to be free. Haylem wanted to have just a little power, scraped from the bowl, or perhaps draped over his shoulder.

Andrew had that already. He had everyone in the palm of his hand every day of his life. When they walked into a party together, one of them was always more prepared to make a friend. It didn't matter that his parents had made him ready for this world and these ways. Because Andrew walked right out of his beaten-up car into a fully funded PhD program. Andrew got invited to be the spokesperson at the local wildlife preserve.

With that kind of security, Andrew wasn't afraid like Haylem was. He had already been to nothing, and he was ready to go back at any moment. Was it really a sin if Haylem needed to buy the same kind of reassurance? Deep within that hole inside, Haylem had poured in bottle after bottle to dampen out the flame of fear. Early on, when his hair did not yet have all the gray peppered in, he had met that fear head on. The fear of losing everything.

And what a waste of time being afraid had been. Because, as he now knows viscerally, you remain afraid once everything is gone. All the things you kept at bay for fear of breaking them have long since found other homes, other places to be when the world inevitably cracks them in half anyway.

Only now could Haylem see that people do not collect each other in an effort to stockpile for an encroaching forever. People play Russian roulette, bringing their hearts closer in an embrace until the barrel rolls too far and one of them dies in the arms of the other. The thing you win is the honor of burying the person you love, sealing their bodies with the cellophane wrap of memory in the hopes that their corpse will kick back alive in the stories you tell.

Although, there were times when even Andrew seemed afraid.

The one time in particular that spun around in Haylem's dark head was of Andrew standing on the pier behind their home. He watched as Haylem let the boat rock away from shore.

He could have been dancing, the way he screamed with his hands. Thumps to the chest, hands at the temples as if trying to stop all the rolling thoughts with his bare fingers. But eventually, Andrew let go. He collapsed onto his knees as Haylem steered the boat away, out across the horizon.

It is hard to say how far he got. No one ever recovered the boat. But Haylem was well on his own when the satellite phone rang for the first time. An obnoxious tone that filled all the air, the phone screamed until Haylem finally peeled himself from the rocking horizon and picked it up.

It is so easy to lose your breath when the house falls out from under you. The boat had just been rocked by a wave when Haylem heard that Andrew was found dead. The feeling that burst open in his heart moved through his legs and into the floorboard, then out across the water. The sound of the waves freezing was like a sword unsheathed. As Haylem was knocked back into a wall, the phone flew from his hand and skidded out across the ice. Each time it rang, there was a part of him that let the cold valley absorb all the sounds.

This time, when Haylem woke up, he heard a softer wail. Climbing out onto the deck and sliding down to the snow-covered ice, he could see a small lump in the even coating several yards away. There was nowhere else to go. No way to pretend like he hadn't seen it. Standing over the unassuming pile, he leaned down and picked up the satellite phone, shaking it gently to loosen the snow and dropping it again on the ground.

He hoped that he had the strength in him to let the phone stop ringing, but from his bent position he clicked the blinking green button.

An automated voice started to speak.

As Haylem heard "car insurance," he lifted his knee and slammed a foot down on top of the phone. The device continued blaring.

Under the drape of this new symphony, Haylem looked back at his boat. As much as he had paid for it, the thing was treacherous. There was something about the hideous green peeking out from under the ice that nauseated him. Maybe this was how to lose the ghost in you? To take it out to sea and watch it wither away under ice when you had no fire at hand. He could feel it pulling at his collar, telling him that home was somewhere over the horizon; out past the ice and snow. The ghost could claim that way out there lay numerous things better than being a man. And with his world chipped like dinner plates across the asphalt, Haylem was willing to listen.

Haylem stomps on the satellite phone again.

-End-

Hayseed, Inc.
By
Roy Christopher

"Do I look inviting?"

She caught his stare before he did. She had the morning kickstart: tall cup of coffee and a cigarette. Todd only noticed that because he craved the same. The sound of her Zippo hit his consciousness like a rock tossed into calm waters. Its metallic slap and the smell of tobacco burning was the only reason he turned and let her presence on the steps behind him fill his vision in rippling concentric circles. He didn't even know if his answer to her auspicious question made it past his lips.

She took a long drag off of the Camel and put her hand on her hip.

"Do I look inviting?"

The winter rain had let up just long enough for the cold to retain its bite. The sky was slate gray, and the only sentiment on the faces he passed on the way to his stop was that of wanting to stay home in warm beds.

"Do I look inviting?"

She looked at him hard, as if she was trying to check his pulse. Just then, the bus lumbered up to the curb. He swore he answered her, but before he could she said, "Well, you're invited," and disappeared up the steps and onto the bus.

He thought he followed her, but he didn't really remember. The last few weeks had been just like the few weeks before that, and the few before that: just weeks that pass seemingly without event. Hearing that Zippo click was the prelude to the first noticeable occurrence since he'd moved here nearly three months earlier.

We needed people to abandon their interests and pursue a goal we could profit from. Something frivolous yet lucrative. Our first few attempts were failures. Politics are needlessly convoluted, and compromise is around every corner. The money comes but only after great efforts. Sports are similar, but there is something physical, tangible, operational about them that politics lacks. We needed our rubes to be able to fake their talents as much as possible. Finally, we arrived at gambling.

There are many established and acceptable ways to gamble representing an array of mysterious skills. It's much easier to fake something if no one really understands how it works. And people are drawn to the unknown. Mystery loves company.

The roulette wheel, the rolling of craps, slots of all stripes: the unknown abounds. But even in the various rule-based and quantifiable card games, there is uncertainty. There are professionals who are untouchable at these games, yet there is always a chance someone new will sit at the table and win. The wildcard. That's us.

We have made sure there was a possibility of a wildcard since the great games began. The hayseed's chance in hell of unearned riches and rewards. In politics, it's possible. In sports, less so. In gambling, we've been holding that door open the whole time. People seem less averse to risk in the winter. People who'd normally be fairly staunch become slightly gullible. The cold wears down their hope and logic just enough. So, as we've figured out the angles to shoot, we've been expanding the operation.

As long as there's the impression that anyone can do it, we are in business. So, we sponsor the hayseeds. We fund them, and we rig the games in their favor. That Blumstein kid from New Jersey in 2017 beat out 120,995 players for the win at the final table. Not good odds for him going in, but those are the numbers we like. We found the kid online, playing poker.

Blumstein's final hand of an ace of hearts and a two of diamonds ended up being stronger than that of Ott, who went all-in with an ace of diamonds and an eight of diamonds. The community cards were a jack of spades, a six of spades, a five of hearts, a seven of hearts and a two of hearts. It was the last card that prompted Blumstein's supporters to erupt. "I'm really happy with the result," he said, "really happy with the deuce because I was playing good." One of those twos was us.

"I'm really happy about how I played tonight," the well-trained Blumstein said. "This is just one poker tournament. It takes variance and luck and playing your best, and all those things came together, and I'm happy to be the winner." He'd have to be. As an accountant, he knows what $8.1 million does to a budget. And so do we. We've even gone global. That Hacham guy in Australia in 2005? He was one of ours too.

In business terms, we're a consulting firm. If a business needs droves of gullible players or pawns with moderate-to-full bank accounts, we can make it happen for one weekend player and make it believable to the rest. Maybe their company needs one success story a year to keep the masses' money moving their way. Maybe they need One Big Win, and the scam is set for history. Either way, we can make it happen.

We are the equalizers. We democratize the illusory stakes of any game. If anyone can do it, you can do it too. We make you believe in yourself.

Todd walked into English and took the first available seat in the back. Two desks over sat the girl from the steps. She was decidedly pale, with short, jet-black hair thoughtfully piled on her head. He pulled out his notebook and tried as subtly as possible to get her attention. She toyed with the tiny troll on the end of her pencil and stared out the window. When the bell rang and she got up to go, he followed.

Her friends surrounded her as they all poured outside.

She introduced him to them as if they'd been talking the whole time. They talked and laughed and hung out from then on. They were holding hands by the time everyone decided to head home.

The way most of us see the world relies on a belief that all the mysteries of life are eventually knowable. Many of our realities hinge on the fact that all will one day be revealed, or that we'll at least get a glimpse at what's really going on as we move through this life, that it's not all just some matrix of coincidences. Our being is bound by time and space, and unrooting anything from that ground requires knowledge from somewhere else.

In one of our toughest and oddest cases, a dad hired us to make his son popular at school. This required a finesse no other case had before or has since. As much as we prefer to work directly with clients and not a proxy, especially a parent, dad paid our full fee and expenses—and the challenge was just too enticing.

High school operates according to steadfast yet unknowable rules. Some famous scientist once claimed that God had a big book of the rules of the Universe, and that every once in a while, scientists were given a glimpse. The rules of high school are in a much bigger book that is much more rarely glimpsed.

There's a group in every high school that seems to have a copy of that book. Remember them? They got away with things that confounded not only you and your friends but your enemies as well. At Elbo High, they were a small, tight group who wielded seemingly unlimited power from the four corners of the school: Norrie, Michael,

Craig, and Sean. They were popular but not in the popular clique. They were into sports but not jocks on any of the school's teams. They were smart but not nerds in any after-school clubs. They were bad boys who shifted between groups and mingled with their members at will. They were untouchable. Every guy wanted to be one of them. Every girl wanted to be with one of them.

The four of them were never seen together. Two of them would be sitting at a lunch table together on Tuesday. Three of them convened at Larry's Barbecue for burgers after school. Two others hung out in the parking lot after the Friday night football game. Students liked to imagine that the ones seen were keeping up their public face while the hidden ones made backroom deals with Principal Carter, Vice Principal Thompson, and Coach Casey for more power over the school.

Knowing all of this, we infiltrated their group and installed Todd.

Of course, he hoped this would happen. Of course, he didn't actually think it would. But here he was, walking home hand-in-hand with a beautiful girl that he'd just lucked upon during a regular school day.

Dreams don't come from staring at screens.
Dreams come from doing things.

He woke up to her singing in the shower. He'd fallen asleep on her couch. He got up and checked the time: 7:21.

Maybe just a little bit
May be just enough.

"What is that you're singing?" Todd yelled through the door.

"Bad Flag," she yelled back. "Why don't you come in here, and I'll sing you more while you wash my back?"

It's like rain you can hear falling,
But can't feel on your skin.
A thirst you drink to death,
But can't get your fill.

Her teeth were her whitest aspect, barely beating out her skin. She had dyed the bobbed mop on her head a shade darker than midnight. All of this was normally exacerbated by the fact that she wore nothing but black. She looked like a photocopy of a photocopy of a photocopy, or a black and white CRT with the contrast turned all the way up.

You drink like you're driving,
And you drive like you're drunk.
Another steering-wheel sing-along
With the body in the trunk.

Naked though, her teeth were the polar bear in her blizzard-snowstorm skin, while her black hair offered the only contrast. The white tile of the bathroom only added to the scene.

She was like a cross between Molly Bloom and Molly Millions. She was never without her dark glasses and was given to soliloquies of great length and thick description. He thought of her as a character being played by someone else. They drank coffee and talked in the waning evening sun.

"I think Thomas Kuhn was just a serial monogamist," she said stirring sugar into her coffee. "See, he's with this one girl for a while for a period of 'normal science'. Then, he meets some other girl, bam! Revolution! Paradigm shift! Then he settles down with his new skeez for another period of 'normal science'." She took a self-congratulating first sip of her coffee. "Say what you want, but it makes more sense when applied to romantic relationships than it does to the progression of actual science."

"Interesting… So, how would your theory cast Feyerabend?" he asked, playing along.

"Total player. That guy got around," she answered without hesitation.

"How about Lakatos?"

"He's a little more tricky, possibly even gay," She improvised.

"Oh, you know sexual preference doesn't have any bearing on promiscuity!" he protested.

"No, but it does make it more difficult to fit him into my theoretical framework," she said grinning.

In many ways, Todd was a model client for us. Nondescript. Nobody. Anybody. If we could make him popular, anyone in the school could be popular.

Successful disruption of a system of this sort requires not only upsetting its natural order but also rearranging its rules. In order to get Todd into this group, we had to make it their idea. Since we owned none of the four, we had to bring in something they wanted and give it to Todd, so they'd want him. To that end, we brought in the one thing that can wreck any stable high school social structure. We brought in The Girl.

The Girl, let's call her Madison, was selected through a rigorous casting process. This role required a believable blend of blemish and polish. She had to be flawed yet perfect, petty yet mature, rugged yet feminine. She had to dupe the four kings of the school by first duping Todd. She had to be desirable to the four kings but also accessible to Todd. She had to have reason to dis royalty but also be convincingly into Todd. Casting also required information about Todd's preferences that Todd might not have been forthcoming about. So, with his dad's signature on a waiver, we hacked his phone and computer, checked his browser history, vetted his friends on social media, and perused his journal. From this dataset, we created a profile. After auditioning hundreds of girls, we got it down to three. Once we explained what the role really was—and why it paid so well—two of them demurred, leaving only Madison.

Madison was pretty but in an everyday kind of way. Model material in some neighborhoods but the girl next door in others. Her beauty was disarming, not flashy. She was also smart. This was key, not only because Todd was kind of a nerd, but also because she had to learn a lot of details to play the part. We needed her to play this thing naturally. We needed her to know things but not act like she knew them. We needed to control her, but we needed her to be autonomous. We needed her to want the same things we did. We needed her to be motivated toward our goals. Sure, the money was supposed to do that, but everyone knows intrinsic rewards always win. We really needed her to actually like Todd.

Madison enrolled at Elbo High a few weeks before winter break. All of the social cliques were well established by then. She was an outsider but being the New Girl would be a boon not a burden. Where others might have accepted their place by the wayside, Madison's looks and swagger leveraged that imbalance, vaulting her to the envied echelons of the social structure of the school. Our plan dictated that on her way up, she take Todd with her.

And it almost worked.

"Do I look inviting?" said the girl on the steps on the television.

"What's this?" he yelled to Madison in the next room. She walked in and looked, plopping down on the couch next to him, one leg draped over his lap.

"This is that pilot I told you about, the one I was in that we filmed a few months ago. I didn't know they were going to actually air it."

"Say, did you do any method acting on the streets in preparation for this role?" he asked, looking her way.

"Yeah, I'd stand on the steps of the building I used to live in, and do the lines to strangers waiting for the bus, why?"

"Huh," he said, looking her over. "No reason."

She was only wearing white underwear and a t-shirt, and when she caught him staring at her thighs instead of the TV, she grinned and added, "Well, do I look inviting?"

As he started to kiss her, sliding his hand slowly up her thigh, she stopped him.

"Hey, tell me something…"

"What?" he said, continuing his advance.

"How did you know I was into you that first day at school?"

"I caught a vibe," he said kissing her neck, sliding his fingers under the hem of her underwear. "Well, that and you were oblivious to Craig and Sean, and they were being their usually charming selves. I put two and two together and hoped for the best."

Our plan ultimately failed. Once we got them together, Todd no longer cared about being popular. Once Madison inevitably broke his heart, he didn't care about anything. He didn't kill himself, but he tried. His dad sued our firm. We settled before it went to trial.

Afterward we went back to our bread and butter: gambling. We even gave politics another go. The variables there are easier to control, and the stakes are much, much lower.

-End-

Sight and Sound
By
Cynthia McDonald

Kane gripped his axe, bringing it down with carefully guided force onto the chunk of wood that stood on end on the chopping block. The log split neatly in half, each piece falling to the side, adding to the pile already haphazardly stacked against the block. His breath steamed out into the frosty air with each exhalation, heavy with the exertion of his effort.

Groping for another large piece from the pile close by, he placed it carefully on the flat surface, feeling to ensure it stayed up before hefting his axe over his shoulder for another blow. Frost clung to the coarse black hair of his beard; sweat beaded on his brow and trickled down his face, running into his left eye. He stopped and rubbed his face on the coarse material of his heavy brown jacket. The right side of his face was badly scarred, and his right eye was gone, the socket invisible under the damaged skin.

Suddenly, he stopped and listened. His trim log cabin was in an isolated part of the dense forest high in the mountains; the silence was unbroken in the depths of winter. There had been a sound, he thought. He thought he had heard some small crunch. It was hard to tell with the continuing crackle of the icy crust that covered the thick snow everywhere around him. That icy cracking crust was even in the trees that surrounded the small clearing around his cabin and the shed where his truck was parked, red tailgate showing through the open door.

Kane shook his head. Maybe a deer, he thought. The squirrels ran on top of the snow, but a deer would break through. Lord knew there were enough of them around to keep him fed, along with the preserved and frozen food he set by every fall from his garden.

Turning back to the chopping block, he heaved the axe again. Wood fell on the stacks. He grabbed another chunk. After another few pieces, he got back into the rhythm. Once all the wood was chopped, he started gathering the split logs together. A post stood next to him, with a rope that led to a neatly stacked pile near the shed. One armful at a time, he carried the wood to the pile, one hand sliding along the rope, and added the pieces to the stack. Once that chore was done, he filled the canvas carrying sack that sat nearby and headed for the cabin, walking with the aid of another rope that led from the woodpile to a post by the cabin door. More ropes led to the shed, an outdoor brick smoker and grill, and another post in the woods that appeared to stand alone.

Before he entered the cabin, Kane stomped his feet to knock the snow from his heavy boots. While the paths along the ropes had been mostly cleared, a recent snowfall had left fresh snow along them, and he didn't want to track it into his home.

The cabin was well-constructed, logs tightly overlapped and notched at each corner. The walls were tight, and any gaps were filled with sealant. As he opened the heavy wood door, heat rolled out and warmed his chilled face. He stepped inside, closing the door behind him. Sliding his gloves and coat off, he hung the coat on a hook on the wall and sat in a chair to the side of the door and bent to unlace his boots.

As he was working on the frozen laces, he smelled something odd. A floral fragrance, light and sweet, wafted into his nostrils, mixed with the scent of bitter coffee he'd been expecting. Instantly he stood, reaching for the shotgun he kept by the door at all times.

He peered around the room with the eye he still had some vision out of, trying to make some sense of the blur which was all he could see.

"Who's there?" he called out. His voice was deep, coarse and gravelly from disuse.

No answer. He breathed slowly and deeply through his nose, smelling the perfume again.

"I know you're there," he growled. "I can smell you."

He moved carefully farther into the cabin. Every inch of the single room was familiar to him, and he was confident he wouldn't stumble or run into anything in here. He continued to look around with his limited vision, trying to find the source of the smell.

Finally, he saw someone. A person was sitting in his chair in front of the fire. Kane raised the shotgun, pointing it at the fuzzy shape he could see and moving closer.

"I won't hesitate to shoot you," he said. "You'd better start talking."

With a start, the figure stood, and he could see their arms slowly rising above their shoulders, fingers spread wide. It looked like the person might be a woman. A small person, in a long dress? That seemed odd, considering the weather and the isolation of his cabin.

Cautiously, the figure was approaching him, arms still in the air. Kane stood still, alarmed but not willing to shoot while they had their arms in the air. And did he want to shoot a woman? He'd been alone so long he wasn't sure what to do. Even a woman could attack him, but he was large enough to overpower a person this small.

As she reached him, she reached out little by little and touched the gun.

"Are you going to say anything?" Kane shouted. "Why are you in my house? Don't touch me!"

The woman pushed the gun down carefully until it was

pointing toward the floor. She put her hand on Kane's arm and pushed it toward the table, which stood nearby. He thought she was indicating that she wanted him to put the gun down. Was she afraid? He supposed she probably was. He knew he would be if he was facing a guy his size who had a shotgun pointed at him. Then again, she was the one who was in *his* cabin, uninvited.

She waved her hand in front of his eye.

"That's right, I'm pretty much blind," he responded. She had to have seen the ropes outside, and with the scarring on his face, it was obvious. He couldn't hide it. Which was largely the reason he'd moved so far away from the outside world.

"Why won't you talk to me?" he asked.

She put a hand over her mouth, then over her ears. He stared at her closely. Then he started to laugh.

"You're kidding me. You're deaf? You can't talk?"

She nodded.

"The first person I meet in years can't even hear or talk to my blind ass?"

She pushed him away angrily.

"Hey, I'm sorry. I didn't mean it. I know what it's like. I just can't believe it. I mean, how are we supposed to *talk?* I mean, really communicate? Hey, how do you know what I'm saying? Do you read lips?"

She shook her head, then took his hand and put it to her ear, where he felt a device behind her ear.

"So you can kind of hear me?" She nodded. "But how will you tell *me* anything? I can't read, and I can't even see what you're doing unless I'm standing this close to you. Hell, I can't even see what you look like."

The woman took his rough, calloused hand and put it against her face. Soft skin met his touch. He felt a long nose with a hoop through one side, full lips, and sharp cheekbones. Her hair was short, standing out from her head in spiky bunches that were somehow still soft. Delicate ears that were pierced with multiple hoops as well, a long, thin neck. Her collarbones stood out when he dropped his hand to her shoulder. She put her hand on his hand to stop him from continuing any farther.

Kane smiled. "Sorry. You don't have to be afraid of me, though. Wish I could ask why you're here, and how you got all the way up here in that dress. It's damned cold out there, and the snow is pretty deep."

She sat down at the table, holding up one leg. Kane reached down, feeling a tall boot on her long, thin leg.

"Ah. Don't you have a coat, though?"

An arm wave at the chair she'd been sitting in when he came in indicated a coat folded over the back. It was a full-length parka when he found it and inspected it. Definitely enough to keep someone warm, particularly if they kept moving. A fur-lined hood drooped behind it as he held it up.

"I guess you were prepared to hike up here. Did you know I was up here?"

She shook her head.

"You just walked up the mountain and got lucky?"

She nodded.

"Why?"

She shook her head and looked frustrated, shrugging. He knew there was a story there that she was unable to tell him.

"Well, we might as well have some coffee and eat something. You drink coffee?" She nodded, and he made his way to the coffee pot, grabbing two mugs and pouring from the pot he'd set to have fresh coffee ready when he came in from chopping wood. Returning to the table, he set one mug in front of her, then sat down with his own.

"Oh," he said suddenly. "Guess I should ask if you like anything in yours. Sugar? I don't have any milk or anything."

The woman shook her head and wrapped slim fingers around the mug, clearly savoring the warmth, before raising it to her lips to drink. Kane enjoyed a long swallow of his own coffee, contemplating her and wondering why she'd come up the mountain if she didn't even know if anyone was up here. It seemed like a hell of a risk to take. She didn't even have any supplies with her. Or did she? He couldn't see well enough to see if she had any bags or anything by the chair she'd been sitting in.

Her eyes wandered about the cabin. It was a simple, one-room setup. Since he'd planned for it to be just for him, even the toilet and shower were right out in the open, with no barrier to separate them from the rest of the room. Kane was a neat person, and he was glad his full-sized bed was made, and he kept his dishes washed after each meal, so it was clean and neat. Then he wondered why he suddenly cared about this stranger's opinion of his home.

She pointed at the light above the table and lifted her hand in a questioning manner. He figured she'd noticed the lack of power poles or lines outside.

"I have a generator," he said, speaking loudly. "It runs the pump for the shower, the lights, and my music. I have a cell phone, but don't know why I bothered bringing it up here. No cell service this far up. I used to play games on it, but I let the battery die a long time ago. I'd rather read anyway."

She suddenly looked excited. Glancing around, she raised her hands as if to ask a question.

"You want to see my books?"

She shook her head. Then she held her finger and thumb up to her face as if making a call.

"You want my cell phone? Guess I can find it, but I'll have to charge it. I'm telling you, there's no service up here." He heaved himself to his feet and went to the set of drawers in the small kitchen area, digging around in his junk drawer, where he tossed the things he used less often. He dug through a mess of pens, decks of cards, and finally found the phone in the back. The charger was wrapped up around some markers, and they fell to the floor as he pulled it out. Sighing, he picked them up.

He plugged the charger into the one of the few outlets he'd installed when building the cabin – it wasn't easy to run wiring through a log cabin. Then he inserted the tiny plug into the phone.

"It'll take a while to charge," he warned her once he'd returned to the table and he thought she could hear him well enough.

"Wish I knew what your name was. Mine's Kane, not that you can say it," he chuckled.

"Hey, why don't I show you around while we wait for the phone to charge?" He stood and indicated she should put on her coat. Then he made his way back to the door and put his coat and boots back on, pulling his hat on his head.

Parka snugly zipped and toggled, the woman slipped gloves on and followed Kane out the door. Grasping his rope, he led her to the shed, showing her his tanks of gasoline, various oils and tools, shelves of chemicals for upkeep of the cabin, chainsaw, and the truck, which he started occasionally just to keep the battery charged. His vision had deteriorated too far to drive anywhere, but he kept it up in case of emergency.

Then he led her to the woodpile, where he showed her the axe, chopping block, and the wood he'd set by. He figured he had enough to last the rest of the winter. Finally, he showed her the grill and took her along the rope into the woods, which led to a pit trap he'd designed to catch game. When he needed fresh meat, he baited the area around the pit trap, bringing in deer. It was no longer possible for him to hunt with his guns the way he had when he'd first moved to this isolated location.

Once they'd returned to the cabin and stripped off their outerwear, he showed her the hinged door in the floor that opened to reveal stairs to the storage area under the cabin. Here he had shelves filled with jars of canned food, most harvested from his garden and the fruit trees planted behind the cabin. Some contained canned meat for those times when he tired of smoked meat or the dried jerky he made in the fall and didn't have any fresh meat on hand. Dried peppers and herbs hung from lines strung along the ceiling. An upright freezer stood in one corner, full of bags of frozen vegetables and meat.

Back upstairs, he opened the refrigerator. He had some fresh venison left from a deer he'd caught a couple of days ago; the rest was in the smoker outside. A couple of venison steaks sounded like just the thing to go along with the stewed tomatoes and canned corn he'd brought up from their sojourn into the storeroom.

As he started firing up the wood stove and seasoning the steaks, he saw the woman tinkering with the cell phone. Suddenly he heard a monotone voice speak behind him.

"My name is Maggie."

He jumped and whirled around.

The woman was standing with the phone in her hand. He thought she was grinning at him. He had the impression of white teeth in a dark face.

"How did you do that?"

Maggie bent to the phone again, typing quickly.

"This phone has type-to-voice software on it."

"What? I don't even know what that is, but okay. If it makes it so you can talk to me, great." Kane was amazed.

"I am so excited that you have this. I have wanted to tell you why I am here and thank you for letting me stay here after I just walked into your home without asking." She smiled shyly as the phone spoke for her.

"I-I, of course, well – you did take me by surprise," Kane said. Then he remembered to slow down so she could hear him clearly. "Were you born deaf or was it an accident like me?"

"I was born deaf, in India," The phone said as Maggie typed. "I had a different name then, but I don't know what it was. My parents didn't realize I was deaf, and we were very poor. They both died of an illness that killed many in our village, and I was placed in an orphanage. My parents came all the way from the United States and brought me here to adopt me. But although they paid for the best treatments, it was too late for me to learn to talk." The dispassionate tone of the phone voice did not take away from the sadness of her story; Kane felt pain in his chest listening to it.

She typed quickly on the phone. "I am not completely deaf. The hearing aids help me hear, but only somewhat, and only when I am close to the person speaking. It was extremely difficult for me to learn English. I also learned sign language, but I am guessing you do not know that."

Kane shook his head as he set a cast iron pan on the woodstove and drizzled some olive oil into it. "No, and I couldn't see it even if I did and you were signing. Thank God for the phone," and he sighed. "We'll have to keep it charged all the time."

Maggie's eyes widened. She bent to the phone. "So, you will let me stay?"

"If you will tell me why you hiked all the way up the mountain, risking your life, not knowing if you'd even find a place to live," Kane said.

More typing clicked from the phone as Maggie's fingers flew over the screen. "Kane, there has been a terrible war. Everyone thought it would be nuclear, but instead it was chemical first, and then biological. A literal Third World War. I left the city with nothing but a backpack full of food, water, and hearing aid batteries, and started running, making my way for the mountains."

She paused for a moment. Then her fingers resumed their typing. "I knew if any place would be safe, it would be the mountains. The higher, the better, right? I didn't want to die in the chemical clouds, or of the diseases that were spreading across the country."

Kane was stunned. He had come to the mountain to get away from people and their cruelty, but he'd always lived here knowing that society was going on below, that the world continued. Now that was all gone? He had already had no family left, but it was shocking to think that all those people were dead.

"I can't believe you made it all the way up here," he said to Maggie. "You have to be one tough lady. And you know what? Maybe it was meant to be."

More typing. "What do you mean, Kane?"

"My vision is failing so quickly. I'll be completely blind before too long, and while I set this place up so I can function without my sight, it's going to be hard. I can definitely use your help, and I'll teach you. I can teach you to shoot, to chop wood, to run the generator. In the summer, we'll grow the garden together. We can do this."

Kane suddenly realized just how lonely he had been for the last few years he'd been living here. Having another person would be amazing, wonderful. He laid the steaks in the pan. They sizzled in the hot oil.

"Oh, Kane," came the voice from the phone. "I can't thank you enough. It was worth walking all the way up this mountain through the snow just to meet you."

He couldn't believe it had taken the end of the world to make him realize how much he had needed a friend.

"These should be ready soon," he said gruffly. Cooking for two, he noticed, was much more enjoyable than cooking just for himself. He was eager to make the food taste as delicious as possible. He opened the corn and the tomatoes, heating each up in its own saucepan.

"Dinner's ready," he announced. Maggie looked up from the opposite corner, where she'd been perusing the bookshelf. Putting a book back on the shelf, she walked to the table, where Kane was putting plates and silverware down.

"Can I help?" She asked with the phone.

"Nope," he answered, setting the saucepans on the ceramic hotpads he'd already placed on the wooden tabletop to protect it from the heat of the saucepans. Then he served the meat, placing a steak on each plate. Once the pan was put in the sink, he sat down opposite her.

Before they started eating, he held out his hands.

"Maggie, I can't tell you how lonely I've been up here by myself. What a miracle it is that you showed up today."

She reached out and took his hands in hers, curling her delicate fingers around his thick ones.

The phone spoke for her. "I'm the lucky one, Kane. If I hadn't found you, I would have died out there in the snow. We might be the last people in the world. It's as if we were meant to find each other."

"I think we were, Maggie. Let's eat."

-End-

For Ibiso
By
Frances Ogamba

The thread I dropped on twitter rolled to far-flung corners. Names that came with their own tongues retweeted and left comments, their anger proportionate to mine. The thread coiled around my daughter, Ibiso, who'd been diagnosed of another living thing: lung cancer.

Before every green thing in Port Harcourt city turned cadaver grey, Ibiso was a contented eight-year-old. Her aspirations were spread out in front of her like the moreen quilt on our windows. Then a murky sheen cased our world, and the sun often bore down with a column too weak to pool radiant on the ground. It appeared as though beneath the sky's skin was a rain too ashamed to erupt.

Something flaky dotted the spread-out laundry and roofs in Rumuokoro, Rumuibekwe, Rumuigbo,

Rumuodumaya, Rumuekini, and everywhere else in Port Harcourt. It lived in the nail buds of the children and made it difficult to recognize the dark bodies they returned with from school. After shuffling through our houses on bare feet, the film of black veneered the soles of our feet. It sat on curtains and on the floors we mopped with dogged persistence to erase this new black tainting our lives.

People discussed it as though its source was a fire raging in dumpsites at the outskirts of the town and would lose strength sooner than we expected. On twitter, mundane topics like *#RedFlags, #BigBrotherNaija, #WizkidXDavido* drowned any conversation about the soot. It felt like questioning it involved dreadful processes, and it'd just be easier to shy away for a time and see if the whole black would just disperse.

A woman named it on the national news, 'the soot'. Her face was lit up with anger that spat on our room walls. She dusted the roof of a car parked nearby and turned her palms to the cameras for everyone to see. Her palmar flexion creases were lost underneath the thick black dust that coated her palms. The local newspapers splashed the name on headlines—THE SOOT MAY TRIGGER HEALTH PROBLEMS. IS THE SOOT A SIGN OF ARMAGEDDON? THE SOOT: THE LAST STRAW?

When I opened a window, I could almost hear footfalls, a distant clatter of tides spilling black dust into the city.

Ibiso's eyes soon began to water, and she could no

longer look sideways or upwards. Fear yanked out my chest. The pharmacist we went to recommended eye drops. Just eye drops!

Then Ibiso began to cough, lightly at first, as if smithereens of her voice were caught, and she only had to clear her throat to free them. Then the coughs dug deeper into her chest and might have joggled her vena pulmonia. She complained,

"Mummy, my chest pains me when I breathe."

She clung to me at midnights, a stunning replica of her father even in the dim light, terrified of another bout of cough. I would hold her slender body against mine when the coughs arrived to rock her body like a piece of ground undergoing a quake.

Ibiso's father died three years after Ibiso was born, three years after he said that he wanted Ibiso but didn't want to be married. My mother had laughed when I told her.

"So, Somi, that boyfriend of yours thinks we are handing over this sweet baby to him, because his manhood can afford to do things we cannot do, eh?"

"Who is giving him the baby? I was just telling you what he said."

"Good girl," she said and bounced Ibiso on her knees. "Ibiso baby, see, your mummy is a good girl, see?" Ibiso's squeals filled the house.

When the news of his death reached me three years

after, I'd been weaned of his memories. That cancerous chunk had been excised. There was nothing left to mourn.

The #JusticeForIbiso trend grew past the rings of twitter and touched the walls of the real world. A woman named Christie, who owned a small NGO, sent me an email asking for us to meet.

It rained on the day we met. It rained as if some cavities in the water bodies had been gouged out, as though the city would be swept away, and we'd be left with a little less than a rubble. The rainwater was the colour of lead. The air was chilly and rammed right into us as we sat in the restaurant Christie had handpicked. Coal Gate Restaurant. Nothing about the name announced food. Christie thumped the table as she spoke, her voice traversed the edge of a scream. Her hair was a cast of wild red — the hair colour of someone who'd survived because of her anger, who made enemies as custom, and tossed light in dark corners. I was the newest preoccupation, and the light in her eyes fluoresced until I was swallowed in the glare.

"I am so sorry about your daughter. So sorry." Her right palm rested on her chest as she spoke, each word arrived bumpy and loud, like slabs being hurled, one after another, into a sinkhole. One strand of red hair hung so dangerously close to her left eye.

"It's okay. Thank you."

She fumbled through her handbag and muttered something to herself. The restaurant was a neat low-key place. Waiters and waitresses moved about, one hovered behind us, clasping a menu book. Christie suddenly looked up.

"Oh, we should order something," she spoke to the young waiter and then to me. "What will you have?"

"Nothing." She insisted and bought us each a piece of meat pie and a can of malt.

"What do you do?" she asked, and her brow pleated into lines. The face of a woman you could never refuse a thing.

"I serve on an administrative role in a primary school."

"I am a midwife," she supplied when I delayed in asking. I was surprised and could not lump the woman before me into the image of a child's first caregiver, the one who spurred women birthing new lives with commands: *Push! Push!* The one who cleaned all that blood and cuddled the baby until its mother was strong enough.

She opened her bag again and rifled through the contents. I wasn't sure why she didn't find what she was looking for the first time. Something jiggled in the bag. Her set of keys for her apartment perhaps. I also wondered if they were car keys. Did she drive? I scanned the parking lot for a car that suited her.

She tapped my arm and handed me a flier. I must have been carried away staring outside. The piece of paper contained information about an upcoming #StopTheSoot march and shunted me into a role I wasn't prepared for. We had become a team. Ibiso was no longer just a girl and my daughter. She had metamorphosed into a movement, an allusion of the fight for which we sought justice. The arms of government were silent, and we'd push until we made them speak. She kept speaking, and it produced a kind of music: the rain cascading down and her talking. I listened hard but barely heard her.

"The soot comes from a local refinery secretly owned by the government. When the refinery flares gas wastes, they solidify into the black powdery substance we know as soot. Only that it is not mere soot, it is something far more dangerous," Christie said.

I nodded.

"Do you see the colour of the rainwater today? Did you hear the warning that nobody should use the water?"

I nodded.

Christie and I created Google documents and WhatsApp groups for volunteers and exchanged private messages on WhatsApp.

Christie

Hey. Somi, I am excited we are in this together, tbh.

21.43.

You

Yeah. It's a good cause. Thank you for everything.

21.44.

Christie

My 1st real fight for social justice. Lol.

21.44.

You

Me too. Hehe.

22.00.

We were leading a war, Christie always reminded me. I'd inherited some of her strength and no longer recognized the woman I became at the marches, the woman full of power who spoke with a voice pervaded by pain and fear of losing her only child. The fury I nursed, that a child full of health and prospects could suddenly be faced with medical verdicts, was divulged at such protests as I chanted: JusticeForIbiso! StopTheSoot! Our marches breathed life into many other situations which needed to be heard: the girl child who was married off at twelve; the young man who was shot dead by a customs official; the lack of equipment at the government-owned hospitals.

The rain poured in endless torrents, taking breathing breaks only in the evenings or for few hours in the night. There were unexpected stretches of sunshine, sometimes, luckily, for a few days before the subfusc trail intersected the sky. Flood water swallowed up porches in some areas of the city, roads in another, a whole community and farm lands in yet another. On the days the rain didn't come, balls of flaming dust splotched the sky. The impossibly grey sky always let something down.

I couldn't tuck away my worry about Ibiso. I watched closely, tailing her as she played as much as her ailing lungs let her: building brick cities with her toys and drawing up faces on a paper with her right hand, the left hand shielding her chest. A terminal illness was heterogeneously savage, especially when it was only scan-visible.

Christie spilled stories of her personal life when we weren't discussing the project; three children who were away in boarding schools, a supportive husband who prodded her on especially when her shine stumbled into a weaker light. I told her of the person I'd very much like to become: a woman leading a glamorous life, who'd be able to give her old mother and her daughter almost everything they needed. I talked about the first time Ibiso coughed up blood, the panic I felt, and the manner the blood stained every kerchief and serviette until there were splotches of red in every cranny of the house. I'd prayed and hoped for pneumonia, or at worst, tuberculosis. Those were curable. The hospital we first went to referred us to another hospital where we were told that Ibiso needed a test, an erythrocyte count. The count was high. It had been 102 or 112. I didn't know what the figure meant. It was only supposed to be lower, and it wasn't.

"Madam, we need to carry out the MRI test on your daughter. Do you know the Crystal Laboratory on Sobo drive, by Egbeda bus stop?"

I didn't know what the MRI entailed, but it was a trouble shooter and was only carried out because Ibiso's lungs were cluttered with the soot. I began to frequently hear and say many terms I'd never known before.

I often wished I could go back to the uneventful life we led before Ibiso's lungs tipped over to the disease. We'd wake up each morning, Ibiso and I, and race each other through chores, laughing.

Christie and I worked together for six months, and our voices grew as loud as Ibiso's coughs. The coughs now poked their claws too deep into her lungs and popped up with thick blood. I was at work, typing the school third term exam questions when Christie's call came in. Her voice sounded hoarse as if she'd been screaming. But I doubted if anything could get her to scream. It seemed her hands were constantly spread out under the sky, expectant.

"Somi dear, we have a mail, an invitation." Her personal email was also our work email. She'd insisted on creating a new one for the project, but I didn't see the need. The stray sun struck through the glass as if coming at me from a gap in the window.

"That's great news."

"Let's meet this evening."

"Okay dear. This evening then."

"How is Ibiso?"

"Fine."

"Okay. Later dear."

We revamped the list of demands over and over, paring down and adding fresh bullet points. Ibiso topped the list, and then many other cases ignited by the soot spilled their insides on the list. I always dreamed of Ibiso's future; my daughter always topping classes, and careers. I'd never imagined having her on the list of people who direly needed saving.

My mother shot me a worried look when I told her she'd spend the following day with Ibiso because I had a meeting. Then she resumed stirring the soup she was making. It rained outside, bold footprints of water and mould sketched her house walls. The flood water, menacingly, had risen to the porch. Ibiso whispered to a doll, the ailment was taking things from her inch by inch. She avoided speaking because it ignited the coughs. Walking, she told me, felt like an inflamed organ inside her was going to burst. She took breathing in slow spurts, and it broke my heart that all the free air around us could not be hers. She always looked exhausted, and I dreaded imagining what was happening in her lungs, wondering if they were endless deserts or a wide corrupt ocean.

I woke up feeling run over by a car. I was to meet Christie at the paved sidewalk of the restaurant where we had met the first time and many times after. I wore an old blue suit, and my body swerved awkwardly underneath it. Christie was already standing at the pavement, her red hair whipped about in the morning wind, and was weirdly tinged by the purple of her earrings. We hugged, and she held on a tad longer. Then she touched my collar and adjusted it.

"They are to close down the source of the soot and foot the medical bills of all the people affected by the soot," she said into the stillness. A reminder.

"You will do the talking?"

"Both of us will," she said. I'd woken up too tired to fight. I wanted to curl up under a duvet, absent from all life, and just snooze. A black Ford Jeep pulled up right in front of us. An imposing hulk. Long and large. It stripped us of the view around us. A door slid open, and a waft of conditioned air greeted our faces. We boarded and the door slid back, shutting us away from the familiar outside world. We'd made a series of tweets about the meeting, and the threads were still live on twitter. A few radio stations were talking about it on their discussion panels. All that awareness suddenly meant nothing in the massive dark belly of the automobile. All my mother's warnings about the meeting came alive within me. I thought about Ibiso and her maroon eyes, which had turned brown in a number of months, and my mother, the bubbly woman who'd lent me a large portion of her strength for the past eight years.

We sped through unknown routes where towns sprang out and spread in a swarming swath across the road. Hawkers and bikes and buses cluttered the highway, and I heard the driver swear at the gridlock.

The car pulled up in a large compound where men and women bustled about in obvious subservience. The world here was all flowers — African Daisy, Bougainvillea,

Alyssum, Amaranthus. It was bursting with a thousand splendid smells and flourished away under a sky that appeared devoid of crusts of soot. Two men who were suited up in black ushered us into one of the buildings and into the elevator. What if we never make it out? The many balconies of the buildings stuck out at the front, and people moving with files and envelopes and trays stopped to stare at Christie and me.

I didn't see the two men at first. What I saw was a large chamber as cold as a mausoleum, with walls layered in beautiful stones, the floor smooth and sheeny like the surface of chinaware. The ceiling was so far up, so far away from the room. Then I saw them seated at a long table. The younger man was light-skinned and looked fortyish. The older man had warts crowding his eye bags. He sagged so deeply in his chair that he might as well spill to the floor. We sat facing them, silent for a bit.

"I am Femi. This is Chief Uche," the younger man began.

"Christie. Somi," Christie said, barely indicating who was who.

"We represent the government and the refinery," Femi said.

"We prefer to speak to the government and the refinery, not to their representatives," Christie fired the first missile.

I could feel the chill in the room thaw. The sound of the air conditioner whistling at one end of the ceiling was petering out. I caught a glint of anger lurking in the chief's eye. I wasn't sure when I was to speak, but I very much wanted to say anything now just to quell the smouldering fire.

"We are the government and the refinery." The chief's voice boomed from across the table, there was an impatient edge to it. He drank something from the goblet before him.

"We want to have a conversation," Femi added.

Christie slid our list across to him. We had clipped the paper respectfully in an envelope. But that attempt at orderliness crumbled in the experimental adornment of the room. Femi glanced through the list, and a wide smile broke out at the corners of his mouth. He passed the paper to the chief, who skimmed though it without any expression on his face.

"That's the conversation we want to have," Christie said when the chief put the paper down on the table.

The chief turned to me, sucking me up in his full glare.

"Tell me about your daughter. I have read about her a number of times."

"She is very ill," was all I offered, not out of malice. I was immersed in the view of the sky from the window facing me. The sun was a generous orange, the hue was close to Christie's hair tint. I glanced at Christie at that moment, her shirt collar stuck out. I was desperate to set something right, to reach out and pat it down. In this room, I was also aware of being the least favoured, the unlucky one.

"We don't need your money," Christie spat out, "We want you to take responsibility for all those sick people. Close down the illegal refineries, then we will take down our posts and the blogs."

The chief resumed drinking from the goblet. Femi passed us a paper each, which had an email address splashed across it in bold.

"The ongoing project at the refinery will last another year or two. There is nothing the state government can do about the soot at present. Send us a mail with your account details if you reconsider. Five million naira for each of you. Right, Femi?" He shrugged and his large shoulder flapped and folded like wings. He was not looking when Femi nodded in agreement.

Christie glared at them. I didn't know where she got all that power from, to hold a room hostage with her eyes.

"Let's go, Somi," she barked under her breath. The chief kept drinking and didn't spare us a glance. Femi followed us to the door and whispered,

"Reconsider."

Christie and I caught different buses home. I walked the short distance between the bus stop and my apartment more tired than I'd ever been. My mother had brought Ibiso home and promised to pass the night with us. When I walked in, Ibiso was asleep. My mother didn't ask how the meeting went. I was grateful she didn't.

I brought out the paper slip with the email address.

I opened the mailbox in my phone and stared at the rectangular box where email addresses went in. Christie had said to me, just as we were about to get into our buses, "You did well, Somi. You are the best partner anybody can ask for." I did not know what she rated, my near-inexistence at the meeting or that I was flexible enough to be bent into this fight in the first place.

Ibiso coughed, still unconscious with sleep, and bloody phlegm drooled to the side of her mouth. She coughed again — the quaky mechanical hum of the equipment that she disappeared into months ago, the sing-song voice of the Indian doctor trying to repress the noise of the machine to get me to hear him shout "No worries, madam. She's safe." The cough racked through her body again and gave the bed sheets a slight tremor, like the earth was going under.

I typed the email address in the address box and then wrote my proposal in the body. I'd publicly pull out of the fight, say that Ibiso was fine and getting treated, leave town. I wanted ten million naira. Ibiso's treatment may take up five or more. The rest would go to finding a town with more sunlight, with brilliant and blue clouds, and less rain.

For a heartbeat, I fantasized staring outside through glass walls bordered by the ocean's blue, surrounded by kitchen walls gleaming white and stain-free. A world so cold and filled with white faces and tongues speaking light and fast English.

My phone rang, and Christie's name streaked the screen. I gave a thought to what she could be doing at that moment; I saw her curl up in her husband's arms, saw her clip her youngest child's nails while the older ones were at the dinner table, probably doing some homework. I compared the beam of her life to mine — her fine husband to the dead one I never had, her healthy children to my Ibiso quivering underneath the duvet, abysmal coughs stealing her away in morsels — and I found mine too weak and hazy. The kitchen door swung open, and my mother appeared bearing a tray of oil and cooked yam. Another door unlocked in my thoughts, the same creaking, the same swing-and-shut, and I circled back to the memory of a light skinned doctor with hairy knuckles prying open an envelope, squinting for long seconds,

Madam, we found some abnormal cells, cancerous.

I imagined Ibiso's insides, convoluted walls of intestines and ribcages, gleaming black like she'd inhaled lungfuls of smoke all her life.

Somi, come and eat first, I heard my mother say. Christie's phone call bore into another bout of Ibiso's cough. The hum of our situation rattled through me and spooked my fingers. I clicked send.

-End-

Nameless
By
Phoenix Blackwood

The girl and her dog trekked through a foggy landscape. Snow and ash covered everything as the mixture fell from the sky. The air was still. Overwhelming silence filled the void. This was welcomed by the girl; she didn't care for noise. The dog didn't have a name, and the girl had long since forgotten her own. She didn't need it here. The two moved along in silent understanding.

Her feet stopped suddenly when she heard a crack. Ice. It was impossible to determine how thick it was or where it ended under the overbearing covering of snow. She didn't know where the ice began, and the only option was to keep going. The fields offered no shelter from the flying bullets and arrows of enemies. There was no place to hide from the mutated beings - Crawlers - that stalked the earth at night. While survivors wouldn't be so foolhardy to land themselves on the ice with the pair, Crawlers had a one-track mind and would chase their prey regardless of the danger in the environment. This brought not only the general danger of a monstrous attack, but also the risk of them breaking through the ice.

Taking a deep breath, she made the calculated decision to cross to safety instead of turning back. She gingerly stepped forward, and her companion cautiously followed her lead, paws padding at the snow gently before putting her full weight on them. Slowly and methodically, they made their way across the ice. Darkness would come soon and usher in the new danger of the monsters. A faint gurgling could already be heard in the distance. As the sun lowered in the sky, the girl began to quicken her pace.

There was the sound of a crack and a shrill yelp as the girl's companion was quickly engulfed in freezing water. The girl immediately dropped to her stomach. She crawled towards the hole where the dog was desperately clawing at the edges of the ice. Her paws took chunks of the frigid substance with them as she flailed. The dog began to sink now that her thick fur was soaked through, bits of ice clinging to the ends. Frost formed around her eyes and mouth as she whimpered and tried to stay afloat. Every pawing motion attempting to climb onto a solid plane broke more and more ice as the girl scrambled to help the dog up. Both girl and dog began to fatigue in the bitter cold. The girl pulled the dog along as they continued breaking away pieces of the frozen pond. When the girl thought she couldn't go any farther, they finally managed to find a solid patch of ground where the dog got her footing and pulled herself from the icy water.

Relief washed over the girl as she flopped down on the edge of the pond. The dog shook her coat frantically, panting as she went. Water flew through the air, soaking the girl even more than she already was. She let out a laugh as she threw her arms around the shivering creature. The dog excitedly lapped at the girl's face. She smiled, but her expression quickly changed as she heard a shrill screech in the distance. She got up, silently signaling the dog to follow.

They made their way through the woods, hyper-aware of every twig snapping or crunch of snow beneath their feet. As the sun finally fell beneath the horizon, they came upon a small ramshackle camp built with sticks and a few tarps. The girl got to work on a fire while the dog shivered against the cold wind. The fire began to crackle and hiss as it started up. She shed her soaking clothes and replaced them with a frigid, but dry, set. Once she laid out the wet clothes to dry, she sat down in front of the fire and rocked back and forth as the dog lay her head in the girl's lap. A small smile formed on her lips as she stroked the dog's still damp fur. With a sigh of relief, she shed the pack she'd been wearing that carried the spoils of the excursion - enough food to last over a week.

Aside from the ice incident, it had been a fairly uneventful mission. Things had seemed eerily calm and empty, which was puzzling as the city was typically pretty populated with Crawlers. Monsters - once human, but now mutated from radiation and fallout of the war. Almost everyone that had lived in the innermost sanctum of the city was killed by the radioactive bomb. Those who had been far enough to survive the blast but close enough to be exposed to a massive dose of radiation were gradually overtaken by the sickness that manifested in monstrous deformation. The city had been peaceful prior to the bombing - it was targeted due to its high population, making for a devastating blow to the community. The girl had lived in the far outskirts and had taken shelter in her family's underground bunker before the bombing. This had protected her from the radiation. She hadn't seen her family that day, but as they worked farther inside the city, she had assumed the worst. After running out of food to sustain her, she emerged to find that the Crawlers had claimed the city.

Pulling a bag of chips from the pack, the girl began munching as she warmed herself by the fire. The fire itself was also a calculated risk - the light could be a beacon for pillagers and Crawlers alike, but it was necessary to survive the cold winter nights. The hope was that she was secluded far enough into the woods that no living creature would find them. That hope was reliant on the cities being a hub for both Crawlers and survivors - the survivors being attracted by the ample supplies that were abandoned within, and Crawlers attracted by the voices of the survivors.

Just as the girl began to settle in for the night, a chorus of gurgling and shrieking surrounded the camp. They were strange creatures with twisting limbs that walked on all fours. Gurgling shrieks were their language. Their faces were gaunt, elongated husks of their former selves. The noises were jarring and irritating, but the girl fought through her discomfort to stamp out the fire and retreat within the makeshift tent with her companion. At first it simply sounded like a handful of the creatures, but the noises became more and more numerous. Soon, it was a loud mob that descended upon the camp. The girl covered her ears and did her best not to make noise as the sounds reached her - causing an internal dissonance that could only be compared to nails on a chalkboard. The dog pressed up against the girl to soothe her, licking her face as tears began to roll down her cheeks.

Branches broke and snow crunched as the Crawlers made their erratic movements through the woods. Limbs twisted with the sound of cracking and popping of joints to echo the snapping twigs beneath them. A few Crawlers brushed up against the tent, peering in with their nearly blind, cataract filled eyes. The girl shook but was otherwise motionless to avoid detection. Her natural silence was an asset. The horde continued passing through, skittering and shrieking for what felt like an eternity. She remained motionless as the noises began to quiet and the creatures passed. Her inner turmoil from the noise began to die down. She sat in silence for a few minutes, then she slowly moved out of the tent. As quickly as they had come, they were gone.

Sucking in a deep breath, the girl stared into the distance. She considered why there had been so many of them. This deep in the woods, there would be the occasional straggler passing through aimlessly. This was completely different. There had been tens, if not hundreds of them that had just passed by, and they seemed to have a destination in their sights. The eerie emptiness of the city earlier in the day must have been tied to this herd. Had something driven them away?

Sounds of a siren rang in the distance - not close enough to trigger the girl's negative response to noise. It wasn't from the nearby city. It was farther off, in the opposite direction. The sound was a distant humming, but with the unmistakable blare that disaster alarms carried.

The girl pulled a sword from her belongings and dared to investigate - she only planned to go so far as the noise was tolerable. Otherwise, she'd wait it out and satisfy her curiosity once the alarm had ceased. She began trudging through the woods with her companion by her side, warily keeping an eye out for any movements of living creatures. A familiar skittering came from behind them, and the girl pressed up against a tree to mask her silhouette - the Crawler paid her no mind and quickly moved on towards the noise. She'd never seen them so laser focused on anything that wasn't food. They were so set on this destination - she was curious to see what could possibly draw their attention like this. The girl walked until daylight broke and the siren ceased. On the horizon, she could see a faint outline of a town much smaller than the city she was used to. She walked closer still. There were no Crawlers in sight - she wondered where they had all gone.

She entered the town with her sword drawn and ready to fight. There was one large building fitted with speakers that was likely the source of the sirens. Otherwise, there were a few buildings scattered around - mostly family houses. A small supermarket sat across from the large building. It looked like it had been a lively little town where everyone had known each other, but it now held an eerie, abandoned atmosphere. Windows boarded up and broken, doors kicked in, supermarket pillaged.

All at once, she noticed the shrieking and hissing coming from the other end of the town. She didn't want to get closer to the antagonizing noises, but at the same time she heard voices - human voices. An investigation was warranted, so the girl sheathed her sword, covered her ears, and walked on. It wasn't as loud as it had been back in her tent, so she fought through the discomfort. After a short walk, she came to the edge of a ravine on the opposite side of the town. Looking down, she saw the horde of Crawlers that passed her tent. Some unmoving, a few desperately clawing at the other side of the ravine, trying to make their way up. It was futile - there were no hand or footholds to be seen for even an experienced climber, let alone accommodations for the frantic and jarring movements of a Crawler.

There was a bridge a ways away that provided the means to cross, but Crawlers weren't sentient enough to figure that out. Their path always ran straight for their prey, regardless of what was in the way. They must've run off the edge like lemmings pinpointed on their target. The talking. The girl could hear a conversation being had at a high volume, and she peered across the ravine to see a field of solar panels. In front of them was what seemed to be a box until the girl squinted harder. A television. Someone had laid a trap for the Crawlers and drawn them all away into the ravine. Upon this realization, the girl ran to a nearby house and pressed herself against the edge. A trap this smart meant survivors were around, and they were almost always unfriendly. She shouldn't have come here.

She began sneaking her way towards the other side of town, back in the direction of the woods, when her companion bolted to the bridge on the ravine. The girl clapped and tried to get her dog's attention, desperate to get away from the danger and the noise. She peered around the corner of the building and saw a figure standing on the bridge, running towards her dog. Fearing the worst, the girl let out a strained scream. The figure didn't seem to notice, as they knelt down in front of the dog and started petting her. Her tail wagged happily, and she turned back to the girl, giving away her position. The figure tensed up, straightened their posture, and drew a weapon from their side pocket. The girl held her hands up in surrender as the figure drew closer - she would have drawn her sword, but she feared retaliation would put her dog in danger. As the figure approached, the light revealed long, curly, copper hair and a worried expression. The dog trotted happily beside her, as if attempting to make an introduction. The stranger was another girl, who looked significantly less threatening as she sheathed the small dagger and silently held out her hands. She signed something that the unnamed girl couldn't understand - without knowledge of sign language, she couldn't tell what the stranger was trying to communicate. The girl gave her a confused look and the stranger then knelt down and wrote "Amara" in the snow and pointed to herself.

This girl had a name.

Amara smiled at the girl, holding out a hand in greeting. The girl avoided eye contact but, judging Amara to be friendly, took her hand and shook it. She wasn't sure what to make of the situation - every survivor she had run into prior had been far more hostile. They would demand for her to speak to prove her humanity and become angry when she couldn't fulfill their request. She realized Amara hadn't said a word either. Questions came rushing to the girl's mind - was Amara here alone? Were there others that would be less welcoming? Was there still danger lurking in this town?

Bringing the girl's thoughts to a grinding halt, the town's siren began its harrowing screech. The girl fell to the ground, desperately covering her ears - this was so much worse than the Crawler's language. It was an unrelenting, powerful noise that shook her to her core. Far beyond the previous nails-on-a-chalkboard discomfort, her insides echoed the screech and tried to burst out of her. She screamed. The dog pawed at the girl, trying to distract her, to bring her back to the world. Unheard by either of the girls, a twisting figure led a group of similar silhouettes at the edge of the town. The dog turned her attention from the girl to the group and barked to try and get her attention. It was no use, she couldn't even hear the dog over the inner turmoil that had overtaken her.

Amara, however, noticed the dog's distress and followed her gaze to the group of Crawlers. Her eyes widened, and she knelt down and put her hand on the girl's back to try and get her attention. The nameless girl responded by pushing Amara away, frenzied by her sensory overload. Amara glanced at the approaching horde of Crawlers and took a risk - she grabbed the girl by the arms and dragged her into the building next to them. The girl fought, kicking and screaming, but not hard enough that Amara couldn't get her to safety. The dog followed along, knowing that Amara was doing her best to help. Once they were inside, the noise was slightly muffled but still piercing through the girl's eardrums. The girl stopped screaming but remained curled in a ball with her hands over her ears. Amara peeked out the window in time to watch the horde stagger by, falling into the ravine in a similar fate as the first pack. Brought into the town by the siren, urged towards the ravine by the blasting television that Amara couldn't hear.

Eventually, the overwhelming sound of the siren stopped. The girl continued shaking, and the dog rested her head on her back. Amara knelt down next to her and patiently waited, unsure of how to help. Slowly, the girl was able to regulate herself and came out of her curled position. She looked up at Amara with a tear-streaked face and sighed. She was tired, overwhelmed. Amara tenderly wiped her tears and gave her a weak smile. The girl sniffed and reached out towards Amara to touch her.

Cracking. Popping. A Crawler approached from the back door of the building. Amara didn't seem to notice. The girl quickly jumped into action, unsheathing her sword. The motion startling her, Amara backed away from the girl - directly into the overgrown limbs of the Crawler. She let out a scream as it encircled her in its arms, making escape impossible. Drool and spit from the monster's grotesque face dripped onto Amara's shoulder. Struggling against the inhuman strength of the creature, Amara's heart raced so hard that it felt like it might explode out her chest. She closed her eyes, not wanting to see the fate she was resigned to. Instead of the bite she expected, the creature's grip released. Amara whirled around to face the monster, which no longer had a head. Black ooze dripped from the other girl's sword as the head rolled to the floor, tongue lolling about. The body fell shortly after, twitching and making a loud thud as it hit the ground. Letting out a sigh, Amara hugged the girl tightly. Uncomfortable at first, the girl tensed up, but relaxed into Amara's embrace after a minute. She exuded a safe energy that made the girl calm - similar to the companionship she had in her dog. Perhaps she'd stay with this girl - the first human that hadn't made her skin crawl to get away. Amara seemed to understand her silence and didn't expect something she couldn't provide.

Amara turned to a dusty drawer and dug around until she found a pen and a piece of paper, and she wrote something. Then, she turned to the girl with a smile. She held out the paper and pointed to the girl. Taking the paper, the girl read the word "Guardian". A smile broke out across her face.

Now she had a name, too.

-End-

www.ingramcontent.com/pod-product-compliance
Lightning Source LLC
Chambersburg PA
CBHW051205190726
48288CB00006B/1813